DEDICATION

For my family, friends, teachers, and everyone who has taught me to believe in the power of my words.

EPIGRAPH

WHAT SAVES US
A Poem by Bruce Weigl

We are wrapped around each other
in the back of my father's car parked
in the empty lot of the high school
of our failures, the sweat on her neck
like oil. The next morning I would leave
for the war and I thought I had something
coming for that, I thought to myself
that I would not die never having
been inside her body. I lifted
her skirt above her waist like an umbrella
blown inside out by the storm. I pulled
her cotton panties up as high
as she could stand. I was on fire. Heaven
was in sight. We were drowning
on our tongues and I tried
to tear my pants off when she stopped
so suddenly we were surrounded
only by my shuddering
and by the school bells
grinding in the empty halls.

She reached to find something,
a silver crucifix on a silver chain,
the tiny savior's head
hanging and stakes through his hands and his feet.
She put it around my neck and held me
so long the black wings of my heart were calmed.
We are not always right
about what we think will save us.
I thought that dragging the angel down that night
would save me, but instead I carried the crucifix in my pocket
and rubbed it on my face and lips
nights the rockets roared in.
People die sometimes so near you,
you feel them struggling to cross over,
the deep untangling, of one body from another.

INDIVISIBLE

A Novel by

JULIA CAMP

INDIVISIBLE
Copyright © 2020 by Julia Camp

FIRST EDITION SOFTCOVER
ISBN: 1622532120
ISBN-13: 978-1-62253-212-4

Editor: Jenni Sinclaire
Senior Editor: Lane Diamond
Cover Artist: Kabir Shah
Interior Designer: Lane Diamond

EVOLVED PUBLISHING™

www.EvolvedPub.com
Evolved Publishing LLC
Butler, Wisconsin, USA

Printed in Book Antiqua font.

Chapter 1

He's made a game of this—standing in front of the mirror, feeling inhuman, trying to feel as little as possible. His vibrant, blue eyes have dulled into a soft gray, and his shoulders slouch as if gravity itself weighs too much to bear. The lines on his forehead have grown thick with worry. He doesn't look like himself, and something about that makes him feel like a stranger, a shadow of the man he once was. Somewhere, somehow, the joy has retreated from his eyes, and he can't recognize himself anymore. He tries to ignore how much that terrifies him.

Sarah comes in, and he looks down, away from himself and her. He puts his tie around the back of his neck and begins to straighten it out underneath his collar. Sarah stands by him for a second, silent, but he can tell that she's thinking—thinking of what to say without making everything fall apart. He can tell by the way she moves that she's debating whether or not to touch him.

She sways, just slightly, back and forth as if being gently rocked by the wind.

"If you can't do this," she says, "there's no shame in that."

"Can't do what?" Charlie asks.

"All of it."

He doesn't say anything.

He turns back to the mirror. For a moment, he wants to think about everything, about his sleepless eyes and terrible posture, but that kind of thinking seems too cynical, so he goes back to attempting to knot his tie. His shaking hands fail him again and again.

Sarah cautiously and gently moves between him and the mirror.

"I got it," she says, and begins to help him with the knot.

He pays attention to how softly she moves, how cautiously and slowly, as if afraid to rattle him even the slightest bit.

She moves the cloth back and forth, carefully and precisely, as if trying to balance a scale, as if trying to make at least one thing perfect. When she finishes, she steps back.

He whispers a thank you, and he runs his fingers through his gelled hair, and tries not to think about anything other than the rising and falling of his chest. He looks in the mirror again, but just seeing himself in that suit makes him want to sit down. Instead, he puts his hands on the counter and leans forward, letting his arms support him, and closes his eyes trying to escape. Sarah doesn't move—he can feel her trying not to even breathe. It doesn't seem fair, how little power she has.

"It's just one day," he says, turning to her. "We'll be fine, right?"

She reaches out and holds both of his hands, letting their fingers interlock as she stands on her tiptoes and kisses his cheek.

For a minute, he finds himself staring at her tight-fitting black dress. He's always thought she looks particularly beautiful in black. Something about the contrast of the darkness of the black cloth against her soft, light-green eyes and long, blonde hair, makes her irresistible to him, as if she can somehow be everything at once.

"You're a good man, Charlie," she says.

He wants to say he loves her, but somehow, as if the words are lost in translation from his brain to his tongue, all that comes out is, "I'll see you there, okay?"

***

The funeral is being held at the very church where Charlie found his best friend, 22-year-old Wesley Andrews, dead. The irony is lost on no one.

"Do you think he wants us to suffer?" Natalie, Wesley's mom, asks Charlie as they sit together on a bench outside St. Ann's, an hour before the funeral begins. It's a beautiful fall day, sunny without being hot, a heavy breeze. Natalie wears a face full of makeup to hide her sleepless eyes, and she promises Charlie she'll be brave so that she won't smear her mascara all over her face. She won't make herself into a spectacle. She won't do anything to take the focus off her son.

Charlie looks into her glazed-over, absent eyes. He's come to know this look, the one she always wears, so disconnected, when imagining memories with her son.

Charlie knows which story haunts her, a story she's told over and over since Wesley's death. In this memory, Wes is a five-year-old boy, and she's dressed him in a white button-down shirt, with ironed khaki pants, and dress shoes. It's a Sunday and time for mass. Wes keeps telling her that he doesn't want to go, and every time she tries to carry him, he slips away from her like a spaghetti noodle. He asks her why they have to keep coming to this boring church. She tells him that this place will give him hope when he has none.

Later, he would fall asleep during the mass and sprawl across the front pew, his head on his mother's lap, limbs limp.

Seventeen years later, Natalie says he looked no different, as he lay across that same pew after shooting himself, dead. That's the memory that haunts her.

"He must have wanted us to suffer," she says.

"He would never want that," Charlie replies. "Never. You know that."

But she doesn't. By committing suicide in that church, Wes had taken away the one place he knew could bring his mother comfort. He'd taken away any chance of her finding hope.

"Did he hate me?" she asks Charlie. "Was there something I did? Did he tell you anything?"

"He loved you," Charlie says confidently. "I know he loved you."

She nods, as if slowly trying to convince herself that Wes could simultaneously commit suicide and love her.

"He loved you too, Charlie," she says.

"I know."

But he doesn't. Not completely anyway.

"Did you know he was struggling like that?" she asks.

There doesn't seem to be a right answer. If he had known, he should have done something more, and if he hadn't, he should have made a better effort to have known.

"I don't know."

"You don't know?"

"I'm sorry."

Sometimes, she forgets that he doesn't have answers to every little thing. Sometimes, she leans on him like a crutch, and he tries his hardest never to break around her, so that she'll never fall.

"Is Sarah almost here?" she asks.

"Yeah, she's coming."

"You two should be together. It's important in times like this."

He nods. The truth is, he's trying not to think—at all—about what he's going through.

"I'll meet you inside, okay?" Charlie stands up from the bench. He leans down to hug her before leaving. "We'll be okay. Try to remember that."

She grips his arm tightly, as if afraid that if she lets go, she might never see him again.

For as much as being at the funeral is itself a living nightmare, what really haunts Charlie is the phone call he'd gotten from Wes the night before he'd killed himself.

***

Charlie's ringing phone woke Sarah and him up, and Charlie stepped outside their bedroom.

Wes kept telling Charlie about how hard it was for him to go to bed at night. He couldn't fall asleep, he said, and when he did, he'd wake right back up thirty minutes later.

Charlie tried to think of the proper thing to say, but he could never quite find the right words. He just ended up responding, "Why do you think that is?"

"I keep seeing them."

"Seeing who?" Charlie asked.

"All the people I killed."

Charlie didn't know what to say to that. He ended up just telling him that it was all going to be okay, that they were going to be fine. They'd made it home.

Of course, that wasn't the truth. Charlie didn't feel like everything was going to be fine, but he thought Wes needed strength, so he tried to give him that.

The other end of the line went dead.

"Hello?" he said. "Wes, are you there?"

For the rest of the night, Charlie sat in bed and tried to convince himself that Wes's phone battery had just died, or that he'd accidently hung up and decided not to call back. He didn't want to face the fact that Wes had purposefully shut him out. Deep inside, Charlie knew that it was no accident. It was Wes's way of saying that Charlie didn't get it. He hadn't made it back at all.

That was the last conversation that Charlie and Wes ever had. Charlie would replay that conversation in his head thousands and thousands of times, wondering if he could have saved Wes if he'd said something different, if he'd offered to come over, or if he'd asked more questions. Those sorts of thoughts were useless though. Nothing was more permanent than the past. No matter how hard Charlie wished differently, he'd have to live with Wes's last words, *All the people I killed,* playing on a never-ending loop. *All the people I killed. All the people I killed. All the people I killed.*

Charlie never knew that Wesley himself would become another person to add to that list.

***

After Charlie leaves Natalie, but before going into the church, he walks away from everyone, toward the parking lot. He wants a moment to himself before the chaos. He closes his eyes and tries to breathe in as calmly as possible.

He pulls out a cigarette from his pocket. He hasn't smoked since high school.

At that moment, Sarah pulls into the church and parks the car. She hates it when he smokes, and she's blown up about it more times than he can remember. She nearly broke up with him when she caught him smoking at senior prom, but that was five years ago.

Now, the cigarette feels like the smallest of their concerns.

As Sarah waits in the car for a few more minutes, Charlie wonders why, but he doesn't think too hard about it. He tries to hide the cigarette when she approaches, but it's no use.

"I wish you wouldn't do that," Sarah says.

"I'm sorry. I won't smoke again."

"Not just the smoking," she says. "I wish you wouldn't hide anything from me."

He can tell that she's waiting for something, affirmation that they're a team, maybe.

"I'm sorry," he repeats.

She drops the subject. "Have you figured out what you're gonna say?"

He hangs his head and stares at the ground. "Not yet."

Wes's mom had asked Charlie to give the eulogy a few days earlier. She said she couldn't even think about it without breaking down.

He didn't even hesitate when asked. He'd do anything to help her.

Since then, though, he hadn't been able to sleep, and he can tell that it worries Sarah half to death. He'd sit at his desk and stare at a blank piece of paper, never attempting to write so much as a single word. Sometimes, late at night, he'd pull out a notepad from the desk drawer and begin to draw. He'd once drawn a portrait of Wes's face, whose eyes were filled with such deep pain. He drew the eyes of a man who couldn't stop thinking about all the people he'd killed. Around Wes's face, Charlie drew hand after hand, all stretched out. Wes's eyes just stared straight ahead, though. He didn't see all the hands.

Sometimes, Charlie wishes he could just raise that picture up in front of the church and let all the people stare at it until they understood. He wishes he could transform that picture into words so that he'd know what to say in the eulogy, but he can't, so he has no idea what to say at all.

He rubs his head, suddenly feeling exhausted, as if he's hung over.

"Headache?" Sarah asks.

He can tell that she hopes he'll say yes because his pain would then be physical, and she could run to the store and get him Advil or tell him to get some sleep.

"Yeah, something like that," Charlie replies.

She nods. "You'll know what to say when you stand up there."

He doesn't believe that, not fully anyway. He knows that she doesn't either, but he doesn't say anything.

"This was never supposed to happen," he says, and something about the obviousness of it makes his words unbearable. He feels uncomfortable and antsy, as if his own skin is the wrong size and he's trying to figure out how to adjust.

She reaches out to hold his hand, but their hands barely touch before they both pull back.

"I'm gonna go get ready," he says.

Sarah nods, and as Charlie passes her, she hands him a piece of gum.

"Thanks," he whispers. He kisses her cheek before leaving, then takes a few steps before turning back. "Hey, Sarah?"

"Yeah?"

"You know that I love you, right?"

The way that he says those words sounds nothing like how he used to say them when he was younger. He says the words as if they might be some tragic result of disillusionment, the way a child asks if Santa is actually real.

"Yeah, Charlie, of course I know that."

***

Charlie goes into the restroom to splash some water on his face and gather himself. He tries to think of something eloquent to say, something that will make Wes's mother feel like she'd picked the right person to honor her son's life, but all he can think of is the fact that his friend is dead, and that Wes had chosen to die. How could there be anything at all eloquent to say about such a thing.

He heads into a stall then, feeling as if he might throw up. He doesn't though, so he heads back out to the church.

Charlie's mom, dad, and sister wait for him in the lobby of the church.

He thanks them for coming.

His mom reaches up to touch his cheek. "I'm so sorry, Charlie."

She goes on to give him a speech about how terrible his situation is and how he has handled it so bravely. She tells him once again how much she always loved Wes and how it's a loss to the whole world to lose him.

Whenever Charlie's mom speaks, he only half-listens. She's a good person, always kind and gentle, but as Charlie grew up, she'd spent all of her time at work or traveling for business. Sometimes, when she came home from those trips, it felt as though she'd been gone for so long that he could no longer remember what it was like to be around her. He loves his mom but in a vague and generalized sort of a way. He couldn't tell you her favorite food or what sort of music she liked, and she couldn't tell you his favorite movie or what number he'd worn on the football field. Over the years, all those unknown facts and missed memories had lodged between them, creating a distance that neither could bridge. Because they didn't—and still don't—really know each other, whenever his mom tries to comfort him or advise him, Charlie feels only ambivalence, along with a twinge of anger.

His father hugs him but doesn't say anything at all. His father is quiet but close-minded, certain about what he believes. He believes that to kill yourself is an evil and selfish act that victimizes the people who love you the most. His father simply and deeply hates Wes for what he's done. If it were up to him, his dad wouldn't even have come to the funeral. He's incapable of understanding the complex blend of love and hate that Charlie has for Wes in the moment, and because of that, Charlie both envies and despises his father.

"Haley, can I talk to you for a moment, please?" Charlie asks.

His big sister, Haley, always knows what to do. Of those in his family, she's the one who really understands him.

Haley steps toward him, and his parents go to sit down.

"I have no idea what I'm gonna say in front of all of those people," he admits.

"Did you talk to Sarah?"

"She told me I'd figure it out."

"You will."

Charlie can feel his own body shaking.

"You're sweating," she says.

"I know."

Haley studies him for a few seconds. "Charlie, when's the last time you slept?"

He doesn't reply.

"You look exhausted," she says.

"You think I don't know that?"

"Don't speak to me like that."

"I'm sorry," he says, and takes a deep breath. "God, I'm so sorry. I haven't been feeling like myself, and—"

"It's all right." She reaches out to comfort him, but he pulls away, as if he knows he hasn't earned the comfort.

"Tell me what you're thinking of saying," she says.

"That's the thing... I can't think of anything to say at all. There's too much that I don't know, and I can't make sense of it. I don't know why he died."

"Stop. Charlie, breathe for a second."

He tries, but he can't.

"Listen to me," she continues. "This funeral isn't about you or what you know. It's not even about Wes, really. It's about all the people listening to you. Do you get it?"

He shakes his head no.

"Tell people what they want to hear. Every single person in this church feels upset and scared and lost, and all they want is for you to be the opposite. Be sure. Be optimistic. Be hopeful."

He looks away from her.

"If you can't feel that way in your heart, then fake it," she says. "It's not time to find all the answers, Charlie. It's time to console."

"I don't know if I can."

He sounds so tragically disappointed in himself.

"You can."

He takes a moment to stare into the church. It's a small, homey, traditional church with wooden pews and stained glass. He looks at the candles and the stations of the cross, and the people dressed in black, but most of all, he imagines what it'll feel like to stand up there at that podium.

"Okay," he replies, looking back to Haley to steal the bravery from her eyes.

***

In the middle of mass, when it comes time for Charlie to speak, he stands under the lights.

Wes's mom, Natalie, looks at him with admiration and faith.

His family sits next to Sarah in the third row. Charlie's mother looks sad, his father angry, Sarah worried, but Haley looks confident.

Inside, he feels like all four of them put into one.

He gives a speech about how we don't always get as much time as we'd like with the people we love. He tells stories about how some of the best moments of his life were with Wes, whether it was winning dodge ball at recess in the third grade or playing varsity football together. He talks about how Wes used to spoil his mother by buying her roses on Valentine's Day, and how he had lunch with her each Sunday afternoon. Wes was a great son. Charlie talks about how honorable and brave Wes had been when he decided to join the army, and Charlie says that he himself never would have enlisted too if it weren't for Wes's bravery. Wes challenged everyone around him to be better, and Charlie believed that he was a better man for knowing him.

That's the version of Wes that the people wanted to see—Wesley the friend, Wesley the son, Wesley the soldier, Wesley the hero.

That's not the version of Wes that Charlie truly remembers. In fact, he started carrying around a picture of Wes in his pocket in order to even remember his smile.

***

On the day Wes died, Charlie was supposed to show up to the church at 6:45 AM to meet him there. Charlie was never religious, but he didn't think anything of the invitation because Wes had always gone to church growing up, every single Sunday, and he used to invite Charlie all the time. Maybe Wes had figured out how to believe in something again.

He was wrong.

Charlie had arrived at 6:45 AM, not a second late, and Wes was already dead. He'd killed himself, and he'd wanted Charlie to find him like that.

Charlie had rushed to Wes's side, and he called 9-1-1. He tried to explain that there was an emergency because his friend was dying.

"Does he have a pulse?" the operator asked.

"I don't know."

"We're sending an ambulance."

"I don't know," Charlie repeated. "I don't know. I don't know."

"What don't you know? Sir? Sir, are you there?"

"I don't know."

He didn't know anything anymore because his best friend, whom he loved more than anything in the world, had shot himself, and Charlie was supposed to know if his friend had a pulse.

There was no pulse. Charlie knew that without checking. Too much blood. There would be no pulse.

He never checked, though. He didn't want to know — not for sure.

Instead, he sat over Wes's body, trying to ignore the fact that Wes's brains had gushed outside of his head. Charlie kept pressing on Wes's chest, over and over, as he cried and repeated, "Why?" — again and again. Charlie tried to resuscitate him because he wanted to believe that, somehow, he could bring back something lost, something he couldn't bear to lose.

A penny lay on the ground beside Wes's body, and Charlie never took his eyes off of it. He focused on that penny. He saw only the penny.

The ambulance arrived and the attendants pronounced Wesley Andrews dead. The sun hadn't even risen yet.

Chapter 2

"When are you gonna start sleeping again?" Sarah asks.

It's been three weeks since Wes's funeral.

"I do sleep."

"Don't give me that, Charlie."

Ever since he got home from Afghanistan, he's had trouble sleeping. There's something about the spinning of the ceiling fan that reminds him of a helicopter, but if he turns it off, the heat of the room reminds him of the desert. He's never free. Things have only gotten worse since Wes's death. These days, he can hardly sleep at all.

He turns away from Sarah and stares at the ceiling.

She says nothing more about sleep, and neither does he.

He adds *sleep* to the list of things they don't discuss—a list that gets longer and longer with each day that passes. They don't talk about the stack of bills on the kitchen counter, or the pack of cigarettes that he tries to hide in his sock drawer, or the penny that Charlie now keeps beside his bed.

One time, she tried to put the penny into their coin jar, but he freaked out, frantically begging her to put it back down, to never touch it again. His whole body shook, and she kept asking him what was wrong, not understanding what she'd done. In the end, she did put the coin back down but stared at him as if he were crazy. She didn't look entirely free of blame, though, and in the end, they *both* apologized. Charlie knew that Sarah had no idea what exactly she was apologizing for, but he could tell by the agony in her eyes that she still meant every *"I'm sorry."*

"You never talk to me anymore," she says. "It was fine at first, but...."

"But now I need to get over it?"

"God, no. Charlie, you know that's not what I meant." Her eyes hold her fear of hurting him and of being hurt by him.

He feels as if he's been thrown into the ocean and is drowning, without even attempting to yell for help. Sometimes he feels bad, as though making her walk around broken glass all the time. Then he feels like the broken glass. He wonders which is worse.

Sarah scoots closer to him, pulls her head off her pillow and rests it onto his, gently kissing his bare shoulder. She then wraps her arms around his chest.

"You're brave," she says, but her words don't feel like a compliment. She sounds sad.

"And that's a bad thing?"

"When you try to handle everything on your own, yes."

Sarah is a private girl. Tough too.

When Charlie first got home from the war, she wouldn't talk about what it was like without him. She pretended they weren't apart at all, as if he'd only gone away for a weekend trip—something casual and common. One night, as they were about to fall asleep, she finally whispered to him that sometimes, when he was gone, she would hold onto his pillow and try to remember the smell of his hair. She held onto whatever part of him she could.

"I just," Charlie says. "I don't want to talk about any of it."

"Then what do you want?"

"I don't know. To move on, I guess."

She takes a moment to think about this and nods. Then she kisses him, moving from his shoulder, to his neck, to his cheek, to his lips.

He kisses her too, but it's more reciprocation than anything meaningful.

She knows it too and stops. "How can we move on when you can't even kiss me?"

She takes her hands off of him, and they're apart.

They just lie in silence, waiting for the air conditioning to stir to life, or for their neighbors' muffled voices to seep through the thin walls, or for any noise at all.

"You know, you don't look at me the same way anymore," she says quietly. "It's like you don't even see me. You look at me like I'm transparent."

Many nights in Afghanistan, when fear started to overcome him, he would take out a picture of her and run his finger over it, again and again. The picture ended up with so many cracks and crinkles that her face was hardly recognizable to anyone but him. That picture always gave him strength. It gave him something to fight for. Sometimes he would think: *If I can just get home, everything will be fine.*

That seems like such a long time ago to him now. It feels like another life.

Sometimes at night, he catches her reading articles on studies of the psychological effects of trauma, and whenever he gets upset, she reassures him not to worry because whatever he feels is normal. She actually uses the word *normal*.

Sometimes Charlie wants to talk to her, but when he tries to put any thoughts together about Wes's death, to find the words, his mind goes blank. It's as if his mind is a computer with parental blocks designed to protect him.

"Are you still happy with me?" she asks.

He sits up in bed. "Why are you asking me that?"

"Why aren't you responding?"

"Because it's the dumbest question I've ever heard. Of course I'm happy with you."

She nods.

"Are you happy with me?" he asks.

"Yes."

She holds his gaze firmly though, as if to acknowledge that it's not a dumb question, as if to affirm that so much has happened lately that any kind of happiness is no longer a given.

"One day, everything will be like it was, won't it?" she asks.

"Yes. God, I'm sorry, Sarah. You know I'm sorry."

He pulls her close and looks at her, his eyes drooping with worry and shame, and her face starts to mirror his.

"I love you," she says, and lets her head sink to his chest. She falls asleep in his arms.

***

Charlie can't sleep though. He never can.

He did sleep once, the night after he'd found Wesley dead. He had this nightmare, which he can't even remember anymore, and he woke up to Sarah shaking him because he'd been crying in his sleep. He was dripping with sweat, and his guts felt as if they'd been ground into mush. He jumped out of bed, ran to the toilet, and threw up everything inside of him.

Sometimes, he thought his heart had liquefied and just poured out of him that night.

Every time Charlie closes his eyes now, he remembers Wes talking about how he could never sleep, and each time that memory pops into Charlie's head, he suddenly feels wide awake. He doesn't know exactly why, but maybe staying awake is the only way he can feel close to Wes anymore. Maybe it's his way of keeping Wes alive. It sounds dumb to him, but that doesn't seem to matter, for some reason. The point is: he doesn't sleep.

Charlie waits in bed for an hour or so, just holding Sarah in his arms, like he always does. Some nights, he decides to draw something, usually something as simple as the ceiling fan, or Sarah's face while she sleeps. Other times, he draws Wes. Tonight, he doesn't draw at all. He can't find the energy.

After enough time has passed, he untangles himself from Sarah, gets dressed, and grabs the pack of cigarettes from his sock drawer. Then, being careful not to wake her up, he slides out of the bedroom.

As soon as he gets outside, he lights the cigarette.

One thing he's always liked about living in Houston is that the city has just the right amount of noise. It's never *too* quiet, such that all he can hear are his own thoughts, but there isn't so much chaos that his instincts make him feel as though he's under attack. Being on those streets always keeps him busy. He likes to watch the passing cars and imagine the lives of the people inside, and he likes to record the amount of time it takes him each night to walk to the bar. He does these things to keep his mind active. He does these things because he prefers them to staying awake at night, alone with his thoughts, watching the ceiling fan spin around and around and around, like a globe.

It takes him eleven minutes and thirty-seven seconds to get to the bar tonight—a new personal best. He decides to drink a little extra to celebrate.

He doesn't speak to anyone at the bar. Some girls come up to him, twirling their hair, smiling, asking him questions, but he doesn't pay them any attention. They leave offended, as if their looks entitled them to something, but he hardly even notices. He just asks for drink after drink.

At one point, someone drops a glass, and the shattering startles him. He jumps out of his chair, and the people around him stare at him as if he's crazy. It takes Charlie a minute to feel safe again. He even looks at his clothes, making sure he doesn't have on a uniform, making sure he hasn't suddenly been planted in the war again. He has to close his eyes for a second to clear his head, to keep himself from reliving what it felt like to be holding a gun, surrounded by dust and sand. He doesn't look at anyone because he knows they'll be staring, that they won't understand.

He orders another drink.

Usually, Sarah is around when sounds remind him of Afghanistan, of the fear that surprises can bring. She always reaches out gently, puts her arm around him, and whispers, *"Everything is fine."* A part of him loves that and appreciates her kindness and understanding, but another part of him despises it. It makes him feel like a child. He hates that he needs comforting at all.

One hour later, the bartender cuts him off, saying that he doesn't look so good and should get some rest. It's the second time this week that Charlie's been asked to leave the bar.

He sits outside, letting the world spin around and around and around, like a ceiling fan.

It takes him a while to see clearly enough to use his phone. Finally, he dials his sister Haley's number.

"Hello."

"Did I wake you?" Charlie asks.

There's a pause on the other end of the line.

"Of course you woke me, Charlie. It's 1:25 AM."

He doesn't say anything.

"You need me to come get you again, don't you?"

"I can take a cab," he says.

He doesn't have the money for that, though. Usually, a taxi ride wouldn't be a problem, but he's already spent so much on drinks that anything else would just make the stack of bills even larger. He's messing up. He shouldn't spend money on drinks, but he can't seem to help it.

"No, no," Haley says. "I'm coming."

***

From the time they were young, Haley loved him fiercely. Charlie's parents had told him stories about how when Haley was five years old, she used to pray at night that her baby dolls would come to life, and she'd wake up disappointed each morning when she looked next to her just to find an inanimate stuffed toy.

Then, one day, their mom woke her up for school and said, "Haley, guess what? You're going to have a little brother."

"You were the answer to all of her prayers," his mom used to tell him. "You could do no wrong in her eyes. You'd cry at night, and we thought your sister would be upset with you, but she never was. She was only worried. Nothing brought her more pain than your crying."

As they grew, she made his lunch, walked him to school, tied his shoes, and played with him outside for hours every single day. The joke in their family was that Haley did more to take care of little Charlie than his mom did, although it was more truth than joke. Haley did everything she possibly could for him.

In return, Charlie loved her back in the same way.

He hates asking for her help, knowing he's taking advantage of her unconditional support, but he doesn't have many other choices, and the truth is, deep down, he knows that Haley will never mind.

***

Haley picks him up, and they don't say anything for the entire ride back to his apartment.

When they get there, she puts the car in park, but Charlie doesn't get out. There's no way in hell Haley will let him leave without talking about it. He waits for her to calm down enough to speak.

"You can't keep doing this," she says.

"I know."

"You keep saying you know, but you keep doing this, so you must be lying to me. Are you lying to me, Charlie?"

There doesn't seem to be a right answer to that.

Silence again.

Charlie is now coherent enough that he's aware of his words and his actions. He's coherent enough to be embarrassed and to know that he owes his sister an explanation.

"I just... I feel like Wes took my life too," he says.

"I'm sorry, Charlie."

He can tell she really means it.

"There's no need to be sorry. The last thing I want is anyone to feel sorry for me. Really."

"I still do."

Neither of them looks at each other.

"I've tried calling you," Haley says. "Have you gotten my messages?"

"Yeah, I'm sorry for not answering. Things have—"

"Don't try to tell me that you've been busy. You've never been too busy for me. Never."

"You're right."

"Then why don't you return my calls?" She keeps her voice soft but demanding. "Cut the bullshit and give me a real answer."

He understands that she needs an answer from him as much as she needs oxygen. He feels guilty all over again, in part because of the way her body tenses when she sees that he's in pain. He wishes he could be okay again, just to end her vicarious suffering.

"You keep calling me," he says, "and asking me to come over to your house for dinner, and I don't wanna go because Anna will be there."

"What? You love Anna!"

"Yeah, I do."

He often feels as if Anna is an extension of himself, as if, without her, he's missing a limb or something. He loves his niece like a daughter.

Haley doesn't understand why that's a problem.

"She's just a kid," Charlie continues, "and I don't know how to explain any of this to a little girl."

"She misses you, you know."

Charlie knows that Anna doesn't really miss who he is; she misses the man he was. Kids know if you're not happy. They're the world's best lie detectors. If he were to see her, she'd look at him with disappointment when he couldn't enthusiastically play games with her like he once did. That would break him.

"Anna got asked to do a presentation at school on her hero," Haley says.

Charlie looks back, not understanding what that has to do with anything.

"She picked you."

He feels his stomach turning, but he doesn't show it. Instead, he just looks back at her.

"She asks me why you don't come to visit anymore. She thinks she did something wrong. Do you get how sad that is, Charlie? She's a five-year-old girl that thinks she let you down."

"She could never do anything wrong."

"She doesn't know that."

He can't think of what to say at first, so he looks out the window and struggles to gather his thoughts.

"I can't explain it," he replies. He feels like a villain, but the idea of seeing her, looking into her eyes, and knowing that he isn't the same uncle, would kill him. "I just can't see her."

Haley stares into his eyes long enough to see that he doesn't have anything left to say, that he's told her everything, and says, "Okay."

Charlie nods.

Between them is a mixture of simultaneous understanding and confusion. Haley can sometimes feel his emotions just by looking into his eyes, and even when he can't articulate what he's thinking, she somehow knows. Often, she can't articulate it either, though.

"Is everything okay with you and Sarah?" Haley asks.

"Yeah, why?"

"You just seem... I don't know. I guess you just seem a little lonely."

Charlie won't look her in the eyes. "Well, I'm not," he says, speaking sincerely and gently.

"Do you love her still?"

He says nothing for a moment, then says, "Of course, I love her."

Haley looks away from him. "Charlie, I know that you're a good guy, the kind of guy who will stay by anyone, through anything. You always have been. You always care so much about everyone else."

He takes a moment to himself, as if trying to reconcile her words with her tone.

"Sarah's the same way," she adds.

"You make that sound like an insult."

"It's not an insult."

"Then what is it?"

"A warning, I guess."

Charlie nods, not fully knowing what to make of that.

"She's a smart girl. She's so smart," Haley says. "You know that, right?"

"Of course I do."

"You can't ever hide what you're feeling from her."

"I'm not hiding anything. What do you think I'm hiding?"

"I don't know, but something," she says. "Otherwise, you wouldn't look so lonely."

"I already told you, I'm not lonely."

After a few moments of Haley's silence, he undoes his seatbelt and gets out of the car. He closes the car door and thanks her for the ride, promising her that none of this will happen again. He turns to walk to his apartment, but Haley rolls down the window.

"Charlie!"

He turns around to hear her final words.

"I really am sorry."

"For what?"

"I'm sorry that nothing feels simple to you anymore."

***

Things haven't been simple in a long time.

About six weeks ago, a week and a half before Wes died, Charlie asked Sarah to come home from medical school by 6:00 PM so they could eat dinner together. She said she would, and when dinnertime came, as he waited for her, he turned the lights off and lit all the candles on the dining table. He made them spaghetti, like they used to eat when they first moved in together and neither of them could cook a thing.

He was going to ask her to marry him. He was ready. He had the ring on the table and everything.

But she didn't come home on time, so he called her, and she said she'd gotten so caught up in studying that she forgot. It just slipped her mind. She asked if they could do dinner the next day instead.

He blew out all the candles, put the spaghetti in the fridge, and went back to their bedroom to wait to tell her goodnight. He waited as long as he could, but his eyelids got too heavy, and when he woke up in the morning, she was already gone again.

The next night, she asked why there was candle wax on the counter. He said he didn't know, and he scrubbed it all off. Nothing more ever came of it.

Sometimes, he could hear Wes's voice in his head saying, "You're lucky, you know. She's everything you'll ever need."

Wes would always grin when he saw Charlie and Sarah, with his big, effortless, million-dollar smile that made everyone love him. That smile was Wes's greatest tool for convincing everyone that he could see some hidden gem in the world that they too should see, and if they were lucky, they could experience the unyielding joy that radiated from his face.

Sometimes, the fact that Wes thought that Charlie and Sarah should be together made Charlie want to fall to his knee immediately, ask her to marry him right then and there, and not waste a single more second away from someone who could be his destiny. Other times, when angry, he thought of all the promises Wes broke, about how Wes just let his own destiny fall apart, like his time with Charlie meant nothing. He trusted Wes's opinion more than anyone's in the world, but he also stopped trusting him at all, and he could never figure out how both those things were true, but they were.

Chapter 3

The next day, Charlie drives to the park to meet Wes's mom.

They meet at the park on Sunday mornings at 9:00 AM. She goes to the park now instead of to church.

Charlie arrives late, after pulling over three times on the way there to catch his breath. He'd woken up with a migraine, and it had only gotten worse with time. He thought about canceling on her, calling to say he was sick, or that Sarah needed his help with something. Anything. Groceries, even. She would have understood that. Charlie is like her son, and mothers understand their sons.

Charlie shows up, though—fifteen minutes late, but he's there.

When Natalie sees him, a smile spreads across her face, as if he somehow holds her entire world. This look of hers always brings him such deep joy and such deep pain.

"I got worried you might not come," she says as she hugs him.

"I'll always come."

Somehow, despite the fear in his heart, despite all the pain, and despite pulling over three times on the way there, he's still sure that those words are sincere.

They sit down on the park bench and remain silent for a while.

"I went back to the church for the first time since the funeral," she says.

"You did?"

"Yeah, this morning."

She doesn't say anything else for a moment, and he doesn't pry. He waits for her to continue.

"Father Dave came to sit with me."

Father Dave is a young priest, only about thirty years old. He's the one who ran Wes's funeral. Right after Wes's death, Charlie had asked him if he'd ever done a funeral for someone who'd killed himself before. He hadn't.

"He talked with me," Natalie continues.

"That's nice."

"No, it wasn't. I asked him if he thought my son was in hell."

Charlie knows little about the Catholic Church —just what he's picked up from Wes and his mom. But even he understands that any Catholic text would say that to kill yourself is a mortal sin. Sometimes, he imagines how much pain that must bring Natalie. She didn't even know that her son was suffering on this earth, yet now her own religion is telling her that Wes, her son, her flesh and blood, is off in some unknown place, suffering for his sins. Nothing could be more painful than that.

"He told me those are questions only God can answer," she says with disdain. "I could see it in his eyes, Charlie. I could see in his eyes that he really believes that my son, my beautiful little boy, is off somewhere, suffering. And I just... I couldn't forgive him for that. Who looks at a mother that way? I'm his mom, Charlie. What sort of a man makes a mother *feel* like that?"

"You don't have to go back there," Charlie says.

Two little boys, both bright blond, take turns going down the slide and racing each other back up to the top to do it again.

Natalie isn't watching the children, though. Instead, she stares at the bright-red monkey bars. No one is there. She's staring at a ghost. "The monkey bars were always Wes's favorite. Have I told you that?"

She has told Charlie that every Sunday, but he doesn't admit it. He's afraid it might hurt her, and he doesn't mind hearing it again.

"He could hold himself on those bars for minutes at a time," she continues. "I remember the first time he tried them, he was only four, and I was just so worried that he would fall. I stood right underneath him the whole time, making sure that if he ever fell, I'd be right there to catch him."

Charlie hasn't heard this story before. There's a new one every time.

"I remember he told me he'd be fine, that I could leave him alone and he'd make it. Sure enough, he got all the way across without an ounce of help."

"He never did want any help, did he?" Charlie says.

"He sure didn't."

"Stubborn as hell."

"I loved that about him," Natalie says.

"Yeah, but I hated it too."

"Funny how that works, isn't it?"

They turn to each other and smile.

Sometimes, Charlie hates being around her because he has to hold the weight of the pain she carries, but this isn't one of those moments. This is one of the times when it feels like they're sharing the weight together. Wes's mom might be the only person in the world who can ever understand what it felt like to lose him. She's the only one who loved Wes as much as he did.

***

Wes was his mother's entire world. He used to tell Charlie stories about her.

In high school, mid-way through her senior year, Natalie Andrews found out she was pregnant. She decided to keep the baby before telling the father anything. She could take care of a kid on her own, with or without any help — she was sure about that.

Wes's dad had offered to marry Natalie, but he was just an eighteen-year-old kid who couldn't understand that babies cry all the time, and it's hard to do homework or go to basketball practice with a crying baby. Within two months of Wes's birth, he left them after putting a note on their refrigerator:

I'm sorry I wasn't stronger.

Natalie never held it against him, though. She never even seemed to mind, never hated him, or judged him, or told him that he'd failed as a father. Years later, when she told Wes about how his father had left, Wes was furious and called his father a coward.

"Lots of people are cowards, son," Natalie had told him. "That doesn't mean he's a bad person."

She always had so much understanding. Anyone who met Natalie would swear on their life that the only emotion they ever saw in her eyes was love.

"Do you think your dad will ever come back?" Charlie had once asked Wes.

"And say what? 'I'm sorry that I loved myself more than I loved you?' You can't just *say* a thing like that."

He did come back, though, twenty-two years later. He came back for Wes's wake.

Charlie noticed him because he was standing in front of the casket for longer than anyone else, unmoving. Natalie then told Charlie who he was.

Wes's father had wept over the body, but he wasn't really crying for Wes. He cried for himself. Everyone else in that church missed Wes, feeling the pain of the realization that Wes would forever be only a figment of the past, but to his father, that's all Wes ever was. He was mourning the lack of memories, weeping for the generalized, unspecific pain in his chest. He cried and cried, the way that Wes had once cried in his arms as a child.

***

"Tell me another story about him," Charlie says to Natalie. Sometimes, the most painful part of losing Wes has nothing to do with what he can remember losing. The pain is in all the memories that he can't recall at all, the moments that disappear into thin air, never to be remembered again.

"What kind of story?"

"Anything."

"Did I ever tell you about the time Wes went hunting?"

Charlie shakes his head.

"Well, since Wes never had much of a father, I thought he should do something boyish, something manly. I never wanted him to miss out on anything that I couldn't give him, so I asked my friend Xavier to take him hunting."

The only time her eyes look full and satisfied anymore is when she speaks about Wes. Whenever she stops talking, the light in her eyes disappears.

"Wes was about five years old, and he was so excited. We went to buy him a camouflage shirt, a sleeping bag, and a tent. I swear, I got him everything he wanted. I spent more money than I did most Christmases. It was a whole two weeks' worth of wages, but if you could have just seen his face... it was worth it. I'd never seen him so happy."

"That sounds like a great trip."

"That's the thing, though. It wasn't. Xavier brought him back two days early, and when I asked what had happened, Xavier said, 'I don't know. I'm so sorry. I don't know why he's so upset, but he's just so... quiet.' See, when Wes came back, he was sad—deeply, deeply sad. I couldn't get him to talk to me about it at all. He was mute. I had no idea what to do. I'd never seen such a silent kid in my life."

She starts speaking more and more slowly, as if trying to solve some sort of riddle along the way. "Anyway, finally, I begged him to tell me what was wrong. I was so worried. I think he could see that worry on my face, because he finally told me. He said, 'I watched the animals die, Mommy. I made them stop breathing.'"

Wes's mom stares up into the sky as if Wes might be there somewhere. "Tell me, how's that the same person who signs up to join the army? How's that the same boy who shoots himself?"

Charlie suddenly wishes that he hadn't asked for another story, because he doesn't know what there is to say about that. He has no responses.

"I don't know," he says. It's the only thing he can think to say, the only honest answer. "He wanted to serve his country."

She looks away from him as if he just tried to fool her. "We both know that's not it. That can't be it."

"What do you mean?"

"My son barely used to look at the flag during the national anthem. He used to get in trouble in lower school for talking during the pledge of allegiance each morning. He was grateful for his freedom, but in an obscure, removed sort of way. My son wouldn't be willing to die for his country. Wes wouldn't be willing to *kill* for his country either."

***

Charlie knows that people join the army for all sorts of reasons. Some people grow up in bad neighborhoods, where they learn how to fight instead of read, and they join because it gives them a way to succeed with their skillset. Some want an education more than anything, so they get the army to help write their college check. Some men are angry and want an excuse to kill, and others would give anything not to kill but get talked into it by their family or loved ones. Some want the glory, the respect, the honor of it all. Some do it because they love America more than anything, and they want to stand up for what they believe in. Most people's truths are not that simple, though. Most people fit into multiple categories or none at all.

Charlie tries to remember the day that Wes told him he was going to enlist.

Wes was always extremely passionate, always moving toward some goal at a million miles per hour. He never abandoned any of his dreams. He'd die before he failed at something.

The first time Wes brought up joining the army, it was in a crowded, loud cafeteria, which made it hard for Charlie to hear everything that Wes was saying as he showed him the brochure. Charlie felt somewhat grateful for the noise, though. It filled the silence, making it less looming and scary.

"Aren't you afraid?" Charlie asked him.

They were seniors in high school, still so young.

"Afraid of what?" Wes replied.

"Of dying."

"Of course, but that's why I have to go, Charlie. All the good things in life are dangerous. That's how you know they're powerful."

All of Wes's dreams were contagious. He had this way of romanticizing anything: glory, hope, war, death. Wes managed to create beauty in abstract concepts, and somehow he could mask the dark side of anything, or at least make it seem trivial. He talked about war the way you would talk about the birth of a baby; he talked of it as if it were something new that was waiting to meet him.

"Don't join," Charlie had begged. "It'll be horrible. It really will be."

"Come with me," Wes said.

Until that moment, they had just been two eighteen-year-old boys, sitting in the cafeteria, eating their third piece of pizza and dreading their upcoming chemistry test.

"I just... I have to know," Wes said. "I have to know if I'm really brave or if I'm just someone who pretends to be."

The idea of joining the army began to haunt Charlie. He would think about it all the time, even when he didn't want to. He thought about it when the teacher was talking, while running, during tests, while drawing, at a family dinner, while kissing Sarah. He couldn't shake it.

***

Wes's mom rests her head against Charlie's shoulder, and he can feel the exhaustion in her body. He knows that, more than anything, she just wants to find enough peace to rest, but there's no way to do that when her world is in such disarray.

"You know, I never wanted to enlist," Charlie says. "It never even crossed my mind. But then, one day, as Wes and I were walking home, he stopped at the front of the school and looked up at the American flag that flew up high, above everything. He didn't stop for long, and he didn't say anything at all, but you should have seen the way he looked at this flag—the same way that you looked at him. He looked at that flag like it was his entire identity. When he turned back to me, he was smiling to himself. That was the moment I told him I'd enlist."

Wes's mom doesn't seem to know what to say to that story.

"I don't know what it was that made him look at that flag like that. I don't know if it was pride or patriotism or belief, but I know that I've never in my life seen anyone who looked so content. I would die to have that look in my eyes. I would kill for it too, and I don't know what that says about me, exactly, but it's true."

Wes's mom isn't looking at Charlie anymore, but finally she whispers, "From the moment he decided to join to the minute he left, he was always so sure it was his path, wasn't he?"

"Yeah, he was."

"Why was he so sure?"

"I don't know."

"But it brought him peace, didn't it?"

"Yeah, it did."

"Do you think he's found peace now?"

"I hope so."

Charlie puts his arm around her, and she leans into his chest.

"Why do you think Meghan didn't come to the funeral?" she asks.

"Meghan?"

Charlie takes a minute to himself, trying to think if that's a name he should know. He can tell from her voice that it is.

"He never told you about her?" she asks.

Somehow, this makes Charlie feel betrayed. He feels weighed down by all the things he didn't know about his friend, things he might never know. There's no point in admitting this, though, so he plays it off.

"I don't know why she didn't come," he says.

"Did they break up? Did he ever tell you anything?"

"I don't know."

With that response, he answers both questions. Part of him wonders if Wes did mention her, if he's just forgotten somehow or wasn't paying attention when Wes talked about her.

"He was so in love with her," Natalie says. "I just... I don't know what happened."

Charlie says nothing.

"It's the lack of knowing that kills me," she says. "I just don't understand when he became so miserable. When did I lose my son?"

She stares emptily at the children who swing back and forth, pushing each other and laughing.

"Will you find out?" she asks.

"Find out?"

"Will you figure out why he died?"

She has this way of looking at him with such belief, as if he's capable of knowing what only God does.

Charlie wants to say, "*I can't.*" He wants to explain that he's not able to do such a thing, but he can see the desperation in her eyes, and the belief that he holds the way to some indescribable truth. She looks at him as if he's the medicine to cure her shredded heart.

Without even thinking, he hears himself whisper, "I'll try."

She leans over and rests her head on his shoulder, and for the first time, he can feel her take deep breaths, in and out.

"You're a good man, Charlie," she says.

Chapter 4

After getting back from Afghanistan, all Charlie wanted was to escape from his pain, a chance to feel like a normal man. In high school, he'd enrolled in courses to earn his certification as a mechanic, so when he got home, he got a job at a shop that was shorthanded. It was a good way to make some money, using his hands, doing tough, physical work. He liked the idea of fixing things, the idea of creating and rebuilding. It felt rehabilitating after so much in his life had been destroyed.

Charlie's always the first one there in the morning. He likes to work in the peace, the isolation, before everyone else comes in. Sometimes, his moments alone are when he feels the most like the man he used to be.

He never told anyone in the shop about Wes. Even the day after Wes's death, he showed up, went to work, and said nothing. No one knew; he liked it that way. He liked how the guys would sit down and talk to him about things that didn't matter. It made him feel like himself again, as if things were normal.

"Good morning, strangers!" TJ, one of his co-workers, calls as he walks into work five minutes late. He has a loud, booming voice that echoes off the walls, and everyone turns to look at him smiling, before they return to their task.

TJ jogs to one of the cars and slides across the hood, grinning from ear to ear as he flies off. A six-foot-tall African American man from downtown Houston, TJ has a way of making Charlie feel young again. Everyone who meets TJ reaches the conclusion that the world is a better place just because he's in it. TJ's presence makes it easier for Charlie to be happy. He's Charlie's favorite part of going to work.

"You wouldn't believe my weekend," TJ says as he walks up to Charlie. "You just wouldn't believe it."

"You look like you won the lottery."

"Oh, I feel like it." TJ rubs his hands together as if the energy in his words needs a kinetic outlet.

"All right, let's hear the story." Charlie stops working on the car engine and turns to TJ as he wipes the grease off his hand.

"Okay," TJ says as he sits down on the hood. "So it's a typical Saturday night, right, and I'm being my lame-ass self getting groceries when I should be at a bar, but I ran out of milk, okay? So I'm walking through the aisles, and I see this girl—"

"Oh God." Charlie laughs.

"What are you getting all bent outta shape for? Just listen!"

When TJ talks, everyone pays attention. The smile never leaves his face. He has a way of telling stories as if each word would be the last he ever spoke.

"So I'm walking down the aisles, and I see this beautiful, stunning girl in the baking section, so I think to myself, yeah, I could use some cake mix."

The other guys start teasing him, but he laughs it off, his enthusiasm only growing.

"So I walk right up to her, and then I realize I haven't even thought about what to say, so I put some cake mix in my cart and walk away."

"Smooth," someone yells from the other side of the shop.

"Okay, okay, not my best work, *but* you can't be on your A-game all the time, right? Anyway, I was walking through the store getting my milk and eggs, but of course, I was distracted still."

Charlie smiles. Everyone has stopped what they're doing to listen. They're not even aware of the way he draws them in. It just happens.

"So I'm walking around the store trying to find her, and it turns out she's still in the baking aisle, so I walk down the aisle *again*. She turns and sees me, and I thought I had something clever to say, but I can't come up with anything, so I just grab another box of cake mix. I'm thinking I'm done for, I've got no chance, when she turns to me and says, 'You know gluttony is a sin, right?'"

TJ is so excited that he can barely get the story out.

"And I say to her, 'If that's the greatest of my sins, I'm not doing half bad.' And she laughs. So we start talking, and it turns out this girl is perfect. Way outta my league! I mean, you should just meet this girl! She's confident, and funny, and so goddamn fine. Also, get this. Are you ready?"

"Ready."

"Loves sports. I mean, she really, actually likes them, not just in that '*Oh I guess I'll watch the Superbowl for the commercials*' type of way. I mean, she knows all the stats, and she actually argued with me about who the MVP of the NBA should have been. Can you believe that?"

"Sounds like a great day," Charlie says.

"And then," TJ practically yells, his voice building to a crescendo with each added detail. "She says to me, 'I have some tickets to the Texans game tomorrow. Do you want to come with me?'"

He pauses and looks around, studying his co-workers' faces, searching for someone with the proper level of excitement.

"Where's your enthusiasm?" he complains. "Did no one hear me? The world's prettiest girl asked me if I wanted to go on a date to the Texans game!"

He's so excited by his own words that Charlie appears as if he won't make it through his own story without running out of energy and collapsing.

"All I'm saying," TJ adds, "is that I don't care what happens to me for the rest of my life. This weekend I learned that there is, without a doubt, a good, fair God watching over all of us."

TJ isn't always the most reliable worker, and he runs late most days, but he has an overwhelming charisma that makes people universally blind to his shortcomings. Of course, this is never something he consciously tries to exploit. His raw, intrinsic enthusiasm makes him a joy to be around.

Of all the things Charlie likes about TJ, what he appreciates most is that TJ never asks too many questions. He has an acute ability to read people, to know when things are wrong, yet he never says anything about it. He doesn't mind when Charlie needs time to himself, time to just listen, time to relax.

"Hey, Magician, Einstein, come take a look at this," says Eric, one of the older guys working at the shop. He's perpetually angry, as if he's unhappy with the way his life has turned out.

TJ and Charlie walk over and examine the engine. Even though they're the two youngest guys, both twenty-three, they were born with the innate ability to know what's wrong with cars. TJ understands engines the way he understands people, with some inexplicable ability to look at them and know everything without even trying. People ask TJ all the time to explain how he fixes things, but he can never put it into words.

"I just look at it and know how it works," he'd say.

The guys at the shop started calling him the magician.

This sort of gift never makes any sense to Charlie, although he admires it. Charlie, while equally effective, sees things in an incredibly scientific manner. He's always looking to learn anything that can help the world make more sense. He has no trouble explaining what he's doing, even if very few people in the shop know what the hell he's talking about.

"I'll get this one," TJ says, as they study the engine. Although the two of them are good friends, they can't work together. TJ follows his gut, Charlie follows his head, and because of that, they never quite understand each other.

"You sure?"

"I gotta keep busy or my excitement is gonna drive you people insane by the end of the day. Gotta wear myself out a little!"

***

Charlie spends most of his day doing standard oil changes, tire rotations, inspections — nothing out of the ordinary.

After Charlie first got back home, everything reminded him of Afghanistan, but at the same time, nothing did. In Afghanistan, he'd learned what it felt like to be worried a hundred percent of the time. He was so deeply afraid, but he never said a word. He handled his emotions with courage and poise. It was just his nature. He looked braver than he felt.

When he got home, he found himself checking over his shoulder all the time, never able to relax. Every startling noise — the backfiring of a car, the sudden crying of a baby, or even an unexpected laugh — made him jump. *Everything* scared him. The only thing scarier than death in a war zone was the anticipation of the boredom that would come after the war. When he got home, Charlie started to mistake peace and calm for boredom, and the boredom made him afraid, made him restless.

He liked his job because it gave him an escape from both boredom and excitement. His days, repetitive yet engaging, meant he didn't have to think too much or too little.

"What do you say, wanna take a lunch break?" TJ asks him.

Charlie checks his watch. It's half past one, later than they usually eat, so he washes his hands and grabs his food.

***

Before Charlie got back from Afghanistan, he'd applied to Rice's engineering program and was accepted. However, when he got home, he didn't want to go.

His dad never understood when Charlie told him that he needed more time off school. He still remembers his father saying, *"You just took four years off school, son. Isn't that enough time to get yourself sorted out?"* Charlie always hated his dad for saying that.

His mom wrote a letter to Rice, explaining that he'd apply again in the future, but that he just wasn't ready to go to college yet. She really played up his commitment to his country, expressing how he just needed some time to collect himself.

"You *will* go back to school, won't you?" she'd asked him.

"Yes, Mom, I will. I just can't yet."

The dean of admissions wrote back to Charlie saying that Rice welcomed him to apply again in the future. He applied again this fall.

Some of the guys in the shop don't like that; Charlie can see it in their eyes. They feel as if Charlie is taking a pit stop in the place where they'll spend the rest of their lives. Although Charlie never acts superior, they see that fixing cars will never be his entire future, and some people, like Eric, can't get over it. Some of the other guys think it's cool, and they look up to him because of his intelligence. Either way, whether it's hatred or admiration, Charlie feels outcast at times. He never feels that way with TJ, though. TJ really understands him.

"I think the inventor of Doritos might be my life hero," TJ says as he opens up his lunch.

"You set some high standards."

"All anyone ever wants is a little flavor in their life, am I right?"

Charlie smiles. "You're always right, TJ."

***

After work on Monday, Charlie goes to his art class. He just started going a few weeks ago, after Sarah had enrolled him in it.

"You should do something you like," she'd said. "Something for yourself."

"Are you sure?"

"Of course."

The truth is, with Sarah in medical school and Charlie saving up for college, they don't have much money. Neither of them wants to ask their parents for anything. Sarah loves her parents to death, but they were never able to provide her with much. Her mom works as a secretary and her father teaches fifth-grade science at a small public middle school. She has four siblings, and her parents struggle to make ends meet. She never wanted to be a burden to them, so she took out student loans as soon as she entered college. Charlie's parents offered to pay for everything for him, but he never liked that either. He wants to make something of himself, all on his own, and even though some people don't understand that, he can't change the way he feels.

The class takes place at Art League Houston, where anyone is welcome to enroll. There are people of all ages, although most are in their early thirties. On the first day, the teacher asked all the students what they wanted to get out of the class. The answers ranged from thinking it sounded fun to wanting to pursue a career in art.

"Do you want to be an artist?" the teacher asked Charlie.

"Oh no, no," Charlie replied. "Nothing like that. I just enjoy it."

Ever since high school, he'd always liked drawing, and he was good at it. He found it calmed him in a way that nothing else did. It provided him a valuable way to withdraw into himself, to find some kind of inner peace. It allowed him to feel connected to the intangible mysteries of the world, like Wes's death and the war, in a way that science and engineering never could.

He always arrives at class early. He did so in high school as well, and middle school, and preschool. His mom used to tell him stories about how he'd cry in kindergarten when they were running late.

"You always wanted to be perfect at what you did," she'd say. "You wanted to be the best."

He still feels that way, but it's different now, less conscious and more habitual. He can't help but show up early, as if he's trapped within himself.

Every week, there's a new assignment written on the board, a new theme. This week, the board reads:

Draw your secret.

Most of the time, Charlie doesn't struggle to think of something to draw. His work is usually decent, above average in the class. He can never create pieces that are quite as abstract as some of the other students, but his drawings are precise and detailed.

Today, he stares at the blank page in front of him as if the picture will draw itself, if he just waits long enough.

He looks around at other people in the class, who don't seem to be struggling at all. Their heads all remain focused, none of them looking up. He feels jealous and slightly angry, although he doesn't really know why he's upset.

"Is that supposed to be abstract?"

Charlie looks up to see the girl next to him staring at his blank piece of paper. "Would you believe me if I said yes?"

"Not a chance," she replies.

He smiles.

She's a pretty girl, with short brownish-red hair that cuts off right under her ears. She has dark brown eyes that ooze sophistication and confidence.

"Don't tell me you're one of those people," she says.

"What do you mean?"

"The kind of person who says they have no secrets."

She has a way of looking through him that makes him feel as if she can see the inside of him, straight under his skin to his bones.

"No, no," he says. "That's not me. I think I'm kind of the opposite."

"The opposite?"

"I have too many secrets. I can't pick."

She'd been playing around with her pencil, but as soon as he says that, she stops and looks even deeper, as if she can see all his secrets if she just stares long enough.

"What's your name?" she asks.

"Charlie."

"I'll make you a deal, Charlie."

"I don't think—"

"I'll show you what I drew, and you tell me a secret—just one of them."

He stares back at her for a second. "Why do you care?"

"Why do I care?" She laughs. "Why do I care about what?"

"About my secrets?"

"Because I'm clearly nosey, can't you tell?" she jokes. "Plus, I'm an artist, and isn't that all art is? A bunch of people's secrets?"

He doesn't answer her question because he doesn't know what to say. He's never thought of it like that, and he's not sure if he believes it or not.

"I don't think that deal works for me," he says.

"Why not?"

"Because I'm not nosey."

"You don't care about my secrets?"

"I don't... I don't know."

"It's my greatest secret."

"But I don't know you."

"You could. One look at this picture, and you could know me."

Charlie stares back at her, slightly confused and slightly intrigued. He smiles, wanting to point out some flaw in her logic, which he knows is there, yet it's hiding under layer upon layer of her certainty.

"I don't know about that," he finally says.

He turns away from her, going back to his blank piece of paper. He says nothing to her for a while, and she turns back to her own work, covering it so he can't see when he tries to peek. He does try.

"Not nosey, huh?" she says, and grins.

"Okay, fine," he says. "I'll accept your deal."

They're sitting in the back of class, whispering so they don't interrupt the other people. It takes him a while to start, as if he's standing at the top of a diving board waiting to jump.

"When I was little," he says, "I really, really wanted to be a rocket scientist. I never really outgrew that dream."

She doesn't seem to get that. "You still want to be a rocket scientist?"

"Yeah, it's what I always wanted. I took all these advanced math and science classes in high school, and I applied to all these engineering programs. I just really want to send something into space."

"Why?"

"What do you mean?"

"I mean, why did you want that? Of all things, why that?"

No one's ever asked him that before. It takes him a while to think about it. "It's just a beautiful idea to me, you know?"

He likes the idea of achieving something so extraordinary through science, through fact. Rocket science is the intersection between the sublime and the tangible, and he has always loved that about it.

She doesn't really get what he means, but she can also seem to tell he doesn't have the words inside of him to fully express himself, so she doesn't push it any further.

"Is that your secret?" she asks. "Your secret is that you're a nerd?"

He smiles. "No, no, you don't get it. See, I have this job as a mechanic right now, and the plan is that after this year, I'm going to get my degree. It's my dream. It always has been, and it still is."

She can't hide her confusion, stained all over her face, with her tilted head and scrunched eyebrows.

"My dream is coming true. I reapplied to Rice, and I have a feeling I'm going to get in. I've applied to other schools too, like Duke and Northwestern, but Rice is just easier with my life right now. It's where everyone wants me to go: my mom, my dad, my girlfriend. They want me close to them, and it's a great school. It's everything I dreamed of."

"You've lost me," she admits. "I don't get it. What's the problem?"

"See, the secret is, when next fall comes, I'm not going to Rice."

"Why?"

"I don't know."

"I thought you just said it was your dream."

"It is."

"Then why—"

"That's just it. I don't understand it at all. I just know in my soul that I won't ever go to Rice, and I haven't told anyone yet."

He feels a vague, unexplainable sense of embarrassment, and he can't look at her anymore.

She stops asking him questions.

"Can I see your drawing now?" he says.

"A deal's a deal."

She pulls out her notepad and hands it to him.

She's drawn a self-portrait, only instead of a typical face, she's turned hers into a hybrid between a tree and a human. The leaves have become her hair, and the lines in the bark outline all her major facial features—her closed eyes, her nose, her mouth, even her veins. It's raining in the picture, with occasional water droplets dripping down the bark, like tears. There are nests in the tree that look almost like hairpins. Hidden low in the corner, on the bark of the tree, there's an engraving with a heart surrounding the letters EL and TH.

"I don't—" he starts to say but pauses for a second. "I don't get it. Are you really into the environment or something?"

"Yeah." She laughs. "My deep dark secret is that I'm an environmentalist."

"I don't get it then. I don't get the drawing."

He tries to hand it back to her.

"You can keep it," she says. "I keep your secret, you keep mine?"

"Will you tell me what it means first?"

"That wasn't the deal. I told you I'd show you the drawing, not explain it."

"And you said that I'd know you after I saw this. I don't feel like I know you."

Class ends, and people start to get up and move around. The teacher makes a few last-minute remarks that no one really hears.

"You will, though," she says, and begins to walk away from him with her books in her hand.

"Wait," he says, making her stop and look over her shoulder. "You never told me your name... unless that's some big secret too."

She grins. "I'm Erin."

"Erin," he repeats.

She walks away, still smiling.

Chapter 5

The rest of the week passes as normal—at least, what normal has become, full of silence, full of attempting to balance excitement and boredom, full of trying to recreate the sensation of normal.

On Thursday during dinner, Sarah says, "Your mom called the house today. She invited us over on Saturday for dinner. Wes's mom and Haley's family are going. I told her we'd come."

"Okay."

"Did you want to go?"

He nods.

"Because we don't have to go if you don't want to. I just thought it might be fun."

"Yeah, it will be."

Their conversation is slow, each sentence stalling in front of the one to come.

"Did I tell you about my test in biochemistry?" Sarah says.

He shakes his head no.

She tells him all about it—every crazy question, how she had to recall the smallest details from the footnotes of her textbooks.

He tries to listen, but lately, when he looks at Sarah, tries to engage with her, he feels angry. He used to just feel disconnected, as though he couldn't remember who she was. Now, he associates her with pain, as if she's somehow to blame for everything that's gone wrong. He knows that's crazy, of course, but that's how he feels. He wishes he didn't, but you can't always change the way you feel.

"It'll be worth it one day, though, won't it?" she asks.

"What?"

"The tests, the quizzes, the stress... it'll be worth it?"

"Yeah."

She holds his gaze for an extra second, and he can feel her reading into his words, so he looks down.

"What about you?" she asks. "How was your day?"

"Fine."

"Yeah?"

"Yeah, it was fine."

He can feel her eyes on him, trying to pull him out of himself, trying to get him to say something, anything. He feels empty, as though she's reaching inside him and finding nothing but glass shards — fragile and sharp. He searches, desperate for something to say, but when he can't find anything, he looks away almost in embarrassment.

Her eyes don't leave him.

He takes another bite, studying his plate as if it's the only thing in the room.

***

Sarah and Charlie stayed together the whole time he was in Afghanistan, but when he'd come home to visit, they found they'd grown further and further apart every time.

At first, it was hardly noticeable. It was just small things, such as how he'd jump if she touched him without warning. He'd laugh afterwards, though, when he realized it was her.

By the end, she'd try to talk to him, but they didn't have anything to say to each other. Charlie didn't want to speak about the war anymore, but it was the only thing he had to talk about, so he remained silent. He couldn't listen to her talk about her life, either, because suddenly her reality wasn't the same as his, and he felt as if everything she had to say was, in some tragic way, irrelevant. Then, at night, he'd want to sleep with her, and she'd tell him to slow down because he felt like a stranger to her.

"I'm sorry," he'd say, all the time, realizing that something was wrong with him.

She always tried to be understanding, as understanding as she could be. She could see in his eyes all the pain it caused him, how mad he was at himself for the anger and sadness he now had in his heart.

"It's okay," she'd say, and then she'd kiss him, slowly, as if trying to calm him down.

He was trying. He really was trying to become the man he used to be.

After Wes died, it felt harder. It felt impossible.

***

"I can't do this anymore," Sarah says.

Charlie looks down for a second, as if the peas on his plate each hold their own individual universe that he must study.

"You don't talk to me anymore," she says, trying to speak gently, not too accusingly. But her voice is also strong and tough—demanding yet empathetic.

"What do you want to talk about?"

"Anything."

"You know that's not true."

"It is. You won't joke around with me, but you don't want to talk about anything serious. You don't want to talk about anything I like, but you don't want to talk about what you like. What do you want from me, Charlie?"

"I don't want anything."

He can see that answer brings her pain.

"You want nothing from me?"

They look at each other for a long time, and he can see how tragic that truth is. He should want everything from her: her soul, her heart, her body.

He looks away.

"Well, I want to talk," she says, and sits back in her chair with her arms crossed. "You're gone all the time now."

"Is that a question or a statement?"

"I hate how you go drinking late at night. I hate it. And the smoking... it's got to stop."

"I know. I'm sorry."

"Are you cheating on me?"

Sarah's asked him this many times. At first, he thought it was because she was afraid of losing him. After a while, he started to wonder if it was something else altogether. Maybe she wanted him to cheat. Maybe she wanted a way out that would be easy and make him the bad guy.

Sarah had told him a few months into their relationship that she only wanted to have sex with one man in her life. It wasn't a religious statement or her family whispering it into her ear. It was out of respect for herself and an act of caution. When Charlie told her he was enlisting, after hours and hours of trying to talk him out if it, she broke down. It was the only time in his life he'd ever seen her cry. She told him that she loved him, that she couldn't live without him, that she wanted to be with him in every way. That was the first time they slept together.

Sometimes, he wonders if that night was her version of getting a ring. Perhaps it was her silent promise to stay with him for better or for worse. She was always the kind of girl to commit to her word and to do the right thing no matter what. That made him wonder if she hoped he'd screw something up so she wouldn't have to be the one to end it. Maybe she wanted a way out. Either that, or he's just being crazy, and she still loves him more than she loves herself.

"Answer me, Charlie. Are you cheating?" she repeats.

He can hear that she's cracking, how she can only be understanding to a certain point.

"No," he says.

"No?"

"No."

"That's all you have to say?"

"You know I'd never cheat on you."

"How am I supposed to *know* that?"

"We both know I'm not like that."

"Did you cheat on me in Afghanistan?"

"No."

"Never?"

"Of course not. I'd never do that, Sarah."

She stares at him, but he doesn't look back. "You were different when you got back."

"Of course I'm different, Sarah. It was a war."

"Maybe I'd understand more if — "

"You don't want stories. You think you do, but you don't."

"Can we talk about Wes, then?"

"What about him?"

"I knew him too, you know. I loved him too. Do you ever think about that?"

He says nothing, and looks down.

They sit in silence.

"I want to talk about the phone number I found," she says at last.

"The phone number?"

"Yes. Who's Rylee?"

"I told you already. She's nobody."

"You've been keeping a girl's phone number buried at the bottom of your sock drawer. That's something to me."

"It's not what you think."

"Then what is it?"

"I'm not cheating on you."

"What's the number?"

"I'm not cheating on you!"

"You're impossible, Charlie."

"I've never even met her."

"Where'd you get her number?"

"From a friend."

"A friend?"

"Yes."

"Who?"

"It's not important. I don't... I don't want to talk about this."

Silence.

They both take a moment to collect themselves, before they say things they don't mean, things rooted in anger rather than reality.

"God, what are we doing?" Sarah says. "We never used to fight."

Their ability to understand each other used to get them through anything. Their whole relationship worked in a way that made fighting unnecessary — until now.

"Things were easier back then," Charlie says.

"I need a minute." She leaves the table and steps out of the room.

***

Charlie and Sarah had made a plan to have a perfect, simple life. They fell in love at the beginning of their senior year. He noticed her first, the way she sat in the front of the classroom, the intelligence in her answers, her modesty, the beauty in her smile. Sometimes, the guys on the football team would say she was hot, but no one ever asked her out. One of Charlie's friends, another guy on the football team, always said he was in love with her, but he'd never found a way to approach her.

"You can't just walk up to a girl like that," he'd told Charlie. "You gotta have something substantial to say."

"And you don't?"

"Hell no. Have you met me?"

One day, Charlie saw her studying in the library after school, sitting with her back to him. He started to go near her but then turned around. He had to do this twice before he worked up the courage to talk to her.

She was so engrossed in her work that she took almost thirty seconds to look up after he sat down. The whole time, he thought about leaving, about how dumb it was for him to be there, just waiting for her to engage with him. So he pulled out a book, trying to look as if he'd just sat down to study.

He was about to say something when she got up and went to the whiteboard, working out a math problem. He started to wonder if she were crazy, if under so many layers of intelligence and confidence, she had no need to connect with anyone else. She hadn't even noticed him.

He watched as she worked on the problem, step by step, filling up the entire board. He copied the problem into his book and worked it out himself. She finished first and sat back down next to him.

A full minute passed.

"We got different answers," he said quietly.

It took her a second to react, as if she wasn't sure he was really talking to her.

"What?"

"The math problem," he said, pointing to the board. "I got a different answer." He leaned slightly closer and pushed his notebook toward her, showing her his work. "Can you show me where I went wrong?"

Her warmth surprised him. He didn't know why, but the way she smiled to herself and moved closer to him, so quickly, wasn't what he'd expected.

"It's a really hard one," she said, as she took the pencil and began to check his work, comparing it to hers on the board behind them. "You're in my class, right? Back right corner?"

"Yeah," he replied. "You can even call me Charlie if 'back right corner' gets too clunky."

"You can call me 'front left' if Sarah's too short."

He smiled, and she did too. She went back to work, and he watched as she froze, slowing down to study his work, and then studying her own.

"You're right," she said at last.

"What?"

"About the problem. Your answer is right."

He'd never, for his whole life, forget the way she looked at him, as though she'd never expected to be wrong; but instead of feeling sad, she looked relieved, as if her own intrigue, her desire to know him, alleviated a burden. He could see something inside her open up to him, just slightly, just the crack he needed to slip in.

The truth was, he'd known all along that he was right, but if she'd sat there, explaining how she'd done the problem, he might never have said a word. He, too, felt a burden leaving him, a sense of comfort, at the simple sound of her voice. Nothing would be the same for them after that. They moved slowly and cautiously, but both could feel the magnetic energy between them.

Years later, as lucky as they felt to have found their better half so early in life, it also made things complicated. They had to coordinate their lives, become selfless, way sooner than most kids.

Sarah was always a careful, cautious girl. Adventure scared her. She wanted to stay in Houston her whole life. She didn't see the need to leave if she was still happy. Her content nature, her ability to love something, even just a city, so fiercely for so long, was part of what Charlie liked about her.

At the same time, though, he felt differently. He wanted to get out of Houston and go somewhere new.

They both applied to the same colleges. When they got their acceptances, they narrowed it down to Rice and Duke. They were such a bright young couple, so smart. That also made things hard. They could see the gravity of their situation, the implications of each different option.

"Let's go to Duke," Charlie said.

"I can't."

"Why? Why are you so afraid?"

"I'm not *afraid*."

"You are, though."

He knew she hated it when he told her how she felt, but he also knew he was right, and he was unwilling to pull back.

"I can't go to Duke. I—I'm so sorry, but I can't."

All these years later, Charlie wonders if that was the conversation that broke them. He knew he needed a change. If he could go back in time, he'd fight her harder. He'd say that he couldn't stay in Houston, that he felt suffocated. He should have insisted that they'd be okay distance-dating, that they wouldn't become another statistic of how hard distance can be. Maybe that feeling of being trapped in Houston was what had really made him decide to go to Afghanistan in the first place. If Sarah had agreed to go to Duke, he may not have enlisted at all. He knows that isn't fair to her, but it's true.

***

After taking a little time to herself, Sarah returns and takes a step closer to him, as if trying to end their fighting. She grabs his hands reluctantly.

"This is all just... I don't know," Charlie says. "It's hard for me to handle."

"What is?"

"How you want to know everything about me."

"You think it's bad that I want to know you?"

"It's not bad. It's just impossible."

"You think it's impossible for me to know you?"

"No one knows anyone."

"That's not true."

"I think it is."

They both stop to breathe.

Sarah lets go of his hands and takes a step away from him. "My God, Charlie, that's the saddest thing you've ever said."

"I'm sorry."

She leans back against the counter and crosses her arms.

"It's just... it's just that I can feel you waiting," he says.

"Waiting for what?"

"For me to get better."

"Of course I'm waiting for you to get better."

"You think I'm damaged."

"You don't?"

Her words bite him, but only for a moment. Her acknowledgement of his broken heart is sharp and poignant. It both relieves and frustrates him.

"I know I am," Charlie says. "But it's not the damage that's the problem. It's the waiting for the damage to be 'fixed'."

He can see her struggling to understand. He knows that she is, above all, a kind person, and it hurts him to say what he really feels. He doesn't want to harm her, but he can't figure out how to say what he feels without everything exploding. The truth is, sometimes she makes him feel he's a shadow of himself, as if the person he is now is just an illusion, as if he's trying to become himself again but can't.

"Do you love me, Charlie?" she asks.

"Stop asking me things like that."

"Do you?"

"Yes, I do. Of course I do."

"Look at me."

He doesn't.

"Please, Charlie, look at me." She gently turns his head so that he has to see her.

She asks him again. "Do you love me?"

He stares into her eyes, trying so hard to see what he once did, looking for the past somewhere in her eyes. "I'm trying to."

"What does that mean? What am I supposed to make of that answer?"

"I don't know, Sarah."

"You don't know?"

"I'm sorry." He can't tell if she wants to cry or yell. "I don't know what you want me to say."

She takes a few steps toward him and grabs his hands. "I want you to say that you're just going through something, but you love me. I want you to say that in the face of everything, you're still sure about you and me."

She moves her hands behind his neck, as if holding onto him physically could somehow bring his heart back to her.

"Everything used to be so simple," he says.

"I know."

"We were so happy. I loved you so much." He feels reluctant to breathe. Each little movement feels hazardous, as if he's standing on ground that's about to break.

"You speak about us in the past tense, Charlie. I'm right here."

He looks away from her, ashamed.

She steps away. "I loved you too, you know," she says. "And I still do, but I can't keep trying to love you enough for the both of us. I need to know if you can love me again."

"I don't know."

"Do you want to love me again?"

"Of course."

She takes a moment to herself, simply to breathe.

"This is all just screwed up," she says. "This isn't how any of this was supposed to go."

"We just need time."

Suddenly, something flashes in her eyes that he hasn't seen before, some kind of unchangeable panic and sadness.

"You act like we have all the time in the world," she says.

"What do you mean?"

"I just need to know if we can make it. I need to know soon if we're going to survive this, if we can get past this." She looks scared, and she never looks scared.

"What's going on?"

"I think we need some space from each other."

"What do you mean?"

"I think we need a few days apart. I can go stay with my parents."

"Come on, Sarah, we don't need that."

"Okay, well, I do," she says, her voice firm and unyielding. "I need some time to think."

"Look, I can try to—"

"No, Charlie, just... just stop. Okay? We need time apart. I don't wanna talk anymore."

She won't look at him now, and she walks toward their room.

He follows her. When she turns to close the door, he stops her.

"I'm just packing some things, okay?" she says.

"Please talk to me."

She laughs at the irony.

He doesn't.

"What's going on with you?" he asks.

She seems to think there's something funny about that, too.

"Oh nothing, Charlie. Nothing."

Chapter 6

The next morning, when he wakes up alone, he realizes how wrong he was. He should have been stronger. He should have been there for her. It's not his right to be selfish, regardless of what he's going through. As much as he needs the people around him, they need him too.

He picks up the phone and calls Sarah, but she doesn't answer. He then calls Haley.

"Hey, it's me," he says.

"I thought you didn't want to talk on the phone anymore," Haley replies, although she sounds relieved, not judgmental or angry.

"I shouldn't have said that. I'm sorry."

There's silence for a moment, and in the background, Charlie can hear little Anna running around and asking her dad where her shoes are.

"Crazy morning?" Charlie asks.

"Aren't they all?"

"I can imagine."

He doesn't say anything else.

"You sound tired," Haley says.

"I am."

"You sound sad."

"I'm all right."

There's something about talking to Haley that feels almost dangerous to him, that makes him want to hang up because of how deeply she knows him. He can't do that, though. Not anymore.

"Anna's presentation on her hero is this morning, isn't it?" he asks.

"Yeah, it is."

"Is she still speaking about me?"

"Yes."

Charlie takes a deep breath. "Does she still want me to come?"

There's silence on the other end.

"What? She doesn't?"

"It's not that."

"I think I'm going to come."

- 47 -

"You *think* you're going to come, or you *know* you are?"

"I know I am." He knows she can hear the uncertainty in his voice; she knows everything he feels, sometimes more than he knows himself.

"Look, Charlie, if you can't do this yet, if you're not ready, don't feel forced. I shouldn't have pressured you into coming if you're not ready."

"I want to come."

"It's not fair to get a little kid's hopes up and not be there. If you tell me you're coming, you have to come."

"I know."

"And you can't be all crushed and sad and tired around her, okay? If you come, you have to at least try to—"

"I will."

"I know that's what you're saying, but—"

"I'll be there, Haley. Okay? I'll be there, and it'll all be fine. Okay?"

Haley takes a moment to reply. "Okay."

"Eight o'clock?"

"Eight o'clock."

Charlie calls in to work and asks if it's okay if he's late. He tells his boss, Anthony, that it's important.

Anthony's dad was a veteran. He's told Charlie stories about how his dad went crazy after combat. His dad was a kind, gentle man, almost passive, before he left, but when he got home, everything was different. He started drinking. He stopped talking. His wife complained about it once, and without even realizing what he was doing, he hit her. He cried and cried afterwards, as if unable to understand how he'd become such a monster. She kicked him out of the house, and he came back home begging for forgiveness. For weeks, he begged, and finally, after years of pulling himself together, changing back to who he'd once been, he asked her to take him back. She did, reluctantly at first, but eventually everything was okay again—not great, but okay. Anthony's dad would tell him stories about the war, and somehow, Anthony found a way to forgive him for hitting his mother, and to at least attempt to understand his father's internal torment. Because of that, Anthony always wanted to help Charlie, as if, by doing so, he was somehow helping his dad too. Maybe he was trying to save Charlie from turning into the kind of person his dad had become.

Anthony tells Charlie to take his time and that he'll see him that afternoon.

Charlie showers, shaves, then goes into his closet and pulls out a box buried deep in the back—his army uniform.

He spends the next ten minutes putting the uniform on and taking it off again, only to repeat the whole process. He hasn't even looked at that uniform for months, and he hasn't worn it since he got back from Afghanistan. Sometimes he feels as if the cloth itself is made of acid, and it takes him five tries before he works up the courage to leave the house.

***

He remembers standing next to Wes in his uniform the day before they left for the war.

Their high school photographer took a picture of them, wearing their army uniforms, on the football field, and the next day an article appeared in the paper about how two high school football heroes had decided to become heroes for their country. It was a big hit, and people loved them for it.

On occasion, Charlie caught Wes staring at his army uniform as if it was his football jersey, as if he expected the back of it to have a huge number 10 and his last name sprawled out across his shoulders.

"You're brave young men," everyone told them.

People came up to Charlie and Wes and shook their hands as if they'd be better people just for meeting those two boys. Sometimes it made Charlie feel sick, as if he were lying to these people by pretending to be braver than he felt. He wondered if Wes felt that way too, or if he really was as brave as he seemed.

"We're going to be loved, Charlie," Wes had told him. "Loved, loved, loved."

He spoke as if he held the world entirely in his hands, as if his destiny was just one step away and everyone who got to witness his greatness was lucky.

Even years later, somewhere in the silence, Charlie can still hear the faint scratching of the words *loved, loved, loved,* trying to claw their way out of the tomb.

***

Charlie gets to Anna's school thirty minutes early. He composes himself, trying to think about nothing at all, to make sure he isn't sad, while waiting in his car until Haley pulls up.

"Uncle Charlie!" Anna shrieks as he steps out of his car.

He kneels down on one leg and outstretches his arms.

When she gets to him, she does his favorite thing, wrapping her little arms tightly around his neck and whispering "I love you" into his ear, over and over, at the fastest possible speed, until her tongue trips on the syllables, and then she laughs.

"How's my favorite five-year-old princess doing?" he asks.

"Great! How's my favorite uncle doing?"

He smiles. "I've trained you well, haven't I?"

She nods, still smiling, and once again wraps herself around him, letting her ear press up against his. She was, without a doubt, the cutest little girl in the world in that moment, with her curly blonde pigtails and her deep, cheery dimples.

"I didn't know you were coming!" she says.

Her comment hurts him, but he doesn't show it. Even after he'd promised to be there, Haley still hadn't told Anna that he'd come. Haley hadn't believed him, not fully anyway. Charlie hates that, but at the same time, he probably would have done the same thing if he were Haley. He doesn't blame her.

"I wouldn't miss it for the world."

"That's what I told Mom, but she didn't believe me!"

"Never listen to that mom of yours," he jokes. "You always know better than she does."

Anna knows better, of course, and that makes her smile all the more.

Within seconds of being around her, Charlie starts to remember all the joy she brings him, and he sees that Haley was right all along. He should have come to visit Anna weeks ago. She has such contagious optimism.

"Cool uniform," Anna says, as she plays with his hat.

"Too bad I don't look anywhere near as good as you do in your little uniform." He points to her blue plaid jumper. "You'd better watch out for all those little kindergarten boys, if you're going to walk around looking so cute."

"Boys are gross, Uncle Charlie!"

"Can I get that in writing to use against you in a few years?"

She laughs, and then stares at him with big, hopeful eyes, as though he holds her entire world in the palm of his hand.

Haley comes over to greet him. She wraps her arms around him tightly but gently.

"You look great, Charlie," she whispers, seeming fully aware of the simultaneous joy and pain that those words bring him. "So handsome."

Before Charlie can say anything else to Haley, Anna jumps up and down with his hand still in hers. "Can we go to my classroom? Can we? Please, please, please?"

"Calm down, Energizer bunny!"

He reaches down and grabs her under her armpits, throws her up over his shoulder, and clings onto her legs to keep her from falling.

As they walk, Anna proudly describes everything about her school. She tells him about the lunchroom where Thomas Greenland always takes two cookies instead of one, about how the water fountains are super powerful and will splash straight into your face if you don't push softly, and about how she got to name the class pet hamster, Peanut.

When they get to her classroom, Anna introduces him to her teacher. The old, gray-haired woman has a tired back and drooping skin, but her spirit is as intact and joyous as ever. She has a huge smile and a gentle approach in her words and movements.

"I've heard so much about you, Mr. Cooper," she tells Charlie. "Anna thinks the world of you."

"Anna's an angel," he says, and he can see from her expression that she thinks so too.

The students observe Charlie as if he's a piece of artwork in a museum, looking at him with intrigue and respect.

The teacher gathers the children, who all sit on a small red rug with blue circles evenly spaced out to mark a spot for each of them. Fourteen kids look up at him with curious, innocent eyes.

It causes his stomach to turn. He feels more nervous looking into the eyes of those little kids than he does looking into the barrel of a gun.

Anna runs over and stands by him, her small hand clutching his, and his fear subsides, at least a little.

Anna starts her presentation by introducing Charlie. She pulls out a piece of paper with words scribbled all over it. It looks as if she had so much to say that she couldn't decide what to include and what to leave out, so she just wrote down everything.

Anna is incredibly bright for her age. She can already read and write, and she has opinions on everything, thoughts that she'll share on every subject. She's a creative and talented little girl, yet she never seems to realize it, and therein lies the magic. It's the unawareness of her uniqueness that makes her special.

She tells the other kids that Charlie is a hero to their country and to her. They all look up at him as if he's someone they want to be, as if they would trade places with him if they could. That look in their eyes makes Charlie simultaneously glad and sorry that he came

At the end of the presentation, she pulls out a photograph. "This is picture of my Uncle Charlie with his best friend, Wes."

***

A few months ago, Charlie had given her that picture, the one Wes and Charlie had taken together the day they left for Afghanistan. They're smiling and have their arms around each other. Strange how simple everything felt, how their faces showed pride and glory and sacrifice.

When Wes died, no one had known what to tell Anna. Without saying anything, Anna assumed that he'd died at war. Wes would usually come visit once or twice a week with Charlie, and Anna adored him. Wes loved to play games with her, like soccer or bingo, and he always found a way to let her win without making it obvious that he'd thrown it. He was incredibly kind to her, and he always managed to mask his pain around her. He never seemed to be the kind of man who was one moment away from blowing his brains out.

Suicide isn't an easy thing to explain to a five-year-old, so when Haley had to tell her daughter why Wes wouldn't be coming back anymore, she just said that he'd died. Haley told Anna that his heart had stopped beating. She didn't know what else she could say.

"Could that happen to me, Mommy? Could my heart just stop beating?"

"No, honey, that won't happen to you."

Of course, there was no way she could really assure Anna of anything. Haley didn't decide who lived or died, but worrying a five-year-old about dying would take away some of Anna's innocence, and loss of innocence has always been one of the world's greatest sources of suffering. Sometimes, lying can be a form of rescue.

***

When Anna finishes talking to the class, it's Charlie's turn. He pulls out an American flag, explains the meaning of the stars and stripes, and gives them a speech about how the United States is the greatest country in the world because it stands for freedom and equality. He tells them he chose to go to war because he wanted to be a part of that greatness. Talking in front of children is easier for him because they buy into what he says without too many questions, without asking about the morality of entering Afghanistan or bringing up politics.

Charlie doesn't speak in front of the class for very long. He's never been exceptionally long-winded. He doesn't see the point.

The questions from the children are mostly innocent and simple. They ask him how old he was when he went to war, how long he was there, if he was ever brave enough to get a medal. They seem collectively disappointed when he tells them he never got any special recognition from the army.

"Any more questions?" he asks.

A little boy in the front row raises his hand. "Did you learn how to use a gun?"

Suddenly, the eyes of all the kids stop roaming around the room and fall back on him.

"Yes, I did."

The boy raises his hand again, and Charlie nods, encouraging him to ask his next question. "Have you ever killed anyone?"

Charlie stares into the little boy's eyes, and he can't tell what the child hopes he will say. Part of him thinks the kid would like him to say yes so that he'd resemble a heroic video game character, but he also knows that little kids never truly want darkness in their lives, whether they know it or not.

Charlie turns to Anna, who looks concerned.

"Let's not ask those types of questions, John," the teacher suggests.

"No, it's okay," Charlie tells the teacher immediately, to assure her that he hasn't been offended. He turns back to the little boy. "No, John, I've never killed anyone."

Anna sighs, clearly with relief.

John looks back down, unhappy, as if he wanted to hear a bloody, gory story — perhaps, Charlie thinks, like the ones he watches on TV late at night when his parents think he's already gone to bed.

Charlie lied to them all.

***

When both of their tours were over, Charlie and Wes used to hang out at night. They would quietly watch sports and drink beer.

After the war, Wes remained mostly silent, like Charlie. In a way, it made them both incredibly self-centered and unable to tell what was going on with each other. Although they hung out, it was shocking how little they exchanged. Perhaps that was why they liked being around each other. It was easy, most of the time. Sometimes, though, Wes would want to talk, but Charlie never felt that he could fully engage.

One time, during the Texans game, Wes asked Charlie if he'd ever killed anyone.

"I don't know," Charlie said. He didn't even look Wes in the eyes. He acted as if Wes had just asked him what he wanted for dinner.

"You don't know?"

"Yeah, I don't know."

"That seems like the kind of thing you'd know."

Charlie shrugged.

"I've killed people," Wes said.

Charlie didn't say anything. He just took another sip of his beer and nodded.

Wes continued, "But I don't remember it, really. I can't imagine it in my head. See, whenever I got an order to fire that gun, I would close my eyes. It made it less real. I would close my eyes, and when I opened them, it was just over. It made me feel disconnected, I guess."

"If you feel so disconnected, why do you think about it still?"

Wes shrugged. "I don't know."

Charlie nodded, knowing that Wes's answers didn't really make sense, but all of war was beyond understanding.

"I had a friend over there. Josh," Wes said. "Good guy, loved football, just like us. Talked about it all the time."

Wes took a sip of his beer, and they watched another pass soar over the receiver.

"He should come over sometime," Charlie suggested.

"Oh, no... he can't."

Charlie looked over at him, to confirm what he thought he understood. "How'd it happen?"

"He was driving a tank." Wes paused for a moment to take another sip of beer. "He was driving a tank, and then someone threw a grenade at them, and it entered the tank. He picked it up to throw it back, but it exploded and blew his arms off, and you can't drive a tank with no arms, so they crashed, and he died."

Charlie didn't say anything. Instead, he got up and grabbed them both another drink.

They watched the Texans advance forward, slowly, yard by yard. Then there was a sack and all the fans grew silent—a suffocating sort of silence.

"I want to go back," Wes whispered finally, so quietly that Charlie wasn't even sure he'd meant to say it out loud.

Charlie said nothing. He just stared at the screen, not reacting to the game at all.

"Did you hear me, Charlie?"

Charlie's brain understood long before his heart. "Go back where?"

"Let's not do this, Charlie. Don't act like you don't know what I'm talking about."

Charlie couldn't believe what he was hearing, so he chose to ignore it. He took a sip of beer.

"I'm sorry," Wes said.

"It's only been two months, and you want to go back there?" Charlie's rage was nearing the point of explosion. It didn't take much to make Charlie angry, not anymore.

"Please try to be calm, Charlie."

"Stop telling me how to feel."

Charlie was worried and shocked, but more than anything, he felt betrayed. "You can't just leave again. We just got home! You're the one who's always telling me that it was a mistake to go."

"Maybe I was wrong. Maybe that wasn't the mistake. Maybe the mistake was ever coming home."

Charlie stood up and began to pace back and forth. Somehow, it helped for his body to feel as restless as his heart. "You just started every sentence with the word *maybe*! You don't know anything! You aren't sure about anything at all! This is another crazy idea, Wes."

Wes didn't say anything. He took a sip of his beer.

"I don't understand," Charlie said, trying to calm himself.

"I know you don't, but please just listen to me."

"Listen to you? Wes, that's all I ever do! Why do you think I went to fucking Afghanistan? I always listen to you! That's the problem! *You* need to listen to *me*, and there's no way in hell you're going back!"

Wes just stared at him, and Charlie felt as if he was center stage with a spotlight on him.

"Don't look at me like that, Wes. Don't look at me like *I'm* the one who's lost my mind."

"I don't expect you to get it."

"Why, though? Why wouldn't I get it? I was there too, in case you forgot. You think I don't get it?"

"I'm not talking about what it was like there. I'm talking about coming home. Things at home aren't the same for me."

"So what? We have different lives! Of course home isn't the same!"

"You just got into Rice, Charlie. You're a genius. You have Sarah. You'll get married one day, and have a bunch of beautiful little kids, and you'll have some great job. You're going to be fine."

"And you won't?"

"I just... I feel like something is off here."

"Off?"

"I feel like... like my life here isn't real. Do you get that? All I want is to feel something *real*."

"Like a bullet in your chest?"

Wes stayed silent.

Charlie didn't speak for a while either. What the hell was he supposed to say? He simultaneously understood and thought that Wes was insane. There's not a whole lot to say to people like that.

"I can't..." Charlie started to say. "I can't go back with you."

"I didn't ask you to."

"I know. I know that." In some ways, Charlie considered that the worst part.

"I don't get what you found in Afghanistan that you want again."

They'd been separated after basic training, so Charlie couldn't speak for Wes's experience; but when Charlie was fighting, he didn't feel any of the things he'd expected to feel. He didn't feel important. He didn't feel honor or glory or pride. He just felt the emptiness of his stomach, the dust on his skin, and the fear in his heart. That was all he'd found in Afghanistan.

"Do you know what you want, Wes?"

"Yes, I know."

"What is it? What are you looking for?"

"I can't explain it."

Wes wouldn't look at him.

Charlie couldn't think of anything more to say, so he picked up the remote and turned the game back on. The Texans had scored and were now winning. It frightened him how much the world continued on in blissful disregard of his pain. That crowd cheered and roared and sang.

Charlie stayed awake as long as he could, but fell asleep before the game ended, and when he woke, Wes no longer occupied the chair across from him. For the first time, it occurred to him that he was completely alone.

***

After the presentation, the teacher invited Haley and Charlie to stay for as much of the day as they wanted. Anna went outside for recess, where she played basketball with all the boys.

"She's the best one on the court," Charlie says, after watching for a few minutes. "Putting those boys to shame."

"I knew you'd be proud of that." Haley laughs.

"Anna's a little basketball badass."

"Charlie, watch your language. We're at a kindergarten."

"Oh, come on, none of the kids are listening. They're too busy having fun."

A few seconds later, Anna turns and darts toward them. "Uncle Charlie, do you want to play?"

"Oh, no, I'm happy, Anna."

"Are you sure? You can be on my team."

"What a generous offer." Charlie turns to Haley. "Can I refuse such a deal?"

"Impossible," Haley replies.

Charlie takes off his hat and goes to play with the little kids, letting them dribble around him and lifting them up so that they can dunk. A couple minutes later, he sits back down with Haley.

"Do you remember when we used to be like that?" Haley asks.

"Naïve?"

"No. Innocent."

"Is there a difference?"

"Of course there is. You know there is."

They stay and watch as Anna laughs and plays with her friends. He's happy there, thinking of nothing but the sound of her giggle, chirping, flying, spinning in the air, like a basketball soaring into the net.

Charlie checks his watch. It's been almost two hours — time for him to leave.

"Anna, I've got to go to work," he says.

"No!" she yells.

"How about I just never go to work again?"

"That's more like it."

She laughs and gives him a big hug.

"Uncle Charlie!" she calls when he's almost out of the gate. "You'll come see me again soon, right?" She looks up at him with evident fear that he'll disappear and never come back.

"Yeah, honey. Of course. Of course I will."

He heads with Haley out to the parking lot. They walk slowly, taking in their time together, although neither says much.

"I needed this," he says.

Haley smiles. "We did too."

"Your little girl is an angel."

"I know."

She has a look in her eyes when she talks about her daughter, as if each of Anna's movements, each bite of frosted flakes, every stop to tie her shoe, each loud sneeze, holds Haley's entire world together. In a world with Anna, she feels no suffering.

Sometimes he looks at Haley and can't imagine what it would be like to try to raise an angel, to try to get someone to grow up without being bitter or cold or cocky or boring. It seems impossible to him, yet Anna is perfect, and he keeps marveling at how that could be.

"I love Anna more than anything in the world," Haley says as they reach the parking lot.

"I know."

"She saves me."

"You don't need any saving."

"Everyone needs saving."

Charlie nods.

"Do you have anyone in your life who makes you feel saved?" Haley asks.

He looks down at the concrete and doesn't reply. He suspects Haley wishes she hadn't said anything, as another few seconds pass.

"I'm sorry," she says. "I shouldn't have asked."

"No, no." He finally looks at her again. "I do. Of course, I do, Haley."

Haley gets into her car, about to close her door.

"That's all anyone ever wants, isn't it?" he asks. "To save and be saved?"

"I don't know. Maybe."

"Yeah," Charlie says. "Maybe."

Chapter 7

On Saturday morning, Charlie calls Sarah as soon he wakes up. They've barely talked the last few days. He's sent her texts saying he misses her, but she's hardly responded. Maybe she doubted whether the messages were true.

"You didn't forget, did you?" he asks. "About my family's dinner tonight?"

"No, I'm coming," she says. "I'll be there at seven." The finality in her voice surprises him.

"You don't want to come home first?"

It takes her a moment to respond. "My mom just wants to keep me a little longer. We're enjoying talking."

"Okay," he says, not sure what to make of that.

"Okay."

She doesn't say anything else, and he's about to apologize when she says she has to go. She hangs up before he can say goodbye.

***

Charlie arrives at dinner around 6:45 PM and waits in his car. When Sarah arrives fifteen minutes later, she parks behind him and approaches slowly, as if walking up to a stranger. She says hello and kisses him mechanically. Without saying anything more, she begins to walk away from him. Things feel just as awkward between them as they did when she left on Thursday night.

"Wait," he says, and she turns back. She's wearing a short black dress and bright red heels that match her lipstick. She's curled her hair, which spirals in ringlets down to her shoulders, and her makeup subtly accents her cheekbones and eyes. She looks gorgeous. He takes a few steps closer and kisses her again, softly and briefly, but intentionally.

They stop to look at each other in the eyes. He feels at peace, but she looks nervous.

"Let's not worry about us, okay?" he says. "Not tonight."

He holds her hand, and she stares down at it for a long time, as if deciding whether it's okay for him to touch her, as if it's the first time their skin has connected.

"What's going on?" he asks.

"Nothing," she says, and looks back up at him. Her face shows the faint hint of a smile, but it isn't real. He's slightly offended that she'd try to fake happiness around him. He always knows when she's being insincere. "We'll be fine."

He doesn't see any point in fighting over it, so he smiles gently back. "Yes, we will."

They walk up to the door together, hand in hand. Charlie's family lives in a big house, so big and showy that it would make some people uncomfortable. He's always secretly hated that about it.

Before he even reaches up to knock, his mom answers.

His mom has always excelled at hosting of any kind. She's hospitable and genuine, which makes her a great businesswoman. She has an unusual combination of kindness and strength. Charlie's always admired that about her, but it also alienates them. To him, she's the master of poise, and he worries that she won't tolerate any of his imperfections.

"Look at my handsome boy," she says as she hugs him and kisses his cheek. She pulls softly on his jacket, acknowledging how nice he looks.

She stands back and admires Sarah. "My God, Charlie, you have the most beautiful girlfriend in the world." She leans in to hug Sarah. "So stunning. Has he told you how beautiful you look tonight?"

They both pause and look at each other, but before he can say anything, Sarah responds, giving the easiest answer. "Yes. He always does."

"Thank goodness my son knows a good thing when he sees it."

"He's a smart man," Sarah says with a smile.

Charlie's dad appears in the doorway behind his wife and greets them formally. "Good to see you, Charlie."

Charlie's dad had grown up poor, with a single father after his mom died in a car accident when he was too young to really know her. He's always wanted to give his children a better life than the one he had, one free of suffering, pain, or hunger. He worked hard, went to law school, and made a life for himself, a life where he could give his children what they needed. After Charlie went to Afghanistan, though, things were different, and Charlie didn't know why. His father never listened when he talked. He'd hardly look at Charlie or speak back, and if he did, he was usually angry.

"Doesn't Sarah look beautiful?" Charlie's mom says.

"She always does." His dad steps forward to hug her.

Sometimes Charlie thinks his dad loves Sarah more than he loves him. Sarah has the kind of life that his father wanted for Charlie. She's in medical school, making something of herself. Charlie's dad loves her drive and how nothing got in her way of taking advantage of opportunities.

"How's school going?" Charlie's dad asks her. His voice is kind, but his eyes never leave her for a second. It's as if he can't even stand to look at his son. Charlie is invisible. There's something aggressive in how much his father loves Sarah, intentional or unintentional.

"It's a dream come true," Sarah says. "A hard, difficult dream that sometimes feels like a nightmare, but my dream nonetheless."

Both Charlie's parents smile. He does too.

"I just got a research position in a lab with one of my teachers who's studying Alzheimer's," she says. "It should be great. It's exactly what I want to do."

Charlie looks at her sharply.

"That's wonderful news," his mom says.

"Really great," his dad echoes. "Those sorts of positions can really open up opportunities."

The doorbell rings and his parents excuse themselves.

"You didn't tell me about the research position," Charlie says. "I would have congratulated you."

"I didn't tell you because you never listen anymore," she snaps at him, saying each word clearly, yet they aren't fighting. There's something disconnected in her voice that concerns him.

"When did you find out?" he asks.

"About a week ago." She tries to walk away, to the door where Wes's mom has just arrived.

"What? We aren't going to talk about this?"

"Since when do you want to talk?"

"Why are you being like this?"

She's always been strong-willed, but she's also usually so reasonable, and she always used to give him the benefit of the doubt when he was going through something hard. He did the same with her in return. It's part of how they've stayed together through so much.

"I thought we said we weren't going to do this tonight," she says. He's never heard her voice so detached.

"You're scaring me," he says.

He waits for her to respond, to tell him there's no reason to be scared. She's about to say something when Natalie appears with Charlie's parents.

The three of them stare at the young couple for a moment. Charlie's mom looks a little white, a little startled. Very few things make her lose her composure, but now she seems uncomfortable. In Charlie's mind, it reaffirms that something's off with Sarah.

Natalie walks toward them. Charlie knows that supporting a mother who just lost her son is bigger than a fight between him and Sarah. Sarah seems to feel the same. The minute Natalie approaches, they both appear fine again.

"Oh, if it isn't my favorite couple," Natalie says. "Look at you two. So young and brilliant!"

"Mainly young." Sarah laughs. "We're working on the brilliant part."

"Thank you again for inviting me," Natalie says.

"Of course," Charlie's mom replies. "You're part of the family."

Sarah won't look at Charlie as she talks to Natalie and his parents. He's relieved when Haley arrives with her husband, Matt, and little Anna.

Charlie shakes hands with Matt, who immediately launches into a discussion about sports, asking if Charlie's been keeping up with the Texans and the Cowboys games. Matt has always been a simple, loyal guy, the kind of guy any father would want their daughter to bring home. Charlie likes that about him. He feels that Haley is always safe with Matt.

Anna walks up and wraps herself around Charlie's leg. When she lets go, he kneels down.

"Hi, Princess," he says.

"Why hello!"

"I have something for you." He speaks softly in her ear while the other grown-ups are busy chatting about work.

"What? What?"

He reaches into his pocket and carefully slips her a Kit-Kat. "Don't tell anyone. We don't want to get in trouble with your mom."

"Wouldn't want that." Anna smiles and winks, promising that her parents will never know.

Sarah looks down at the two of them. She seems to have overheard their whole conversation. She's smiling slightly, but when her eyes connect with Charlie, he sees a brief expression of pain.

"I think Sarah's busted us," he says to Anna.

Anna looks up at Sarah and tries her best to cover the candy bar.

Sarah turns to Charlie, and when he smiles at her, she finally seems to relax. She looks at him the way she did when they first met. She bends down to their level, distancing herself from the adults.

"How much did you see?" Charlie asks.

"Too much," Sarah says.

"What's it gonna cost us to keep you quiet?"

Anna looks at her, awaiting her answer.

"I'm afraid I have a steep price," Sarah says.

"For this type of crime, not surprising," Charlie replies. "Just give it to us straight."

"Wait," Anna says. "I'll make you a deal."

"It better be good. I don't settle cheaply."

Anna pulls out from her little purse a small flower that she's picked, probably from the front yard. It already looks half dead, but she's clearly proud of it.

"Wow," Sarah says. "Beautiful."

"I'll give it to you," Anna says.

"In exchange for lifelong secrecy, of course," Charlie says.

Sarah pretends to think about it for a moment, then sighs. "How could I pass up such a beautiful flower? You leave me no choice."

Anna smiles and hands it over.

Anna's always loved Sarah. She used to ask Charlie almost every time she saw him when they were going to get married. She'd tell Charlie that Sarah should have been a babysitter instead of a doctor, because any kid would love her. She was always so serious about the suggestion, and he laughed every time.

Charlie and Sarah stand up.

"You're different around Anna," Sarah says.

"In a good way?"

"Yes."

"You're different around her too, you know."

He wonders if that's a bad thing, if they need someone else around to make them feel like themselves.

***

At dinner, Charlie sits between Natalie and Sarah. Across from them, Haley sits next to Matt and Anna. Charlie's parents sit at the heads of the table. His mother has set the table beautifully.

No one in Charlie's family has ever been religious, but usually when Natalie comes over, she says grace before dinner. It seems a sensitive subject today, though, whether they should ask the mother of a boy who died in a church if she wants to say a prayer. There's an awkward silence, as if no one knows how to begin dinner without her prayer. Everyone looks at one another.

Charlie turns to Natalie, and he can see on her face the realization that the others are waiting for her to speak. She looks as if she's about talk, maybe to say that she can't do the prayer today, that she no longer prays. However, Charlie senses that it would crush her to have to say that, to announce her pain.

"Would anyone mind if I said the prayer today?" he asks.

Natalie looks down, her face briefly ashamed but then relieved.

"That'd be great," Haley says. Everyone agrees.

Charlie realizes, as soon as he volunteers, that he has no idea what to say. He's never said a prayer in his life. Just saying the word "God" out loud gives him pause. It isn't that he's against religion. If someone asked if he believed in God, he might even say yes. He's just never quite got used to the idea of talking to someone he can't see.

"God, thank you for the delicious food," he says. He pauses, trying to figure out what other sorts of things people normally say. "And thank you for all the people we love who are here tonight. Every moment is a blessing."

No one says anything, as if they're all so acutely aware of the truth of his words that they're only halfway uplifting.

Charlie can't come up with anything else to say, but feels that what he's said is too short.

"Amen," Haley says, freeing him. She gives him a small smile, as if acknowledging what he's done. Like her mother, she has a way of always being gracious. She can see effortlessly what other people need and help them out.

"Amen."

Everyone picks up their forks and knives and stares down at their food, silent for a moment. His mother's made steak with mashed potatoes and green beans. It was Charlie's favorite meal growing up.

"I hope you made some extra plates of this, Mom," Haley says as she takes her first bite. "We all know that Charlie will eat at least two plates."

"Two?" Charlie says, picking up his fork. "At least three."

"Trying to get fat, son?" his dad asks.

Everyone glances up at Charlie's dad. He's staring at Charlie, his face stoic and stern.

"I'm only kidding," he adds, letting a slight smile creep into his face, as if trying to erase the impression that he was being rude. It's the first time he's looked Charlie in the eyes all night.

"Well," Matt says, "if I could eat this every night, you can bet all your money I'd take my losses being fat."

"Oh, me too," says Natalie.

Charlie looks away from his dad and turns to Sarah. She usually has a way of diffusing his tension when he's around his father. Sometimes, he uses her as a shield.

She reaches under the table and puts her hand above his knee, only for a second, as if trying to provide some comfort, but she doesn't look at him.

Haley begins a conversation with her parents about her work, stories about crazy patients and all the dumb things people do to get sent to the ER.

"We're looking at the charts, right," she says, "and we see there's been an injury from roller blading. So we walk into the room expecting to see someone the size of Anna."

Anna smiles proudly.

"But we walk in, and instead, it's a forty-five-year-old man. No kids. No wife. No one was forcing him to try it. He just decided one night he wanted to try to roller blade down this hill. Said he was bored. He fell on the way down and broke his arm. Clean break. Here's what makes the story good though. He tells us that he'd do it all over again. Says he had more fun in those ten seconds than he's had in the last ten years. The whole time we're putting on the cast, he's talking about how we should all try it."

"I'm not sure if that's funny or sad," Matt says, and laughs.

"Both, for sure," Haley says.

Charlie smiles and turns to Sarah. She has an absent expression.

"What do you say we try it out?" he whispers to her.

"What?"

"Roller blading."

"What are you talking about?"

"You weren't listening?"

She looks as if her mind is on another planet. She isn't even eating.

"I'm, uh..." She seems to snap out of it. "I'm sorry."

"What's going on with you?" Charlie asks quietly, trying to figure out where her head is.

"So, Sarah," his dad says. "Tell us more about this research you're doing."

She seems happy to stop talking to Charlie. She takes a second to compose herself, and she starts describing her research. She talks about the long hours, the difficulty, the rewarding aspects of it.

Haley and his mom both appear to realize something is wrong between them. Haley looks as if she's getting ready to do damage control, thinking of how she can make them both comfortable again. Charlie's mom doesn't know anything about their problems after he got back from Afghanistan; he's never told her. She just looks confused. Natalie, Matt, and his father seem completely oblivious.

"She's such a smart girl," Natalie whispers to Charlie as Sarah talks. "You're a lucky man."

Natalie looks so content. Her expression makes Charlie feel as if Wes isn't dead. He doesn't fully understand it himself, but he doesn't dare hint that anything is wrong between him and Sarah. He wouldn't want to ruin her image of perfection and peace.

"I am lucky," he says, although he's trying to decode Sarah's words rather than really listening to Natalie.

"I bet you're excited for Charlie to be applying to Rice," his dad says after they finish discussing medical school.

There's a short silence.

"What do you mean, Dad?" Charlie asks.

"I just mean I bet she's happy for you. Can she not be happy for you?"

"I am," Sarah replies. "He'd do great there."

"That's not what you meant," Charlie says, looking directly at his dad.

His dad takes a sip of his drink. "What are you talking about?"

"Do you really hate what I'm doing right now that much? Are you really so ashamed of me?"

"Who said anything about being ashamed?"

"Don't give me this."

"Give you what?"

Sarah interjects quietly. "Stop it, Charlie."

He looks down at her. Suddenly, he sees it. She's not on his team anymore.

"Give you what?" his dad repeats.

"Nothing," he says, now only looking at Sarah. "Nothing, Dad."

***

For the rest of the dinner, Charlie doesn't say anything. He listens as the others discuss their work and talk to Anna about how she's just started playing basketball. They reminisce over funny stories, like when Matt first met the family and couldn't stop sweating, and how Haley used to tell everyone when she was little that she wanted to be a puppet collector when she grew up. Charlie feels distracted, but as he disengages, Sarah engages.

After an hour or so, Anna starts to yawn.

"Wanna go to sleep, honey?" Haley asks.

Anna nods.

Haley gets up to take her to the couch, when Charlie rises.

"I'll take her," he says.

He picks her up and brings her to the couch, where he sets out a pillow and lies her down carefully. He gets a blanket and tucks it tightly around her.

"There you go. Snuggled up nice and cozy." He leans down to kiss her. "Goodnight, Love."

"Wait, Uncle Charlie, aren't you going to tell me a story?"

"A story?"

"Mom and Dad always tell me one."

He looks back at the table, about twenty feet away, and debates whether he should stay or go back.

"Scoot over," he says, and slides next to her on the couch.

She smiles.

"Okay, so uh, once there was a little boy named Jack." He has no idea where he's going with this. "And Jack had a toy that he loved more than anything in the world."

"What was it?"

"A bear."

"What color bear?"

"Uh, just standard. Standard brown bear."

She nods, encouraging him to go on.

"But one day, he lost the bear."

"Oh no."

"He just went to bed, and the next morning, it was gone."

She looks confused and sad. "Did he find him?"

"No."

"Did he get a new bear?"

"I don't think he wanted a new one."

She doesn't seem to understand the story.

"That's the thing, though," he says. "If you ever lose anything you love, anything you really love, it can't be replaced."

"So was Jack sad?"

"At first. But he was okay."

She considers this, not looking at him. "I think he finds the bear again later."

"You do?"

"I do."

She looks up at him, seeming saddened by his story. He wonders what's wrong with him, why he couldn't tell the child a happy story like anyone else would have.

"He finds that bear," she says. "I'm sure of it. Sometimes things that are lost come back."

He doesn't say anything for a moment and stares at the floor. "You're right, honey," he says, although he isn't sure if he means it or not. He leans forward and kisses her cheek, then stands up and turns to go back to dinner.

"Uncle Charlie," she says. He turns back around. "Are you a sad man?"

"What?"

"Are you sad?"

He kneels beside her. "No, honey. Who told you that?"

"No one."

He looks down and sees the worry in her eyes. "I'm fine, Love. I promise."

"Okay," she says, a small smile now on her face. "I just don't want you to ever be sad."

***

When dinner is over, Sarah walks right by Charlie's side as if everything is normal. She even reaches out to grab his hand. He takes it, but he can tell she's doing it because people expect it.

When they get to their cars, Sarah takes a step back from him. She behaves as if looking at him makes her feel something like disgust.

"Are you leaving me?" he asks.

"What?"

"Is that what this is about?"

"What *what's* about?"

"You sound like my father. Don't play dumb. I know you're too smart for this. You know what I'm talking about."

She glances down, and when she looks back up, she seems nervous. "I don't know what you're going to say."

"If you're leaving me, just tell me." He starts to feel as though he wants to cry, but tries to convince himself not to. "I get it if you don't love me—"

"I'm pregnant."

They both freeze, Charlie's mouth still open. Neither of them moves or speaks for a moment.

"You're pregnant?" he asks eventually.

She doesn't say anything, but her eyes start to cloud with tears and turn red around the edges.

"You... you can't be pregnant," he says.

She steps back, shaking her head. "Really romantic, Charlie. That's just what I wanted to hear."

She begins to walk away from him.

He tries to grab her hand.

"Don't touch me."

"Please, Sarah, I didn't mean it like that. I—I just need a second to think about it."

"You need a second? It's a baby! We're supposed to have a baby together, and you want time? For what? For some fake reaction? For you to plan how you *should* feel?"

"No. No, that's not what I meant."

"It is. At least admit it. You're 'too smart to play dumb' with me."

He doesn't argue with her. "What are you thinking?"

"Thinking?"

"Yeah."

She looks confused. "What do you mean? I'm thinking about everything!"

"Look, I'm sorry, okay? I... I...."

"I'm leaving," she says. "I have to go."

"Please don't."

"I'm going back to my parents' house."

"Come on. Don't do this. Come home with me, please. We can talk about it there."

"I can't do this. You said we weren't going to do this tonight."

"I wouldn't have said that if I'd known. We need to talk about this."

"Not tonight. You don't want to hear any more of what I have to say tonight."

"Sarah—"

She closes her car door, shutting him out.

"Please, Sarah," he says. "Please talk to me."

She drives away.

Chapter 8

Charlie doesn't hear from Sarah for over two weeks. He's been calling her, every hour, for the last fourteen days. He's left hundreds of voicemails, all saying the same thing, begging her to pick up the phone. He's said he's sorry, over and over.

He even drove to her parents' house a few times, but whenever he knocked on the door, her father answered. He usually likes Charlie, but he's also a stern, protective man. Charlie doesn't know what Sarah's told him, but he looked as if he was one second away from killing Charlie.

All her father would say was that Sarah wasn't home — nothing more. Charlie never got anywhere. He begged, and begged, and he would even point at Sarah's car in the parking lot, as if to call her father out on a lie, but her dad never cared. He just repeated his words, *Sarah isn't here.*

Eventually Charlie gave up on dropping by her house when it proved pointless.

During these two weeks, Charlie continued going to work, as always. He listened to TJ ramble on about anything and everything — sports, food, the perfect girl that God had put into his life.

One time, TJ asked how Sarah was doing.

Charlie thought about telling him everything. If he'd told the truth, he would have explained that he could hardly sleep at night, that he felt an emptiness within himself that made it hard to feel anything else, even tired. He also had trouble eating. He felt sick to his stomach, and the worst part was, the future didn't seem any brighter. There wasn't a simple answer in sight. How could he fix their relationship if Sarah wouldn't even speak to him? He'd give anything to hear her voice.

The reality was that Charlie couldn't tell TJ. He didn't know why, but he just couldn't. He said that Sarah was fine, and TJ said, "You're damn right she's fine," and then laughed.

Charlie laughed too. It was all he could do.

However, TJ seemed to notice that something was off. Charlie could tell by the way TJ would glance at him occasionally when he was working, as if trying to figure out what was wrong, as if Charlie could be analyzed and understood like a car, as if he could be fixed like an engine. Maybe he could be.

Regardless, Charlie never said anything, and TJ never asked. Instead, TJ just accepted that he'd have to do most of the talking, which really wasn't out of the ordinary. He never got mad when Charlie looked dazed or when he had to repeat parts of his stories. He was incredibly patient.

One day when they're having lunch, Charlie decides to try to talk to TJ.

"Can I ask you something?" he says.

"Oh wow, that mouth of yours *does* actually move. Thank God. I was thinking it was gonna rust and I was gonna have to spare some oil."

Charlie gives a little laugh and TJ smiles back. He looks down, playing with his food for a moment before speaking. "Are you... are you afraid of anything?"

TJ stops eating his sandwich. "What sort of a question is that?" he yells. "Hell yes, I'm afraid of things! If someone tells you no, they're a goddamn liar or they're just flat out stupid!"

Charlie smiles.

"You want to know something?" TJ asks.

"What?"

"When I was a little kid, I was scared to death of mannequins. Actually, I think I still am! Those things are scary as fuck."

"Mannequins?"

"Yeah! I mean, some don't even have faces! Who makes a human figure and then doesn't put on a face? Plus," he adds, "their bald heads kinda remind me of Voldemort. Does anyone else think mannequins are freaky?"

The guys in the shop all shut him down immediately.

"I'm just saying. I have a real appreciation for clothes being on hangers, not some fake human!"

TJ's answer initially felt out of place to Charlie, but then he found it unexpectedly calming. It made him feel as if fear was something ridiculous. In some ways, it was exactly the reaction he needed.

***

After work, Charlie goes to his art class. When he gets to his desk, he finds a brochure about an art exhibition next month. The teacher explains that it's a way for all the students to show off their work to their families, friends, and anyone else who wants to see their pieces. Charlie hides the brochure in his notebook. Art has always been more private than public to him, and he thinks trying to make it something for everyone to see would ruin it. The idea scares him, too. It would be like letting people read his diary. He also knows, though, that's the whole point of art, sharing what he doesn't want anyone to see.

Before class begins, he gets out his notepad and pencils, setting everything up in the exact order he likes. He looks around, at the couple in front of him who won't stop holding hands and gazing into each other's eyes, the stoner who always seems to be tapping his thigh, the old man in the front row who looks so content, as if being in this class is the only thing he wants in life. Everything is just how he left it three weeks ago. That upsets him for some reason he can't explain.

"Hello, ditcher," Erin says.

Charlie looks up, startled to hear anyone addressing him. He turns away from his work for a moment to see her, as if needing to confirm that she really was talking to him. "What?"

"You've missed the last two weeks of class." She sits down next to him.

He takes a deep breath, trying to engage with her, to joke back, but it feels difficult. "Stalking me now?"

"Oh yeah. You now know that I'm nosey *and* a stalker. I'm clearly a real gem."

She begins to get her stuff out, quietly getting ready for class. She glances over at him a few times. He ignores her and draws on his notepad, just scribbling down meaningless garbage.

The assignment on the board reads:

Draw someone you hate.

Charlie continues to draw lines and patterns, squiggles shooting in all directions, not really creating anything at all. He doesn't know what to draw. He feels that he's never clearly hated anyone or anything in his life, and that hate is much too mucky an emotion to express.

"If that's a person," Erin says, looking at his scribbles, "I think he needs to go see a plastic surgeon." She smiles and seems to be waiting for him to smile back.

He does, but it's half-hearted. It's as if he can't feel any joy since Sarah left.

Erin studies him, as if his face can explain why he isn't laughing, why he can't return her joy. She doesn't seem to find what she's looking for and turns back to her work.

Charlie, curious, looks over and sees her drawing a man with close-shaven brown hair and circular glasses. He's laughing and holding a cigarette, the smoke turning into clouds above. He's handsome and beaming, not the kind of man that anyone would hate. Charlie considers asking her about it, but he can't find the energy. He goes back to his own work.

He doesn't talk for the rest of the class. Erin tries to make a few comments to him— how some kid in the front row looks like he's falling asleep, how the teacher's voice sounds different today, how she thinks the clock is slightly off. He isn't too responsive, even though he wants to be, and eventually, she stops trying.

"What is it?" he says, when he catches her glancing at him.

"You always have the same look on your face."

"Yeah?"

"Yeah."

"And what look is that?"

The playfulness in their voices is gone.

"You look...." She stares into his eyes as if searching for an adjective. "I don't know. You look like the world is falling apart around you."

She suddenly seems embarrassed to have been so honest. He doesn't know how he feels, except that he wishes she wouldn't look at him so deeply.

They sit in silence. When it's almost the end of class, she turns to him.

"I'm sorry if I shouldn't have said that," she says.

"I'm not mad. I'm just distracted today."

The teacher dismisses the class. She makes another announcement about the art exhibition coming up, but Charlie hardly listens.

They start to load up their things into their bags. Erin packs up her stuff first, and when she's done, she puts her backpack on and looks back at him.

"So, is it?" she asks.

"What?"

"Is the world falling apart around you?"

He stops putting away his stuff for a minute. Erin has such kind eyes, such dangerously kind eyes.

"It's either falling apart or coming together," he says, "and the problem is, I don't know which it is."

She takes a moment to think and then nods. He's surprised that she seems to understand, or at least attempts to understand. She looks sympathetic. He isn't sure if he deserves that or not.

He stands up, and they begin to walk out of the classroom.

"Can I ask you something?" he says. "I know it'll sound dumb, but I'm gonna ask you anyway."

"I love dumb questions. They're actually the only kind I think I'm capable of answering." She smiles, hoping he'll smile too, that he'll laugh at her jokes. He wants to laugh. Sometimes he feels as though Erin is trying to bring him back to life, and each bit of joy is a push on his chest, trying to resuscitate him, to bring back something dying.

"Do you ever worry that you're gonna hurt someone? That no matter what you do, no matter how much you wish you weren't, that you're going to hurt someone?"

Her eyebrows scrunch together. "Hurt someone?"

"Not *physically*," he says. "I just mean... I don't know. I don't know what I mean."

They step out of their classroom and begin walking toward the exit.

"Charlie, I have a lot of talents, but mind reading isn't one of them."

They walk in silence for a while along the long, narrow hallway. Charlie pretends to look at the artwork on the walls, trying to figure out what to say.

Outside, it's growing dark. Charlie stops walking, and she mirrors him. He finally looks her in the eyes.

"I found out I'm going to be a dad," he says.

She looks completely composed, hardly reacting at all. Her calm manner makes him feel safer.

"And I don't know what to do about it," he says.

"What do you mean?"

"I mean, sometimes I feel like *I'm* still a kid. How am I supposed to raise one? I don't... I don't know what to say or do or anything. I think my kid would be messed up or something, and it'd be my fault."

Erin grins, although she tries to hide it.

"Why are you smiling?"

"I'm sorry. It's just that you're too hard on yourself."

"You don't know anything about me."

"I know you're a good guy."

"No," he says. "I was a jerk to my girlfriend, actually."

"Really?"

"Yes."

"Because you don't seem like the jerk type."

He looks down at his shoes.

"I've met quite a few mean guys in my day," she says. "And you know one thing they all have in common?"

He doesn't respond.

"They don't think they're mean."

He looks back up at her. "I told her I wasn't sure if I loved her. She was pregnant with my child, and I told her *I* was going through something hard. Who does that?"

"Do you love her?"

Ever since Sarah told him she was pregnant, his love for her has seemed so obvious. He loves her to his core.

"I've always loved her," he says.

Erin nods. She seems to be searching his eyes for something, but he doesn't know what. "You can't be mad at yourself for everything that you feel."

"I can when I'm being an ass."

"No," she says. "Not even then."

He knows she's trying to get through to him, but he can't grasp what she's getting at.

"You can't reject what you feel, or nothing will ever be real. Do you get that?"

There's a long pause, as Charlie doesn't know what to say.

She looks as if she realizes that she's given him too much to think about, that he's emotionally spent.

"It'll be okay," she says. "All right?"

He nods. "Yeah. You're right. I know you're right."

She studies him again. He can tell she wishes he could see things more clearly, yet she also understands he can't. He's stuck, and because of that, there's nothing she can really do. She tells him she'll see him next week, and after they say their goodbyes, she begins to walk away.

"Hey, Charlie." She turns back. "For whatever it's worth, the world isn't falling apart around you."

She glances at the sky and the trees, as if each thing is a mystery waiting to be solved or adored. She seems to find some hidden beauty and meaning in all of it.

"How do you know?"

"Because the world isn't yours to destroy."

He can see he's supposed to take solace in those words.

He does.

Chapter 9

The phone call comes later that night.

He's in bed, sprawled diagonally, thinking how miserable it is to have so much room. He misses Sarah, the way her heavy breathing sometimes made it hard for him to fall asleep, the way she'd kick him in her sleep and never realize it.

When they'd first moved in together, he'd told her she was the world's worst sleeper, and playfully threatened that unless she improved, they'd need to get twin beds.

"I swear," he'd said, "You grow limbs at night and find a way to cover ninety-five percent of the mattress."

She laughed and put her arms around him.

"I'm sorry," she whispered. She scooted closer to him and put her hands in his hair.

Sometimes, when Sarah looked into his eyes, a slow, subtle smile would spread across her face. At these moments he could tell that she loved him endlessly, that just the sight of him would make her beam with joy. She always had a million plans, things she wanted to get out of life, and that look made him feel as though he was one of the things she wanted most. His face always mirrored hers, and in those moments, he knew he was the luckiest man in the world.

When his phone rings, he hopes it's Sarah, finally calling him back. It's nearly two in the morning, and he thinks that, just maybe, she too feels that the bed seems empty without him.

He almost doesn't answer when he sees the unknown number. Nothing would be worse than the disappointment of thinking Sarah wanted to speak to him only to find that things were the same as before.

He answers anyway.

It's a nurse calling. At first, she has to repeat herself a few times for him to understand what's happening. He feels paralyzed, as if the blood inside him has stopped moving.

"Sir, are you there? Sir?"

He doesn't realize that he's stopped breathing until, suddenly, he feels as if he's drowning and has inhaled water.

"I'm coming," he says. "Right now. I'm coming right now."

***

He drives over one hundred miles per hour down I-10. He can hear the nurse's words, playing over and over again in his head, but it's all disjointed and fragmented. *Late, concrete, lucky, scrunched, blood, car accident.*

For a few moments, he thinks about slowing down. Anna's voice pops into his head, telling him not to go so fast. It's foolish to be driving so dangerously, weaving in and out of cars, the pressure on the pedal only growing as the speedometer ticks up. That isn't enough to stop him, though.

***

When he gets to the hospital, he runs to the front desk.

"Natalie Andrews," he says. "I'm here to see Natalie Andrews."

He wishes the lady at the front desk would type faster. He starts to hate her for how slowly she seems to move.

"She's in surgery," the woman says.

No matter how much information he asks for, she just repeats the same things he already knows, that there was a car accident and Natalie's in critical condition. He asks what specifically is wrong, what surgeries are being done, whether Natalie will be okay. He gets no answers, and the woman asks him to sit down, saying they'll update him as soon as they know more.

Something about sitting in that chair makes him feel as though he's back in Afghanistan. He stares at the plain, white walls. There are a few other people, scattered about, but he tries not to look at them. He doesn't want to acknowledge their pain. It'd be too much. One more ounce of suffering might break him, so he just stares at the white walls.

When he can't take the waiting anymore, he picks up the phone and calls Haley.

"Charlie, are you drunk—"

"No, no," he says. "There's been an emergency, Haley."

Instead of waiting for Haley to come, after explaining everything to her on the phone, Charlie leaves the waiting room. He goes outside where he smokes a cigarette and tries not to think about anything at all.

It's quiet out there. For a while, he stares at the parking lot, studying the hundreds of cars, realizing just how many people are inside, waiting to be saved. Despite his best efforts to ignore his own pain, at times he slips up, and he wonders if Natalie is dying on a table inside the hospital. He looks up at the stars, and there seems to be something cruel and brutal inside their beauty. He remembers Erin's words, about how the stars in the sky should be proof of everything being a part of something grand, something bigger than his pain. In the moon alone, maybe he should be able to see proof of beauty within darkness, but he can't help thinking it's proof that there's darkness in the face of beauty. He tries to think about something else.

***

Thirty minutes later, Haley arrives with Charlie's mom. His dad doesn't come. Charlie doesn't ask why; he doesn't want to know.

Haley and Charlie sit down while their mom demands answers from the staff, answers she doesn't get. She starts to get angry. Charlie can see how his mom is used to being in control, and the lack of power eats at her. He says nothing as she complains.

"This is ridiculous! I want to speak to a doctor immediately!"

After a few minutes of listening to her yelling, the nurse surrenders and agrees to find someone.

"Will she live?" Charlie's mom asks when the doctor arrives.

The doctor is a stoic, skinny blond woman, and Charlie has a hard time reading her.

"There are many risks with surgery—"

"I'm not looking for the political answer," his mom replies. "I'm asking you, in your professional medical opinion, will she live?"

"Ma'am, I'm not in a position—"

"I'm not asking you to be God. I'm not going to hold you to whatever you say. I just want to know, human to human, what do you think?"

She continues asking question after question, getting nowhere. In a way, Charlie appreciates it. He loves how his mom never backs down from anything, and he thinks, maybe she'll be able to get something, any kind of information. The idea of knowledge, good or bad, comforts him. But then again, part of him wishes his mom would just come sit down.

***

Four hours later, a woman with short, blonde hair walks up and introduces herself as one of the hospital's orthopedic surgeons. She asks them if they're Natalie's family.

"Yes," Haley says.

All of them stand.

The doctor explains that there was a car accident. Natalie Andrews was driving on I-10 around 2 AM when suddenly she crashed into the concrete traffic barrier. There was a witness, a lady driving near her. Apparently, everything looked perfectly normal until they approached a curve in the highway, but instead of turning, Natalie's car just kept going straight and crashed. The car was scrunched, like an accordion, upon impact. The medics had to saw the car apart to get to her, and blood spilled onto the road, along with shards of the car, as if someone had smashed a glass of red wine.

The surgeon uses the word "lucky." She says Natalie was lucky because she avoided any major head trauma. Her life was, instead, endangered by the amount of blood she'd lost. The majority of Natalie's injuries were to her lower body, particularly her right femur, which had snapped in half and jutted through her skin. Charlie tries not to picture any of it. He pretends she's talking about a stranger, which seems to make it easier.

"You can take some comfort in knowing that she was in shock," the doctor explains. "She didn't feel the full extent of her injuries."

"She wasn't in pain?" Charlie's mom asks.

"Not to the degree you'd imagine."

Charlie wants to ask so many things. What on earth was Natalie was doing in her car so late at night? She wasn't drinking—they knew that from her blood report. None of it makes any sense.

"Was there anything medical that might have led to the accident?" Haley asks.

Charlie wonders if Natalie had a seizure, or something that rendered her incapable of turning the wheel.

"Of course, it's hard to know what really happened, but she doesn't have any signs of neurological impediment."

For a second, there seems to be something ironically cruel in that statement. According to any medical examination, Natalie Andrews's brain was completely fine. Of course, that couldn't be more of a lie. Charlie wishes she'd had a seizure or something. The alternative was that Natalie crashed her car because she was too distracted simply to turn the wheel. Either that, or she just chose not to turn. Charlie can't help but wonder if this was all her grand attempt to be with her son again.

He keeps that thought to himself.

"We were able to give her blood transfusions, and we operated on her leg. She won't be walking any time soon, and she'll require—"

"Excuse me." Charlie speaks for the first time in hours. His voice is gentle and quiet; he's afraid of his own words. "Are you telling me she's fine?"

"Well, she's not fine—"

"She's going to live though?"

"She's alive. She has a tough road ahead, but—"

He doesn't listen to anything else the doctor says. He takes a step back from his family and lets go of Haley's hand.

"Charlie, what are you doing?" she asks.

He looks around, and it seems as if everyone in the waiting room is staring at him. His chest pounds, and he doesn't move or speak.

"Are you okay?" she asks.

Without replying, he turns and walks out. He begins to run as soon as he gets to the hallway. When he gets outside, he turns a corner to make sure he's alone.

Then he closes his eyes and lets himself cry.

***

He doesn't sleep for the next forty-eight hours.

At first, they're not allowed in Natalie's room, but after a while, the doctors let them in. Charlie sits by Natalie's side, never letting go of her hand. Haley comes in every once in a while, and Charlie can tell she wishes he'd sleep or take a break to eat a full meal. She never says anything, though, because they both know he'd never leave Natalie.

She's hardly recognizable with her swollen face and scar-ridden body. There's a particularly deep cut along the right side of her face, and he can't help but think that, for the rest of her life, she'll remember this day every time she looks in the mirror. Somehow, that feels like the cruelest part of the whole tragedy—how there's never any escape from the past.

Haley puts her hand on Charlie's shoulder.

"You smell," she says. "You should shower."

He doesn't reply.

"Please, Charlie—"

"Why do you think she was driving that late at night?" he says. For once, he takes his eyes off Natalie and studies his sister's face. He sees that she's just as tired as he is. Whether she's more worried about Natalie or him seems to be a toss up.

"I don't know," she replies.

Charlie goes back to staring at Natalie's cuts. He tries to remember each one, the design of them, the patterns.

"I called her," Haley says.

"Who?"

"Sarah."

Even attempting to think about Sarah in that moment feels overwhelming. Of course, he's never really stopped thinking about her. She's permanently engraved in the back of his mind, and truth be told, he's thought about calling her many times. The problem was that he didn't know what he'd say when she answered. He felt he'd caused enough problems and she didn't deserve this additional burden.

"What'd she say?" he asks.

"She wants to talk to you."

"I... I can't leave. I'll call her later."

"She's here."

He turns his attention to Haley.

"She's outside."

Charlie's eyes move to the door. He studies it the same way he studied Natalie's scars, as if this moment is something he'll remember forever, as if there's some importance in it that will influence the rest of his life.

"Get up, Charlie," Haley says, although the command in her voice is filtered through love and kindness. "You need to go talk to her."

He knows she's right.

He stares back at Natalie. Her skin looks almost blue in his hand. Haley sits down and takes Natalie's hand from him. She looks at him steadily, as if to assure him that he can trust her never to leave Natalie alone.

Charlie gets up and walks to the door, but stops for a second, trying to think of something to say to Haley. Nothing he comes up with seems adequate, so he leaves in silence.

***

Sarah is sitting in the waiting room, staring at the floor. Charlie hesitates, not sure what to do at first, then goes and sits next to her.

She looks at him. Her eyes are red, and her face shines with the residue of tears. She's still and expressionless. For a moment they look at each other as if acknowledging that only silence can articulate everything that's going on. Then they both look away and just sit, side by side, for a while.

"When I got back from the war," Charlie says quietly, "I thought I was done losing people." He lets himself look at her again.

"You aren't going to lose her."

He knows she's trying to comfort him. He thinks about telling her she's being naïve, that she doesn't know that for sure. But he also knows it takes strength to have that kind of faith, to share that kind of belief with anyone. He knows Sarah's a smart girl, that she's fully aware that it's a promise she can't necessarily keep. For her to comfort him, to put aside logic and pretend to be sure everything was okay, takes a lot of love.

"What about you?" he finally says.

"What?"

"Am I going to lose you?"

As soon as the words leave his lips, he feels hollow inside. He feels as if adrenaline is rushing through his whole body, and something about it makes him want to throw up.

Her face droops, her eyes heavy and sad.

"No," she says. "You could never lose me, Charlie."

He lets himself breathe.

"I shouldn't have left," she adds.

"I shouldn't have given you a reason to leave."

She puts her hand in his and leans her head on his shoulder. "We still have so many problems. This doesn't change that."

"I know."

"I wish we could just fix everything, but—"

"I know."

Without saying anything else, without trying to plan the future and figure out what this moment would come to mean, he lets his head rest on top of hers.

"Just come home," he says. "Please, just come home."

Chapter 10

The next few hours pass slowly and painfully. Charlie is suddenly acutely aware of the weight that individual moments can hold, as if each second is physically heavy and needs to be carried. It's exhausting, and he starts to feel that he'll never be able to breathe fully as long as he's sitting in that waiting room.

Finally, Natalie's sister, Hannah, arrives.

"I can take over," she says. "Really. I've got it."

Hannah is a quiet, kind, simple woman who married a farmer when she was twenty-two, and moved to a town in the middle of Nowhere, Kansas. Charlie can see she doesn't fully understand the gravity of everything that's happening, but that obliviousness rescues her, keeps her unfailingly strong. In a way, he admires that about her, but it also makes him nervous.

"Charlie," Hannah says. "You don't need to worry. I'm gonna stay in Houston as long as she needs. Why don't you take a break?"

When he doesn't move, she reaches out and hugs him. "Thank you for what you've done for our family, but you don't need to carry this burden anymore. Okay?"

Charlie says nothing.

"Okay?" she repeats.

"Okay," he whispers back.

***

Charlie stands in the middle of the waiting room, unable to force himself to go.

"Do you want to leave?" Sarah asks, breaking a long silence.

"I don't know," he says, looking at her as if she has the answer.

He feels an unyielding anger. He's not sure whom the feeling is directed toward, but he thinks he's angry with Natalie. He's mad that she was out late at night, driving when she should have been asleep, and he can't understand why she didn't turn the steering wheel. At the

JULIA CAMP

least, she was reckless, and at the most, suicidal. The idea of looking Natalie in the eyes and asking her what happened feels unbearable. He's not sure he can handle any answer at all.

"Honey," Sarah says quietly, "I wanna go. Will you take me home?"

He can see she isn't doing this for herself; she's asking for him. She's saving him from the decision. He feels the burden leave his shoulders, and suddenly, the passing seconds don't carry so much weight anymore.

He nods. They exchange a long look, silently acknowledging what she's done. She gives him a soft smile, gently puts her hand on his shoulder, and kisses his cheek before standing up. Then she goes to explain to Haley, Charlie's mom, and Hannah, that she needs to go home and that Charlie is going to take her. She's gracious, polite and sensitive.

When he's hugged everyone goodbye, left the hospital, and got into his car, he turns to Sarah and whispers, "Thank you."

She pretends not to know what he's talking about.

***

Things at home are different for the next few days. Sarah doesn't start fights or repeatedly ask Charlie what's on his mind.

Instead, she reads all about pregnancy on the Internet. He doesn't even know what she's spending all her time researching until, one night, she asks, "Do you think I eat enough vegetables?"

He sees that her screen is filled with information about the importance of nutrition during pregnancy. "What have you been looking at?"

"Just some basic things."

He looks more closely at her screen and sees how many tabs she has open. She rotates between them all, quietly reading about diet, exercise, strollers, breastfeeding, baby names.

After a while, she asks, "What kind of stroller shocks do you think would be best?"

The look in her eyes frightens him, a look that suggests he should have an opinion. She's always been the type to over-prepare, and he can tell that reading article after article makes her feel safer, as if everything is under control.

In a way, though, Charlie can feel her disconnecting from him. He sees that deep down, although she'll never admit it, she doesn't have the energy to think about him as much as she once did. Sometimes, he

- 84 -

steps outside to smoke a cigarette, and she never says a word about it anymore. She stops questioning him about what Rylee's phone number is doing in his sock drawer, and she goes to bed long before him, no longer staying up as late as she can, waiting for him to fall asleep. He doesn't think badly of her for it. He understands that she has to live in a world that's primarily her own, even though it scares him too. Her lack of questions somehow feels worse than the constant interrogation.

***

At work that week, Charlie finds himself talking more than usual. He isn't sure why. He gets there early, starts work, and says good morning to everyone as they enter. The routine feels peaceful to him. He feels more like himself, the person he was in high school, so long ago, before the war. The simple act of greeting people embodies hope, a belief that he can return to the man he used to be, someone undamaged, who could one day be a father.

There are times, while he works, that he wants to stop and talk to TJ about everything that's happened. He wants to talk about Sarah, and his baby, and the accident, but he knows that telling TJ would change everything. TJ might filter the things he says in attempt to be sensitive or gentle, or he might think Charlie needs special treatment. There's nothing Charlie wants less, so instead, he just sticks to routine conversation and works on the engines. When the guys ask where he's been the last few days, he says he had the flu, and no one asks him any more questions.

As Charlie becomes more engaged and friendly, TJ becomes the opposite. He's just one notch quieter and more reserved. It's so subtle that when Charlie asks another guy at the shop about it, he doesn't know what Charlie's talking about. It's clear to Charlie, though, how TJ keeps to himself slightly more, not always looking around for someone to talk with or tease.

One morning, as Charlie checks the tires on a '94 Plymouth that came in the day before, TJ comes over to bring him a rag. TJ hands it to him in silence and begins to walk away. If it were anyone else, it would have been a normal exchange, but TJ is never quiet, or passive, or anything short of extraordinarily extraverted.

"You all right?" Charlie asks.

TJ turns back, as if confirming that Charlie was really talking to him. He looks surprised by the question.

"Yeah," TJ says.

In the brief moment before TJ turns around, Charlie can see something behind the surprise in his eyes, a twinge of vulnerability, as if he knows he just got caught. For the rest of the day, TJ goes back to being his loud self.

"Could you work any slower?" he yells at Tyler. "At the rate you're going, cars won't even exist by the time you're done fixing that engine. Scientists are working faster at creating a teleportation device."

In those moments, as they all laugh, things feel normal again, but whenever TJ looks at Charlie, there's a moment where his smile freezes, as if he's on autopilot rather than expressing how he really feels.

Charlie decides to drop it, to let his friend keep to himself whatever he wants. TJ would grant him the same courtesy.

At lunch that day, when the two of them are alone, TJ says, "You know that girl I was telling you about?"

"You mean the perfect one that you haven't shut up about?"

TJ smiles a bit, but looks down. "Yeah, that one." He clears his throat and refuses to look Charlie in the eyes. "We aren't together anymore."

"Oh." Charlie knows he should have something else to say, but he can't think of anything that's not a cliché. It seems pointless to say the first things that popped into his mind, like 'You'll find someone new,' or, 'It's her loss.' Instead, he just says, "I'm sorry."

"Wanna know the crazy part?" TJ says.

Charlie nods.

"I broke up with her. I'm the one who left."

"What? Why?"

TJ smiles and shakes his head. "Because apparently I'm out of my fucking mind."

Of course, that isn't really any answer at all, but that's all he says before he stands up, throws away his trash, and goes back to work.

Chapter 11

Charlie spends a lot of time in the next few days thinking about Sarah, Natalie, and Wes. Occasionally, when he thinks about being a dad, his chest tightens, and he finds himself wanting advice. Sometimes, for a second, he thinks of calling Wes. In those moments, when his heart reacts before his brain, he feels as if his chest is on fire.

Lately, when he thinks of Wes, he remembers Natalie telling him about Meghan, Wes's girlfriend who didn't come to the funeral. He wants to talk to her. She might have some more insight into what happened with Wes. Most of the time, he feels sure he wants to know more about Wes's state of mind, but sometimes he wonders if the answers would be worse than the unanswered questions.

One day after work, he sits down at his computer for a long while, staring at the screen. He takes a deep breath and turns it on.

He had made the mistake of going on Facebook once after Wes's death. The whole world had reached out, post by post. Part of him appreciated the support because it confirmed that Wes had mattered, that he was important to everyone and not just to Charlie. But he'd also felt slightly angry, looking at all the people who'd never miss him as deeply. It didn't feel fair. He'd closed the tab and shut his computer. Sarah would sometimes tell him that he should read the posts, that maybe he'd take comfort in what everyone else had to say. He got her point, and he even thought she might be right, but he never logged on again.

He intends to just go to Wes's friends, search for Meghan, and not look at anything else. But, of course, that doesn't work. As soon as he types in Wes's name, he sees a picture of the two of them together, and he can't look away. He remembers that day, Wes's twenty-second birthday, right after they got home. It was at the beginning, when things were still good, when they were just happy to be away from the gunfire, not fully aware of how the horror wasn't over. Wes has his arm around Charlie's neck, in a bit of chokehold, and in the picture, they're both laughing. The bartender in the background is pouring drinks and people mull around them, trying not to get in the way. There are huge bright gold balloons labeled 22. Sarah had bought them. He remembers how he couldn't see out the back window the whole time he was driving to the party because of those huge balloons crowding the backseat, and he'd complained about it. But when they got there, and Sarah handed him those balloons, he wasn't even slightly irritated anymore. He still remembers the way Wes smiled and hugged her.

Charlie puts his head down next to the computer for a second. He doesn't cry, or even want to. Instead, he fights the urge to talk out loud, as if speaking to that picture would bring Wes back to life.

He lifts his head again and clicks on Wes's pictures. He's in so many of them. Sarah is too, sometimes alone with Wes. He felt lucky to have the two people he loved the most in the world be so close as well. He comes across a photo of the three of them at a high school football game, the screaming fans in the background, the two boys in their uniforms, Sarah smiling in the middle. Looking at that picture makes him acutely aware of how insensitive he's been to Sarah. While he was trying to get over Wes, she was too, and he's been incapable of helping her, of dealing with anything other than himself.

He scrolls away from the old pictures and looks at the most recent ones. There are pictures of Wes playing football with kids. He knew Wes had gotten into coaching little kids when he got back from the war, but he'd never really stopped to picture it. It's painful, looking at the way the kids smiled at him in the photos, the way he was smiling. It doesn't make any sense that Wes could feel this way and then choose to die.

He keeps scrolling until he finds a picture of Wes with a girl. She's beautiful. She has a long, slim body, like a ballerina, and she leans into him and puts her head next to his. She has light-brown eyes and thin, blonde hair in ringlets that stops just above her shoulders. They look as though they're at a park, with big trees and a kid throwing a Frisbee in the background. There's a blanket on the ground behind them. He hopes it's theirs—the idea of them sitting down and having a picnic comforts him. Wes looks happy with her.

After studying the picture for a while, he clicks on her name. Meghan Wallis. In her profile, he sees a phone number.

Without giving himself time to think or back out, he punches the number into his phone and presses the call button. His heart accelerates with each beep as he waits for her to answer.

"Hello," she says.

"Hi," he replies, suddenly startled by the sound of his own voice, realizing he's just set a plan in motion, a plan to search for a truth that he hopes will heal him.

***

Meghan agrees to meet him. To Charlie's surprise, she knows who he is. Wes had talked to her about him. She doesn't say whether the stories were good, or bad, or both.

She chooses to meet him at a bar, later that night. It's about thirty minutes away, and he drives the whole way in silence. His head already hurts from his internal voices screaming different, unanswerable questions. The last thing he needs is any more chatter adding to his headache. Plus, when he's in the car, he usually listens to a CD, but the CD is Wes's, and lately, it's been hard to hear. Wes had put all his favorite songs on it, and in high school, he'd play air guitar and scream at the top of his lungs from the passenger seat. "Bohemian Rhapsody" was the first song, and he'd play it again and again. Charlie always begged Wes to shut up, although they both knew he never really meant it.

When he pulls up to the bar, he realizes he's sweating. He'd forgotten to turn the air conditioning on in his car. Usually, he would have noticed the discomfort of sitting in the heat, but now he feels uncomfortable all the time when he thinks of Wes, and the line between internal and external discomfort feels blurry. He doesn't even notice anymore. He wipes the sweat from his forehead and goes inside.

He takes a deep breath as he enters. It's very dark and loud, with half a dozen crowded pool tables near the entrance. People smoke cigarettes and cheer while watching whatever sport is on the television. He's come about thirty minutes early, thinking he'll get a couple of drinks in before meeting Meghan. He could think more about what to say, practice wording, practice making sure he's always sensitive. When he gets there, though, he sees Meghan already sitting at a table. She's staring at her drink, lost in her own world, not cheering along with the other people who are jumping up and down while screaming about a referee's decision.

She sees Charlie and does a double take, as if thrown off by him being there so early. He sees her take a deep breath, and she nervously tucks her hair behind her ears as she stands up.

She looks slightly different than he expected. She's just as pretty as she was in the pictures, but she looks stronger and better built in person. Her eyes are piercing rather than soft like he'd imagined. He reaches out his hand and introduces himself. He isn't aware of how sweaty his hand is until he touches hers and feels how dry it is.

"Sorry." He wipes his hand on his pants. "I feel like I just ran a marathon or something."

His heart is racing, but then she chuckles and smiles at him, and he relaxes.

Her demeanor is different than he expected, more passive. She's confident but quiet and unimposing.

"I have to admit, I'm a bit nervous," she says. Her voice is tender and gentle, and Charlie can immediately see what Wes liked about her. She's genuine and unintentionally charming. "Kinda a silly thing to be nervous about, isn't it? I mean, sitting down and getting drinks isn't exactly terrifying, right?"

"Well, I've been out of my mind all evening, trying to figure out what exactly to say, so if it makes you feel any better, we're in the same boat."

"The same rickety, sinking boat." She laughs, keeping the words from shriveling into something dark.

He smiles. He isn't afraid anymore, and the shakiness in his voice is gone. He's aware that she just made him relax in one of the hardest conversations he'll ever have, and he appreciates it. She has a kindness emanating out of her that makes him comfortable.

She takes a sip of her drink. "So tell me, what was the result of those hours of thinking? What exactly did you figure out that you wanted to say?"

He'd had a whole speech lined up. He was going to start with small talk of some kind, something to ease them into the conversation, and then he'd say something eloquent; but looking at her now, he can't remember anything he'd planned to say. He knows, after only speaking to her for thirty seconds, that she has the rare talent to make people feel as if they've known her forever. He didn't need a speech.

"Did he seem sad?" he says. "Did you know he was so sad?"

The simplicity of the question strikes him as particularly tragic, and he can see she feels the same. Without knowing it before walking into the bar, he realizes this was the only question there was at all. Somehow, everything else was wrapped inside.

"No," she says softly. "God, no."

They both look down at the table and Charlie starts to wish he had a drink.

"I loved him," she adds. "We only dated for a few months, so I know it's hard to believe, but I really loved him."

To anyone else, the fact that she didn't know he was sad and that she loved him might have seemed unconnected, but he got it. He believed she really loved him because she saw those two things as painfully related.

"He never... he never told me about you," Charlie says quietly, as if ashamed. "We grew apart in the last few months, but I still don't get it. I don't get why he didn't tell me he had a girlfriend."

As soon as he finishes his sentence, he wishes he hadn't said it. It's an unfair thing to say, and he doesn't know how on earth he'd respond to that if he were her.

"He didn't tell a lot of people a lot of things, apparently," she says, her voice holding no anger, only factuality and understanding. "He talked to me about you, though. He worried about you. A lot, actually. He talked about how he thought the war really messed you up. He said you never wanted to talk about it."

Charlie doesn't know what to make of that. The irony of Wes worrying about him tears him apart, cell by cell, his skin burning.

Meghan goes on to tell him about her life and how she met Wes. She had gone to college at A&M, where she was an All-American basketball player, and she never stopped loving the game. It haunted her that her career was over. She said it felt as if she'd lost a limb, as if a part of her was suddenly missing and would never come back. Without basketball, she'd never be the same. She couldn't face losing it, so she started volunteering, coaching little kids, and she loved it. She met Wes while she was working there.

"He loved football the same way I loved basketball," she says. "It made us feel like we understood each other in a way that other people couldn't. I really think we did. I *thought* so anyway."

He knows the look on her face, the way her insides tighten when she speaks of him, the way she feels she can't breathe, the feeling of betrayal deep in her bones. She doesn't look him in the eyes.

"I thought we had everything, and then one day, he just broke up with me."

"He broke up with you?"

"You didn't know that?"

Charlie shakes his head.

"About a month before he died. It was a weird break-up. He told me I was 'too perfect.' I thought that was a line or something. I thought it was the 'it's-not-you-it's-me' sort of thing. But the longer I talked to him, the more I could see that he meant it. He actually thought I was 'too perfect,' and he didn't mean it as a compliment. It was the real reason he didn't want to date anymore."

"What's that mean?"

"I don't know exactly. He told me that I felt more like a myth than something real. What am I supposed to say to that? 'I'm sorry?' 'I promise I'm real?'"

Charlie doesn't know what to make of that, either.

"Whatever he was telling me was the truth, though. I don't understand what was going on in that head of his, but whatever it was, it was true to him. I'll hand him that. He wasn't a liar. Sometimes when people sound that crazy, that irrational, that incoherent, it's how you know they're genuine."

Charlie doesn't think he could accept that sort of irrationally as something human. He sees the unknown as too ugly and scary to really be acknowledged.

"What can I say, I always saw the best in him. I loved him. I really did." She stares down at her drink as if there's shame in that.

Charlie tries to change the subject. "He told me he was going to re-enlist. Did he ever talk to you about that?"

"Well, yes, until he applied to coach."

"Applied to coach where?"

"He applied for the assistant coaching job at his high school. He was really excited about it. He thought he'd found his path, I guess, but then he didn't get it and he was crushed."

"How on earth would he not get that job?"

Meghan shrugs.

Wes was the best player in the history of the program, and the head coach was the same man who'd coached Wes growing up. Charlie would have bet all his money that Wes would have gotten that job.

"It destroyed him, though," she says. "Not getting that job just... broke him."

They're quiet for a while as he tries to understand everything she's told him.

"Can I ask you something?" she says.

"Of course."

"Did he ever say anything to you about someone named Rylee?"

"Rylee?"

"It's probably nothing. I just was wondering. He used to keep this piece of paper on his dresser, and it had her name and phone number on it."

Charlie knows exactly what she's talking about. It's the same piece of paper Sarah's asked him about time and time again.

"Did you ask him about it?" he asks.

"Oh, of course. I thought he might be cheating on me. I brought it up, and he told me that wasn't it, that I wouldn't understand. He begged me not to worry about her, but he also never told me who she was. It was weird."

"Do you think he was cheating?"

"Was he the cheating type?"

"No, I don't think so." He pauses for a moment. "But I also didn't think he was the type to kill himself."

She looks up at him, heavily and painfully. "You know, I used to think he'd come back to me one day. I used to think he'd realize he made a mistake and show up at my doorstep. I don't know if I thought I'd take him back, but I just... I never thought I'd actually never speak to him again. I don't even remember the last thing he said to me."

***

Later that night, when they're outside the bar and about to say goodbye, he asks her to wait. He runs to his car, turns it on, and hits the eject button on the CD player. He runs back to her.

"You should take this," he says.

"What is it?"

"It's all of his favorite songs."

She stares down at the CD as if touching it would be dangerous, as if there's a fifty-fifty chance it's covered in a layer of acid.

"You'll never get to speak to him again," he says, "and I can't... I can't do anything about that. But I can tell you that if he were fine and happy, like he once was, like he was so often, he'd be singing these songs, terribly, at the top of his lungs."

Standing there, holding out that CD, makes him feel shaky, as though he could crumble.

"I can't take that from you," Meghan says softly.

"Please," Charlie says. The CD is too painful for him to keep himself, but it also comforts him for someone else to have it. The vague idea that Meghan could imagine Wes and keep him alive, at least in some small way, makes him feel less alone. And then, there's the simple truth that he hates how Wes hurt her, and he wants to do anything he can to ease her suffering. "Please, take it."

She reaches out and takes it. Wes had written his name on the CD, and she looks at his handwriting as if it means everything.

"He told his mom he was in love with you," Charlie says. He hadn't planned on telling her that, but the words just poured out. "I don't know what you're supposed to make of that, but he did love you."

He thinks his words will upset her. He thinks they'd upset him if he were in her shoes. Instead, though, a little smile appears on her face.

"If he loved me, I did all I could. Right?"

"Yeah." He nods slightly to himself as he looks away. "You're right."

He gives her a hug goodbye and goes back to his car, where he sits for a while in silence. Then he turns on the radio and drives home.

Chapter 12

Sarah starts spending more time at school, and when she comes home, she goes straight to bed. She's kind to Charlie, and always kisses him first thing when she gets back from studying, but it's routine and passionless. He thinks about bringing it up with her, but she's never still, never around, long enough for him to feel the moment is right. There are other times, though, when she laughs, when she shows him something funny or shares a story, where things return to normal, as if the world has been put back on its axis. Those small, simple, moments carry Charlie.

One morning, he walks into the kitchen for breakfast and finds her sitting at the table with a bowl of ice cream. Before he can say anything, she stands up, walks to him, and gently puts her hand over his eyes.

"You didn't see anything," she says, laughing. "We never speak of this again, okay?"

"Was that chocolate chunk with sprinkles?"

She takes her hand off his eyes, and they both look back at the ice cream on the table and smile. "Do you want a bowl?"

The growing smile on her face makes her eyes narrow.

He offers to make her breakfast and takes a carton of eggs out of the refrigerator. He'd never liked scrambled eggs until he met Sarah, but she made them all the time, for just about any meal. The first time she had him over, she made him scrambled eggs for lunch, loaded with cheese on the top. He never had the heart to tell her he didn't like them, so he ate every bite, and now, years later, he realizes that he's never once mentioned that he doesn't like eggs. Instead, he keeps making them for her. He eats them too, every time.

"Hey, you haven't showed me any of your artwork lately," she says, out of the blue.

"Oh." Her interest surprises him. "Well, I could if you wanted."

"Yeah, I'd like that." She takes another bite of her ice cream.

He cracks the egg. "There's this gallery opening coming up on Friday, actually. It's just a student show. Not a big deal really."

"Why didn't you tell me about it?"

He shrugs as he cracks another egg and throws the shell in the sink. "I don't know. I wasn't really planning on going."

He pulls out a fork and starts beating the eggs. He's still working when he looks up to see Sarah turn slightly away from him. It occurs to him that this isn't about his artwork at all.

"We could go, though," he says. "I'd love to take you, actually."

"Really?"

"Yeah. We could make a night of it."

She smiles at him, and her smile doesn't fade as she looks back down at her ice cream. He knows she's never particularly liked art, that she doesn't fully get it. Her brain is wired to think scientifically, and she once joked that she could hardly tell the difference between the paintings at her lower school and van Gogh. She'd never go to an art gallery if it weren't for him. He's about to say that she doesn't really have to go if she'd rather do something else, but then he looks down at the eggs on the stove and doesn't say a word.

***

That night, when Charlie's alone watching ESPN while Sarah's at school, he gets a phone call from Haley. She explains that she has to work the night shift at the hospital and Matt was working late, so she dropped Anna off at their parents' house. Their mom was out of town, and their dad had promised to watch Anna, but he got called last minute to go to a business dinner. It was supposedly very important. The clients were from out of town, and this was the only night they could meet.

"I'll watch her," Charlie offers, before she even has to ask.

She apologizes, again and again, saying she didn't mean for it to be at such short notice. She asks if he's sure and goes on about how she respects his time, but he cuts her off.

"I'm already on my way out the door," he says. "I love watching Anna. It's no big deal."

"Are you—"

"You've done me about a million favors. It's about time I start repaying them, isn't it?"

Still, she thanks him about ten more times before hanging up the phone.

***

The traffic on his way to get Anna is heavy, and he's a bit later than he'd expected. He knows that will worry his dad. There's nothing his dad hates more than being late to anything. When he gets to the house, he jogs to the doorway, takes a deep breath, and knocks.

When his dad answers, he's already dressed for dinner in a suit and a green tie that he's adjusting as he opens the door.

"Anna, are you ready?" he yells immediately. Charlie can tell that he's in a rush by his voice and the way he keeps tapping his pocket to make sure he has his wallet and keys.

Anna's voice echoes from somewhere in the distance, saying she's looking for her shoe, and she'll be there in a second.

The two of them stand in silence for a moment.

"Thanks for coming to get her," his dad says. "I'm really sorry. I didn't know about the dinner beforehand."

"It's all right." Charlie looks down at the floor, trying to come up with something else to say. He's ashamed to realize how hard it is just to stand in the same room with his dad. He'd rather be with a stranger.

"Anna, you coming?" his dad yells again.

"One second!" she chirps back.

Charlie looks up and something about his dad seems different. His eyes look heavier than usual, with bags underneath them, and his skin looks drier and more crinkled than it once had. The ends of his eyes droop down at the ends, making his eyes more concealed. He's thinner, too. In fact, upon a second glance, his suit looks slightly too big, as though he's shrunk. Charlie decides not to say anything about it.

"How... how are you?" his dad asks. "You doing all right?"

"Yeah. Yeah, I'm good."

"I heard about Natalie's accident."

"Yeah." Charlie nods.

His father looks down at his shoes for a second. "I would have come to the hospital, but—"

"Don't worry about it, Dad."

In the silence, Charlie can hear Anna running around upstairs, frantically and loudly, gliding from one end of the house to the other.

His dad looks down at his watch, and Charlie can see he's getting ready to come up with an excuse to leave the room. He's thirsty, or has to change outfits, or something. He's been pulling the same move for years now.

"I forgot my phone," his dad says.

Charlie doubts that's true, but he doesn't call him out on it and lets him walk back toward his bedroom.

***

Charlie and his father haven't always been so estranged. When he was young, his dad bought him a baseball glove for Christmas, and the two of them would go out into the front yard and throw a ball back and forth for hours. His dad was a quiet, simple man, who never had much to say, so they'd just play catch under streetlights in silence. Charlie's arm would be exhausted after a while, but he'd never ask to go inside. He loved it too much, valued the time too highly, to be the one to stop it. His dad must have felt the same way because he never asked to go inside either. They'd wait until Charlie's mom called them to come inside, saying that dinner was getting cold. His dad would always smile and put his arm around Charlie on the way into the house. He'd put his glove on Charlie's head like a hat, and Charlie always laughed.

It was when Charlie told him he was joining the army that things changed. His dad became distant and angry, at the time when Charlie needed him most, and deep down, Charlie isn't sure if he can ever forgive him for that. He gets the feeling that his father feels the same way, that he'll never forgive Charlie for enlisting. They're at a stalemate. Sometimes, it feels as if they're still standing in the front yard, throwing the ball back and forth in silence, neither of them willing to be the first to break the silence with an *I'm sorry*.

***

His dad comes back two minutes later. Charlie can tell he's about to go into some speech about how he finally found his phone, how he never expected it to be where it was, but Charlie cuts him off.

"I have something to tell you," he says. "It's important."

There must have been strength in Charlie's tone because his father's head snaps up, and Charlie can see that he's nervous.

"Is it about school?" his dad asks.

"Sarah's pregnant, Dad."

He's never seen his father so still. It frightens him a little, how unmoving he is. His eyes look straight at Charlie, and it's the first time in a while that Charlie feels as if his dad really sees him.

Charlie doesn't know how he expected his dad to act or what he thought he'd say, but he sees how, suddenly, his dad isn't in a hurry anymore, how the business dinner is nowhere on his mind.

"You're gonna be a father?" his dad says quietly.

"Yeah," Charlie says. "Yeah, I am."

Before his father can say anything else, Anna runs down the stairs, greeting Charlie with a flurry of hellos. Charlie turns away from his dad and squats down. Anna runs into his arms.

"Rocket!" she yells. "Do the rocket!"

Still squatting, he pretends to call NASA over an invisible intercom that he holds in his hand. He counts down, 3-2-1, and lifts her high above his head, saying "Blastoff!" as he zooms around the kitchen. When he sets her back down, she's dizzy and laughing.

He looks back at his dad, who hasn't moved a muscle, whose face hasn't changed. He can't tell what he's thinking, but he hasn't taken his eyes off Charlie.

"You ready to go, Anna?" Charlie asks.

She nods and runs over to tell her grandpa goodbye. She hugs him, but he barely moves.

"All right," Charlie says. "Let's go. I'll even let you ride shotgun. Don't tell your mom."

Anna giggles and runs to the door. Charlie can't help but smile as he watches her. He turns back to his dad, who now won't look at him and stares straight at the floor. Part of him feels sorry for his dad. He can tell that he's desperately looking for something to say—a feeling all too familiar to Charlie. Maybe it's something he got from his dad.

"You don't have to respond," Charlie says. "I just thought you should know."

With that, he turns and walks out the front door. Anna talks to him the whole way to the street, her hand in his.

As he gets into his car, he sees his father through the window, still standing there, unmoving, as if staring at Charlie's ghost.

***

On the way home, Charlie tells Anna he'll make her anything in the world for dinner. She thinks for a moment before deciding on macaroni and cheese. They stop at the grocery store and buy two boxes of noodles shaped like Scooby-Doo characters. When they get to his apartment, Anna insists that she knows how to make it all by herself, that her mom taught her. Charlie tries to help, but she's determined to do all the preparation on her own, apart from stirring on the stove. When it's ready, they sit at the table, eating macaroni, talking about her day at preschool.

After dinner, Charlie helps her with her ten minutes of homework. Then he makes popcorn, and they sit down in front of the TV together. He lets Anna pick the movie—*The Incredibles*. She picks it every time. He's already seen it three times with her, but he doesn't mind.

"You know, Uncle Charlie," she says during the opening credits, "my birthday is in a week."

"One week, huh?"

"I'm gonna be six. Can you believe it?" She looks up at him smiling, shoving popcorn into her mouth.

"Well," he says, "Your birthday might just be the best day of the year to me."

"My mom told me I can have a birthday party. It's at a bowling alley. She said I can invite ten friends."

"Ten? That's a lot of friends."

"Will you come?" she asks. "I picked you first."

At moments like these, he doesn't know what he ever did to deserve such kindness. It's the kind of thing that makes him want to believe in God, to go pray every Sunday in a church.

"Of course," he says. "I wouldn't miss it for anything in the world."

She smiles and goes back to staring at the screen. A little while later, she lies down, puts her head on Charlie's lap and falls asleep. After a few minutes of sitting there, watching her breathing, the peace is so overwhelming that he falls asleep too.

***

When Sarah wakes them up it's late, nearly one. She kisses Charlie's cheek and tells him Haley is at the front door. Anna's head still rests on his lap. Gently and slowly, he picks her up, and her eyes flutter open for a second and then close again as he carries her on his shoulder. Haley thanks him again and again.

"I'm the one who should be thanking you," he says. "It was a great night."

He sets Anna carefully in her car seat booster, making sure her head stays safe as he leans down to put her in the Toyota. He buckles her in and steps back to take a look, checking if there's anything else he needs to do to keep her safe. He adjusts the seatbelt, making sure it's tight enough. He brushes her hair out of her face, then leans down one more time and kisses her cheek.

"She looks most like you when she sleeps," Charlie whispers.

"You think so?" Haley asks, grinning.

They both look at Anna for a moment in silence before Charlie says goodnight and goes back inside.

***

Sarah is already in bed when he gets back to the apartment. When he comes into their room, she turns to him as usual. She kisses him and then closes her eyes again.

"Sarah," he whispers.

She mumbles, "Um, hum," keeping her eyes closed all the while.

He takes a deep breath. "Do you think our kid's going to look like us?"

Sarah smiles a bit and laughs. "Well, I sure hope so."

He doesn't say anything. He thinks about what it'd be like to have someone who looks like him roaming around the world. All of a sudden, the idea of being a father becomes less abstract, almost tangible, and he can picture his life full of cheering about correct addition problems and debating how much milk is ideal for macaroni.

Sarah turns, as if watching him think. "Why do you ask?"

"Do you remember when we were in high school and I took that crappy job as a waiter?"

She smiles for a second and opens her eyes. "Yeah, of course I remember. Why?"

"Well, I just... I never told you why I got that job."

She looks up at him, her eyes opening slowly as she sits up and brushes the hair out of her face. She blinks a few times and rubs her eyes. The two of them lean against the backboard of the bed.

"Okay," she says. He can see she's trying to figure out the reasoning behind the seriousness in his voice. She looks nervous. He feels nervous too.

"I was saving up for a ring."

Her face is frozen as she looks at him, although in her eyes he sees something different, that one of her walls has come down.

"The point is," he says, "I've known for five years that you're the one I want to be with forever, and I just... I just need you to know that I still feel that way. I want all of this: you, me, the baby."

He looks down for a moment at the blankets and takes a deep breath before looking back at her.

"I'm sorry if I ever made you feel like you were on your own," he continues, "but you're not, okay?"

She studies his face. He can see from the way she's looking at him that she's trying to read into everything he's saying, trying to see if he's still the same man who worked at Chili's to buy her a ring.

"I had this plan," she says quietly. "I was gonna go to medical school and do research, and by the time I was thirty, I wanted to be a part of something big. I wanted to cure Alzheimer's and study cancer, and now, at night the only research I do is about cribs and diapers."

"I know."

"It's not what I planned."

"I know."

She pauses and lowers her voice, as if ashamed. "I don't mean to sound selfish, but this... it's just not really what I wanted."

He reaches out and takes her hand. "I'm sorry."

"There's nothing to be sorry about. I didn't mean it that way."

For some reason, that doesn't make him feel any better. They're both carrying a weight, something almost physical but indescribable. Maybe it's the weight of everything they can feel coming but can't yet hold.

"I don't really know what I meant," she says. "I think I just mean that I'm scared."

He nods, still looking at her. He feels scared, too, all the time, and he knows that she knows that. As they look at each other in that moment, the only thing that's certain is how afraid they are and how much love is buried inside of that fear.

"We're gonna be good parents, you know," he says.

"You think so?"

"Yeah," he says. "Of course I do."

Her shoulders relax, and she scoots closer to him. He does the same. She leans forward and kisses him softly before putting her head on his chest. "I think we're gonna have a boy."

He wonders if she's right, if one day he'll be standing in his front yard playing catch with a little boy who never wants to go inside.

Chapter 13

The next day, Charlie is working on an engine when his boss, Anthony, asks to speak with him. Anthony keeps to himself most of the time, and hasn't ever asked to speak with anyone, as far as Charlie knows. Charlie feels worried, knowing Anthony wouldn't call him in over nothing.

"Charlie, what the hell did you do this time?" TJ jokes.

Charlie looks over his shoulder at TJ and smiles, trying to brush it off and not automatically assume the worst.

Anthony's office is a small room outside the garage where he takes phone calls and manages the business. It's a plain room, with only a single picture of his wife and his twin sons with their missing teeth and big smiles. The walls are blank and tan. Papers cover the entire surface of the desk. The simplicity of the room makes Charlie's blood pressure increase.

He sits down in a wooden chair with only a bit of cushion. Anthony loosens his tie as he sits, and he uses his sleeve to wipe the sweat from his forehead. All the guys in the shop joke that Anthony constantly looks as if he just got done swimming with the amount he sweats. His bald head doesn't help, the way the water rests on his entire head in little beads, shimmering under the lights.

"What's going on?" Charlie asks.

"How are you feeling, Charlie?"

"Feeling?"

"Yeah, you said you had the flu last week when you missed work."

For a moment he's tempted to tell Anthony the truth about everything that's been going on in his life, but he doesn't. He doesn't say anything about Natalie's accident at all. Instead, he talks about how Sarah brought him soup and how he's been feeling worlds better since his fever broke.

"You've been sick quite a few times lately."

Truthfully, Charlie hasn't given it much thought. Wes's death, Sarah's pregnancy, and Natalie's accident have all taken their toll on him.

"I'm sorry if that's been a problem," he says. "I didn't mean to cause any trouble."

"I know," Anthony says. "I get it. I really do."

Anthony always has an unbelievable amount of sympathy, sometimes to the point that Charlie doesn't think he deserves it. Part of him thinks Anthony knows everything somehow, how his world has been crashing down, how he's never really been sick once. Something about the tone of Anthony's voice, the sympathy combined with the inquiry, makes him feel as if he's trying to be a lie detector. Of course, Charlie doesn't say that. He just nods.

"There's no problem right now," Anthony adds. "Okay? I just... I just want to make it clear that you can't miss any more work on such short notice. It makes it impossible to staff the garage. You get that, right?"

"Yes, sir."

"I'd have to let you go if you keep doing this. Okay?"

"Okay," Charlie says. "I understand."

Anthony wipes the sweat from his forehead again. He looks as though he's about to stand up when he opens his mouth and then shuts it again.

"Charlie, is there anything going on with you?" he asks at last.

"Going on with me?"

"Yeah. Is there anything that I should know about? Anything that could get in the way of you doing your job?"

Without giving the question too much thought, Charlie says, "No, sir. Everything's just fine. I won't miss again."

Anthony nods, appearing to accept that answer, and sends Charlie back to work.

On his way back, though, Charlie looks through the office window to see Anthony looking down, leaning on his desk with two hands. After a moment, he wipes the sweat again and turns to go back to work. As he sits down, they lock eyes briefly. Charlie's vision is partially obstructed by the blinds, but he can read the look in his eyes. Anthony had called him into that office to fire him, but he just didn't have the courage or insensitivity to do it. After a moment, Anthony takes a deep breath then gulps, their eyes never leaving one another.

Charlie nods, then goes back to work, determined to demonstrate that he'll never let Anthony down again.

***

Charlie works hard, making sure to be extra focused, for the rest of the day. He turns off his phone and hardly takes a lunch break. When TJ comes over to talk to him, he doesn't let himself get distracted, continuing to work as TJ tells story after story.

"Anthony scare you straight or something?" TJ asks, laughing, as if the idea of Anthony being intimidating is too ridiculous to consider seriously. "What'd he do? Threaten to send you to his barber?"

Charlie laughs, although he still doesn't take his eyes off the engine. "Believe it or not, I'm not sure that a bad barber is really my biggest concern."

"Well, hell, it should be." TJ touches his own hair, emphasizing how great it is. "See how bouncy and playful it is? Girls can't resist this shit, man."

Charlie smiles. "You think Sarah would leave me without my great hair?"

"Naw, if she's willing to date an ugly ass like you, she's not too concerned about looks." TJ laughs, proud of himself, before he turns away, talking to Charlie over his shoulder. "Stay focused, man. Can't have you getting fired. Wouldn't want the second smartest guy here gone."

"I hate you."

Charlie goes back to work, thinking that he'd hate nothing more than leaving this place. He likes being there. He feels good again when he's around TJ and the guys. In a way, it worries him, because every time he starts to feel too at home, he imagines the promotional letters, sitting on his kitchen counter, from Rice.

***

At the end of the day, when he gets to his car, he sits down, puts the keys in, and turns on his phone. As his cell powers on, he adjusts the air conditioning and rolls down the windows. When he looks back at his phone, he sees many missed calls from Natalie. There's a message too, but he doesn't listen. He thinks about Natalie, though, just as he has every time he's gotten in his car since the accident. Sometimes, the longer he sits at the wheel, the more he feels a vague guilt for what happened to her. He doesn't know why, but when he starts to feel that way, he usually turns the car on, blasts the radio and goes home.

Today is different, though. Instead of driving home, he drives to his high school.

He intends to talk to his high school coach, to find answers about Wes that Meghan couldn't give him. Wes not getting the coaching job doesn't make any sense at all, and he feels entitled to an explanation.

It's the first time Charlie's been back at the school since he graduated. As he pulls in, he notices how different the place looks than it did in his memory. The grass is duller, the buildings smaller, the brick dirtier. This place used to feel as if it held the entire world within itself, and he can't believe how tiny it seems now. Still, though, he feels content and safe as he drives through the parking lot because that school holds his past. That comforts him. He knows if he brought anyone new to the school, they'd never see anything exceptional, but those walls are where he met Sarah, and the field is where he had the time of his life playing football with Wes. He watches some of the boys walk past, heading to their cars, laughing. He feels as if it was both just yesterday and a million years ago that he was one of those kids.

He parks the car and heads out to the football field. The field itself, without a doubt, is the nicest part of the school. The inside of the school could use a new coat of paint and a carpet that wasn't put in during the '80s, but a brand new turf field with red and white bleachers towers proudly above the buildings.

Charlie sits on the bleachers, which are chilled from the cool air, and watches the practice. He knows it's nearing the end because the boys are running sprints, Coach Terry's favorite way to end practice. The whistle blows like clockwork every thirty seconds.

He notices one boy far ahead each time as they run suicides. He's strong, lean, and fit. With every passing set, the gap between him and the guy in second grows. The boy reminds him of Wes.

***

Wesley Andrews, at age seventeen, had one of the brightest futures of any young man in the country. Every scout agreed he was one of the best running backs in the state. He wasn't the biggest guy—about six feet tall and 180 pounds— but he was fast as lightning. No one could catch him. He struggled in school, getting straight Cs, but his IQ for sports was unparalleled. He played with the mindset of a professional. Every recruiter who saw him play said that, with the right training, he might even have a shot at the NFL. Wes had scholarship offers from every school in Texas that he could dream of, schools that could give him a real future. He could go anywhere he wanted—UT, A&M, TCU, SMU. Even Notre Dame and Michigan sent letters of interest after seeing his tapes.

His stardom seemed surreal to Charlie. He'd known Wes since they were young, and to him, Wes wasn't a star, but the guy who liked too much jelly on his PB&Js and looked ridiculous when he tried to dance. The magnitude of what was waiting in his future never got in the way of Wes's humility, though. He never acted entitled to anything or superior to anyone, but always maintained a genuine, unwavering kindness. He never took credit for what he did, always thanking his coaches, his teammates, his mom, and God. He had a great life: a beautiful girlfriend, a sport he loved, a future as bright as the stadium lights. He believed his life was the result of gifts that were out of his control—talent, love and support. He always told Charlie it wasn't him that was special, but the people around him. What he didn't realize was that saying that, and really meaning it, was what made him special.

The only issue anyone ever had with Wes was that he wanted his dream in a way that was blinding. He thought about football twenty-four seven, and nothing was more important than the feeling he had on the field. The intensity of his passion drew people to him, but there was also an unspoken understanding between Wes and others that they could only ever be the second greatest thing in his life. His friends never minded, though. Wes never lacked energy around anyone. Football fueled him.

But sometimes this passion led to fits of anger that only those closest to Wes could fully understand. He could never fathom how everyone else didn't love football as completely as he did. He was the kind of guy who came into the weight room before the sun could even bench-press the darkness and turn night into day. Not only was he the most naturally talented player, but he worked harder than everyone else, so that no one could catch up to him. Charlie always respected him for how hard he worked—everyone did. But Wes never thought there was anything special about his behavior. Playing football was just in his DNA, and he assumed it was like that for everyone, as if loving football was part of what it meant to be human.

One time, a kid showed up to morning practice after a party the night before, and he was slow and lethargic. Wes hated him for that, and before the coaches had a chance to handle the situation, Wes walked over, ready to fight, yelling about how stupid it was for him to put anything above the team. Charlie had to pull him away, telling him to calm down.

It was the first time Charlie had ever seen fury in Wes's eyes, and for a moment, he wanted to just let Wes go, let him do whatever he wanted to the kid.

"Don't do anything stupid, Wes," he said.

The whole team had frozen as they watched Wes, awaiting his next move. Wes looked around at the other players and then back at Charlie, still angry.

"Please," Charlie said. "Cool off."

Wes took a deep breath, looked down, then walked over to his teammate. "Get off my fucking field," he said to the kid, and then he went to fetch some water, taking time to calm down.

Nothing, though, would compare to Wes's anger after his injury. On the first game of his senior season, a few days after he'd committed to the University of Notre Dame, Wes stepped onto the field full of hope and plans for what the season would hold. The crowd boomed, cheering for him wildly. Right before the whistle blew, Wes looked over at Charlie and smiled as if he knew a secret, as if he knew that this cheering crowd was just the beginning for him.

But only a few plays into the first quarter, Wes got the ball on third and seven. Charlie watched Wes run as hard as he could, only to be sandwiched by two linemen, who both slammed into him from opposite directions. His right shoulder shattered on the spot. He flew to the ground, hit his head, and was knocked out cold.

The X-ray of his shoulder looked like broken glass, shards of bone everywhere. The doctor said it was best that he was delirious, otherwise the pain of his injury would have been unbearable.

Charlie knew the worst part for Wes was never the physical pain. In that one moment, he lost the game he loved the most. His concussion was so bad the doctors told him if he played again he'd risk his life. They also said his shoulder might never fully heal, and he'd be lucky just to be able to raise his arm.

A few days later, when Wes was healthy enough to speak and sit up on his own, he begged the doctors, again and again, to let him try to play one more time. He told them that the risk, whatever it was, would be worth it to him, that he didn't care if it put his life in danger. He said that keeping him off the field was just as dangerous, because he'd never be okay again. Charlie remembers the way his eyes were wilting and his whole face suddenly looked blank and lifeless. Without the passion, without football, pulsing through his veins, he was a different man.

"Tell them, Charlie," Wes said at last, making eye contact with him for the first time since the accident. "Make him understand. Please."

Charlie had never seen Wes so vulnerable. In that moment, he wasn't the All-American football star, but just a boy who was losing what he loved more than anything in the world.

"You can't do something that'd put yourself in danger," Charlie said. He'd never forget the way Wes looked up at him, so betrayed, so alone. He looked at Charlie as if they were strangers.

Five years later, Charlie can't help but wonder if that was really the moment that Wesley Andrews died.

***

After practice, Charlie walks up to Coach Terry as he's putting away the footballs. It takes Terry a moment to react, the shock of seeing Charlie followed by immediate joy. He smiles and throws his arms around Charlie, pulling him close.

Coach Terry is a reserved man, unlike almost every other high school coach in Texas, but that's what makes him different, special even. He has an unyielding belief in his players, and at some point, his faith in his athletes becomes contagious. It's a deep, unspoken respect that makes his players profoundly loyal to him.

"It's good to see you," Charlie says as he hugs him back. "How've you been?"

They'd seen each other briefly at the funeral, but Terry had just nodded, saying nothing. It wasn't out of character for Terry to be quiet, so Charlie had thought nothing of it. Sometimes, Charlie thinks Terry is incapable of answering questions about his emotions, as if his feelings are too private and too real for him to articulate.

After a moment, Terry's smile deflates. Charlie knows why. Charlie loved football, but not in the same life-altering way that his friend did. Wes's love for football made him a coach's dream come true. Terry had coached him since he was four, and Wes would have said that he loved Terry like a dad. They couldn't have been closer. Coach Terry had a wonderful, beautiful family with three little girls, but Charlie knew there was a special place in his heart for Wes. Wes was family too.

"Oh, I'm fine," Terry says. There isn't any weakness in his voice. Charlie knows that in his coach's eyes, no matter how old Charlie gets, no matter what he's faced, Terry will always see him as a boy who dreamed of winning a state championship. Terry won't show any weakness. He's there to support Charlie and nothing else. He won't speak of the way Wes's death hurt him. "How are you?"

"I'm good," Charlie says.

Terry looks down at his feet for a second before looking back at Charlie. "I've been meaning to call you, actually."

"Yeah?"

"Yeah, I meant to call you after the funeral."

Charlie nods, trying to figure out what to say about that, but can't think of anything. Terry looks as if he wants to say more, but he doesn't.

"I... I just came here to ask if you knew anything," Charlie says.

"Knew anything?"

"If you knew anything about why Wes did what he did."

Standing here in front of his coach makes the whole situation feel more real. He can tell by the way Terry tenses up and looks down at his shoes that he feels that way too.

"The night before he died, he called me," Terry says. He looks down at the ground for a moment and then back at Charlie. "He told me he'd just gotten off the phone with you. I could tell something was wrong, but it was the middle of the night, and my baby girl was sleeping. He sounded crazy."

Charlie nods, remembering Wes's voice on the other end of the line, the frantic, nonsensical mess about the ghosts he saw.

"He kept... he kept telling me that 'she didn't deserve this,'" Terry says.

"Who?"

"I don't... I don't know. I don't remember."

"Was it Meghan?"

Terry shakes his head slowly. "I don't... I don't think it was that. Something with an R maybe?"

"Rylee?"

Terry's face lights up. "Yeah, Rylee. He kept saying he finally told her it was his fault."

"What was?"

"I don't know. He just kept telling me that it was his fault. I asked him what he was talking about, but he never answered. He mentioned a friend, though. Someone named AC? Did you know someone with those initials?"

"No, I didn't."

"Wes said he was sorry. He told me he had to tell AC that he was sorry."

With everything that Terry doesn't know, Charlie can see the worry spread on his face, and the desperate wish that he did know. He looks as if the fact that he didn't know was what killed Wes.

"Did he talk to you a lot after he got home?" Charlie asks, trying to get Terry to focus on a specific question, something to keep Wes's voice from repeating in his head.

"When he applied for the coaching job, yes," Terry says. "The letter you wrote was great, by the way."

"What?"

"The letter of recommendation that you wrote for him, for the coaching job. It was beautiful."

Charlie thinks about telling him that he didn't write the letter at all, that he doesn't know what he's talking about.

"You said a lot of nice things about him. Hand-written and everything. I already knew Wes was great, of course, but it helped when giving information to the board to have as many recommendations as possible. My word can only do so much."

Charlie wants to ask a million questions, but he can't figure out how to get the answers without admitting his total confusion. Maybe that's what he should do, but he thinks of how fragile Terry's heart must be, and how knowing Wes lied to him could ruin his perception of the boy he loved like a son. Maybe it was already ruined, but for Charlie to say anything felt unfair, even cruel.

"Since the funeral, I've been carrying it around," Terry says, putting his hand on his back pocket for a second. He laughs a little, as if there's something crazy about keeping the letter of recommendation of a dead man in his pocket. Maybe it helped him feel as if some things had gone right, that not every relationship had been a disaster.

"Can I see it?"

Terry looks confused. Charlie knows, as soon as he says the words, that his request doesn't make any sense. Why would he want to see a letter that he wrote? But Terry doesn't seem to expect every emotion or request to make sense at such a time, so he pulls out the letter and hands it to Charlie.

After one glance, Charlie recognizes the handwriting. Wes wrote it himself.

> Dear Coach Terry and Staff,
> I can't think of anyone who'd be a better assistant coach than my friend, Wes Andrews.

Charlie stops reading, too angry to continue. If Wes had asked, Charlie would happily have written something for him, and it would have been better than whatever Wes came up with to say about himself. Charlie would have been honored to recommend his friend, and he doesn't get how Wes wouldn't have known that.

He tries to hide his anger as he hands the papers back to Coach Terry.

"It's a shame," Terry says. "It's a shame things didn't work out. I think he would have been really happy coaching here."

Charlie can't believe the school board wouldn't have picked him. Wes's recovery had gone better than any doctor could ever have predicted. He had no permanent cognitive setbacks from his head injury, and he regained almost normal range of motion in his shoulder. He could even throw the ball, at least well enough to help out at the practices. Wes knew more about football than anyone else, and he loved the program. It made no sense that they wouldn't hire him.

"Why didn't it work out?" Charlie asks. "I'm sorry if that's pushy. I just want to know what you think."

Coach Terry looks confused. "Well, I don't know. Your guess is as good as mine."

Charlie's eyebrows scrunch together as he tries to work out what to make of that. "Why would my guess be as good as yours?"

Coach Terry looks lost. "I mean, if anything, I thought you would be the one to know."

"Me?"

"Yeah."

"Why would I be the one to know why the school didn't hire him?"

Terry's face changes completely, from confusion to shock. "That's what he told you?"

Charlie doesn't know what to say. Wes hadn't told him anything. He was just going off what little information Meghan had given him.

"Yeah," he says, believing that Meghan wouldn't have lied to him about what she knew. He could see it in her eyes, how each detail was painfully true.

"Well," Terry says. "I don't know what to tell you. Wes came into my office about two months ago and said he saw we had a position for an assistant coach opening up. He said he wanted the job more than anything. I told him I thought he'd be perfect for it. He applied, got the job, and then declined it."

"What? Why?" Charlie can't stop himself from thinking out loud.

"I don't know. It made no sense. He just came in here, looking completely defeated, and told me he couldn't accept the job. He said he wanted to more than anything but couldn't."

"And you didn't ask him?" Charlie feels bad the minute the words leave his lips. He knows it's an unfair thing to ask. Terry looks at Charlie as if to see whether he really expects him to respond to that.

"He looked so... closed off," Terry finally says.

In that moment, Charlie can see on Terry's face that he blames himself for not asking more questions. It's a horrifying sight, and Charlie hates himself for coming to the school at all.

"I'm sorry," he says. "I shouldn't have asked that."

Terry just keeps looking down, not saying anything.

"None of it makes sense," Charlie continues. "He loved football. He would have loved being a coach. He had nothing keeping him from taking the job. I don't know what he was thinking that day, but there wasn't a reason for him to pass it up."

Terry nods, seeming to only half-hear Charlie. There's a different look in his eyes now, as if he's had a realization. "I guess it wouldn't have made sense for him to accept it."

"What do you mean?"

There's only sadness in Terry's voice. "I mean, why accept a job when you know it won't matter?"

"Won't matter?"

"Why accept a job when you know you'll be dead in a month anyway?"

Terry doesn't seem able to function anymore. He looks as if no matter what Charlie says, he'll never hear a word.

Charlie thinks about trying to tell him that he misinterpreted everything, that it's not his fault at all. He believes that, of course, but he also knows it won't work. He knows Terry won't hear a bit of it.

"This shouldn't have happened," he says. "That's all there is to say about it. Nothing else. He should be standing here, and that's not on anyone but him. All right?"

Terry doesn't move. Instead, he looks down at his watch and says his wife is making dinner, and he's got to go home. It's an excuse to leave, and they both know it.

Charlie hugs him before he turns to go. There's something different about it, though, a certain disconnect, walls between them.

"Hey, Charlie," he says.

"Yeah?"

"If you ever, ever need anything, any time of day, you call me, okay? Promise you'll call me?"

"Yeah," Charlie says. "I will."

He knows that what he's really promising is that he'll never kill himself.

Chapter 14

The rest of the week passes with a cloud of heavy tension in the air. Charlie can't get his conversation with Coach Terry out of his head, and the constant weight of self-blame weighs down on him. He knows that, more than anything, he needs things to return to feeling normal, to feel good again.

On Friday, the night of the art exhibition, he hopes the event will hold everything he needs. It'll be a distraction, a break, from trying to piece together the crumbs that Wes left. Instead of staying late at the shop, as he has all week, Charlie goes home at five, showers, and puts on khaki dress pants and a light-blue, button-down shirt. It's been a while since he's dressed up. He looks at himself in the mirror and stands up tall. He thinks of what Sarah will look like in her dress and smiles.

Sarah had planned on coming home to get ready, but she was working in the lab, and it ended up taking longer than she'd expected. She set her things out on the bed, though, and asked Charlie to bring them so she could change at the school and they could go from there. He agreed to meet her at the lab.

***

Charlie's been to the lab with Sarah before, so he knows where to go once he gets inside Baylor's research facility. Walking past all of it makes him feel young, younger than he wants to feel. He couldn't explain what any of the machines inside the rooms do, but he wishes he knew. He's always loved science. It makes him sad, for a moment, thinking about what his life might have been like if he'd never enlisted. He could have been one of the students, huddled around a microscope, talking about experiments and worrying about tests.

When he arrives at Sarah's lab, he looks in through the glass walls. She's sitting at the table with a guy, both concentrating on the papers in front of them. Charlie can't get into the room because he doesn't have a key. He tries to think of how he can grab their attention. He's about to knock when the guy says something, looking up from his paper, and a smile spreads across his face. Sarah laughs and so does the guy. Charlie's always loved her laugh, the way her whole body sways and her hair falls in front of her eyes, so at first, he smiles too as he watches them. The longer he looks, though, the more his smile starts to feel heavy. He doesn't know why, but he wishes he hadn't seen them laughing together.

Part of Charlie just wants to stand there and watch, as if looking for something, but he can't figure out what, so he knocks on the door.

Sarah looks up, still smiling from the guy's joke, and sees Charlie. She stands up and comes to the door.

"Hello, honey," she says.

"Hello."

Suddenly, the guy is looking down at his papers rather than at Charlie, and he takes a moment to write a few more words before looking up. The closer Charlie gets, the more he notices about the guy — medium build, dark features and a pleasant smile. He has kind eyes. Charlie doesn't know what he thinks about that.

"I brought your clothes," Charlie says.

"Thanks, Love." She glances back at the guy. "Hey, I hate to ask you this, Charlie, but Max and I just need a few more minutes to finish up this lab, and —"

"No, no," Max says. "You go. I'll finish up here and send you the data when I'm done."

Sarah starts to argue with him. "It's not fair for you to have to do more of the work —"

"Is she always this difficult with you?" Max laughs, looking Charlie straight in the eyes now. He can see the joy on Max's face, the way he thinks her arguing is genuinely ridiculous and endearing.

"Yeah," Charlie says, turning back to Sarah, who puts her arm around him and smiles up at him. "I hate to say she is."

"You two are the worst," she says. "But thank you, Max. I'd really appreciate that."

Max looks at her for a second and then back down at his paper. He taps his pencil. Charlie can't figure out what to think of it all.

Sarah grabs Charlie's hand and turns to the door. She thanks Max again on the way out, and Charlie can't help but notice the way he sits up a little straighter when she says his name.

Charlie considers asking her about it, but when they get out the door, she's already speaking a million miles per hour about how excited she is for the gallery, how she's been looking forward to it all day, and bringing up Max seems beside the point.

***

The only thing more beautiful to Charlie than the gallery setup is Sarah in her silver, long-sleeved dress. She wore that same dress long ago when she first met his parents, and she looks just as pretty now as she did then, with her understated make-up and confident disposition.

They walk hand in hand down a path lined with trees and illuminated by lights above. The walkway leads to a giant gallery in the lobby of an auditorium, three stories high with walls made of glass. It's a gorgeous venue, and the closer they get, the more crowded it is.

"You didn't tell me it'd be like this," Sarah says, looking around, amazed at it all, as they walk inside. The whole place is bright, with white walls, wooden floors, and chandeliers that hang from the ceiling. The artwork is displayed on the perimeter, and there are tables where people are drinking and talking as they take breaks from walking around. A gentle buzz of voices constantly rings, keeping the volume inside low but never completely silent.

"I didn't know," Charlie replies.

After waiting a moment to take everything in, they begin to walk around.

Every piece in the exhibit is amazing. Some are abstract, some realistic, some interpretive, but each one tells a story. Charlie's always loved that about art, how you could wonder what it means and never find the answer. It also drives him a little mad, though.

Sarah stops in front of one piece, staring at it for longer than the others. Charlie had walked past it at first, but when Sarah stops, he comes back to look. It's a man lying in bed next to a woman, but it's hard to tell whether he's really there. He's drawn with light strokes, making him faint and almost invisible, unlike the girl. The blankets don't look as if they're on top of him in the same way they're on the girl. It's hard to tell whether they're resting on him or below him.

"It's like he isn't even there," Sarah says. "What do you think it means?"

"Charlie?" he hears before he can answer. He looks up and sees Erin.

She looks different than before. He's never thought of her as the type of girl who'd blend in at a formal event. He couldn't have pictured her in a dress, sipping wine, talking to people who go to galleries in their free time. She wears a bright red dress that makes her stick out, as if she's not afraid to be the center of attention, and on her right shoulder there's a tattoo of a compass. He's never seen it before.

"I see you found my drawing," she says.

"This is yours?" he says.

"I'll try not to be offended by the shock in your voice." She smiles and points under the picture where there are business cards with her name, number, and email address. "Can you believe this? I mean, what do you think? You think we get any big enough fans to really take these things?"

Their teacher is clearly behind the cards. She always looks to go the extra mile, to make the students feel their work is important.

"I think your work is great," Sarah says. She hasn't taken her eyes off the drawing.

Erin becomes fully aware of Sarah for the first time. She shifts her attention from Charlie and smiles. "You think so?"

"Absolutely," Sarah replies. "Granted, Charlie can attest that I might know as much about art as a kindergartener, but I'll be your first fan for whatever it counts."

"Counts for everything," Erin says. "I'll even give you this fancy business card, no charge. You can have one too, Charlie."

"How generous," he says.

Charlie waits for the silence to hang for a second, and then he formally introduces them to each other. He tells Sarah that Erin is in his class and how they've become friends over the last few weeks.

Within a minute, the two women are deep in conversation. Erin asks Sarah what she does and follows up with questions about her research and schooling. For some reason, Charlie finds it strange to watch them talk. They're similar in a way, both enthusiastic and passionate. Erin tells a story about her grandfather who passed away from Alzheimer's a few years ago, and Sarah goes into detail about a clinical trial on the use of estrogen in the prevention of neurodegenesis, something she wants to study that might one day be useful in Alzheimer's research. Erin hangs on to every word she says. It's as though they already have the foundation to be best friends. Charlie gets the feeling that he could walk away, and they might not even notice.

He finds out all sorts of things about Erin. She'd just moved from New York. She'd been trying to be an artist there, until one day, it all became too much, so she went to the airport and decided to go somewhere far away, somewhere different, somewhere that she'd have an entirely new life. She flew to Houston, Texas, and got a job teaching art at a local high school. She loves it, but she isn't sure whether she'll stay or go back to New York.

"Sometimes I feel like I want to see the whole world," she says, "but other times, I feel like I just want to be somewhere that's going to be my home forever. You know?"

Sarah doesn't respond immediately. Her face suddenly gets more serious, as if she's trying to think about a million things at once.

Charlie wonders what it is about Erin's statement that makes her stop to think, and he feels worried. He can see, though, how she notices that she's paused too long.

"I get that," she says. "It's a dilemma."

But then she looks at Charlie and her eyes linger in a way that makes him suspicious, as if she's just been caught lying.

"What are you thinking about?" he asks, trying to get some kind of explanation, not letting her look go unnoticed.

"Nothing," she says, although her eyes migrate to Erin, as if she doesn't want to talk about it in front of anyone else.

Erin seems to notice it too, and looks slightly uncomfortable. She changes the subject. "Have you gotten to see your piece yet?" she asks Charlie.

When he says he hasn't, Erin offers to walk them to it. Sarah follows behind Erin, and he trails a few steps behind. He wishes he knew what exactly what was going on, but when he stands in front of his work, Sarah stops and reaches her hand out to take his.

To Charlie's surprise, there are a few people huddled around, looking at his work. He'd drawn a man tossing a penny in the air. The look in his eyes is both hopeful and dark as he watches the coin spinning through the air. There's an inexplicable pain in his eyes that's dominating and enticing. The drawing is titled *Fate*.

"It's amazing, Charlie," Sarah says as she studies it. He can tell she really means it, her face now mirroring the man in the drawing, as though she's on the verge of a choice and everything rests in that coin toss.

"Thanks," he says. Erin hasn't taken her eyes off it either.

"How'd you think of drawing that?" Sarah says quietly, so that only he can hear.

"Wes used to make all his big decisions by flipping a coin," he says.

Wes saw random chance as something more than arbitrary. To him, it was the intervention of God in some inexplicable way. He used to keep a special penny in his pocket, and any time he didn't know what to do, he'd flip it. Wes even admitted that when he couldn't pick between Notre Dame and the University of Texas, he pulled out a coin. It was just what Wes did.

Charlie has been trying not to think too hard about how he found that coin next to Wes's body, heads up. He's never told anyone about it before. He didn't really plan on ever telling anyone, but something about those strangers looking at his drawing makes him feel like it isn't a secret.

"Oh," Sarah says, looking away from the drawing for a second, then back at it. She looks as if it's the saddest thing she's ever seen. Charlie doesn't know if that makes him feel good because someone finally understands what he hasn't been able to put into words, or if he wishes she'd forget what he's just said. "Well, it's unbelievable, Charlie. Really."

She stands there, unmoving, for the longest time. Her reaction makes him sadder; he wishes she wouldn't feel his pain so deeply.

Erin looks at the drawing too, without saying a word.

"Do you wanna keep walking?" he asks. "There's a lot to see, and we don't want to stand here all night, do we?"

He smiles, but Sarah hardly reacts at first. It takes her a moment to drag her eyes off the drawing.

They say goodbye to Erin and keep walking around, looking at the drawings, stopping to talk to some of the artists. They run into Charlie's teacher, an energetic, spunky, middle-aged woman with big hoop earrings that fly all over the place when she speaks, her hands buzzing through the air as if they're on fire.

"Charlie's great," she says. "His work is fantastic."

Charlie can tell she's excited to meet Sarah.

After an hour or so, before they're about to leave, Sarah goes to the restroom. Charlie feels isolated for a moment when she goes, not knowing where to go or what to say to anyone. Instead of waiting around, he goes back to Erin's piece and studies it, trying to understand all the details. The longer he looks at it, the more he realizes how much the girl in the picture looks like Erin. She even has a tattoo of a compass on her right shoulder.

"Just can't keep you away, huh?" Erin says, appearing behind him.

"Who's the guy in the picture?" he asks.

"What makes you think he's someone real?"

"Because the girl is you."

She stares at him for half a second, as if deciding whether to acquiesce, and takes a sip of her red wine.

"Who's the guy in your drawing?" she asks.

She seems to know he won't want to answer, because she takes another sip of her drink, signaling a pause. For a minute, he feels as if she's won. Then suddenly, as he looks at her, part of him wishes she knew everything.

"He's my best friend," he says. "At least he was. He shot himself after we got back from Afghanistan."

He feels as though Erin is the type of girl that always knows what to say, who's never caught off guard, but her face suddenly turns blank. She takes a moment to compose herself, trying to come up with the right thing to say.

"I was the one who found him," Charlie adds.

"I'm sorry," she says at last.

"It's all right." Of course, nothing could be less true. He thinks about saying something more, but nothing comes to mind.

She looks at him for a moment, and he can see her imagining everything, running through what it must have been like for him to find Wes dead. It's a look he's seen in Sarah's eyes many times. She's searching for a way to connect with him again, a way to keep his past from wedging between them.

"His name was Tyler," Erin says after a pause.

"Tyler?"

"Yeah. He's the one I drew."

Charlie can tell that Erin sees this as an exchange, as though revealing something about herself is the only way she can make things balanced again between them.

"He was my boyfriend in New York," she says.

"So you left him to come here?"

"No," she says. "More like he left me, so I came here."

Erin's eyes have a preoccupied look, as if she's more worried about telling the story correctly than gauging his reaction. It takes some of the pressure off him, letting him relax instead of scrambling to try to come up with a good response.

"He was an artist too, and I used to love that about him. It made me feel like I'd been connected to him my whole life through that passion. It was as if every day I'd spent loving art, I somehow spent loving him too. Does that sound crazy?"

He shakes his head. "I get that."

She has a way of speaking that makes him feel similarly, as if he's known her his whole life. He feels guilty for it, as though it's a betrayal of Sarah, but of course that's absurd. He can't help that he doesn't want her to feel sad.

"I don't know. I just thought he loved me like I loved him, but he didn't, and that's all there really was to it."

He silently studies the drawing again, the way the girl looks down, her eyes not quite shut, unable to rest fully. "I wish everyone in the world could see your art."

When she doesn't reply, he looks away from the drawing and back at her. She looks happy, and his expression mirrors hers.

"What?" he says, with a smile slowly growing on his face.

"You don't even realize the kindness of those words, do you?"

For a moment they look at each other, both content, and he feels nothing but calm. Something about that makes him want to look away, and he does after a second.

"What's the meaning behind the compass tattoo?" he asks.

She looks down at her own shoulder, as if reminding herself that it's there. "I don't know." She's still smiling to herself. "I guess I just believe that people always find their way."

"You think so?"

"Yeah, I believe that more than anything." She has a kind of radiance when she speaks, as if each word is booming with truth and authenticity. "Don't you?"

"Yeah, of course I do." The funny part is, he doesn't even have to think about the answer. Her faith feels contagious.

Charlie looks up to see Sarah coming out of the bathroom and starting to look around for him.

"I've gotta go," he says.

Erin's also noticed Sarah, and immediately takes half a step backward, as if physically acknowledging that he should be with Sarah. "It was nice running into you."

"You too."

He takes a few steps away but then turns back to her. "Erin, for whatever it's worth, Tyler was an idiot."

He doesn't wait for her to respond before he turns around and walks to Sarah.

***

As they leave, Sarah tells him she had a great night. He talks about all her reactions to the different works, how she did a good job pretending to be a critic. She laughs, but she seems slightly distracted. She takes longer than usual to formulate her responses, her mind roaming through the worlds of a hundred paintings.

"You never told me about Erin before," she says after a while.

"Oh," he says, surprised by her comment. "I didn't think there was much to say."

She nods and looks down at their feet as they walk. She scoots closer to him. "She's pretty, you know."

"What do you mean?"

"Nothing." She's still looking down. Her tone isn't accusing; it sounds as if she's just stating a fact and doesn't know what to make of it. "I just mean that I think she's pretty."

Charlie doesn't know how he should react, so he says, "No one in the world is as beautiful as you are."

She smiles at him but doesn't say much else, as if he's somehow missed the point. She drops the subject, though, and they walk all the way home hand in hand.

Chapter 15

On the day of Anna's birthday party, Charlie spends the morning working on a Chevy Malibu with a leaking exhaust system. He arrived an hour before anyone else. He'd woken up before his alarm went off, but the day was so full of promise and expectation that he'd found it hard to go back to sleep.

For Anna's party, he promised Haley he'd bring the cake. He went to Memorial Bakery and had them specially make a cake with the Incredibles on it. He knew she'd love it. He put Anna's cake in the refrigerator at the shop with five sticky notes saying "Do Not Eat" all over it—an unnecessary and endearing precaution.

The party would start at 5:30 that night at the local bowling alley. The party was originally at 3:30, right after Anna's school ended, but she pushed it back, just for Charlie, so he could go first thing after work. He told Anna and Haley many times that there was no need to modify their schedule, that they shouldn't center their plans around him, but they insisted, and truthfully, he appreciated the gesture. He wants to be there, watching her run around with her friends, cheering when she knocks down pins, telling her to slow down on the cake consumption without meaning a word of it. He's been looking forward to the party since the moment Anna invited him.

Everyone at the shop notices that Charlie's in a good mood. TJ asks him about it. Charlie tells him about the party and how he got Anna a new basketball as a gift.

"Can I see it?" TJ asks.

"No way are your greasy hands touching her present!"

TJ laughs. "You just won't let me see it because you know you'd never stand a chance if a game broke out."

Charlie can tell that TJ likes it when he's more relaxed, and that he wishes Charlie would always speak so freely. TJ asks about Sarah, saying she hasn't been around the shop lately, that she should stop by and join them for lunch, like she'd done so many times when Charlie had just gotten home from Afghanistan. She could hardly bear to be away from him back then.

"Sarah's good," Charlie says.

"Good?"

"She's good. We're good. Everything's good."

TJ looks at him, suddenly appearing to realize that "good" doesn't mean things are only "neutral" or "fine" to Charlie. It means things are at peace. He smiles.

"We're going out to dinner tonight, actually," Charlie says. "After the birthday party."

They've made plans to meet around 7:30. They'd have a nice meal and things would feel right.

"Sounds like you have quite the day ahead," TJ says.

"I'm a lucky man, aren't I?" Charlie's amazed how easy everything feels, how simplistic his joy is.

"Hell yeah you are, pretty boy." TJ's smile mirrors Charlie's.

What Charlie doesn't tell TJ is that he's made a reservation at Carrabba's, the Italian restaurant that he took Sarah to on their first date. Lately, there have been moments when he wishes she could be his forever, when he thinks back to their first date and realizes she's the only one he could ever need. He doesn't know for certain if tonight's the night, but just in case, he has the ring in his pocket.

***

Over the last few days, Charlie has felt better. He's been more aware of his own fortune, how lucky he is. After the art exhibition, things between him and Sarah have felt different. She hasn't stopped talking about his artwork, and he's started showing her more of it. He used to want to keep it to himself, but he doesn't mind showing it to her anymore. He likes it, even. In return, she's started telling him more about medical school, about the jobs she wants, about how she's debating her specialization. Sometimes, to Charlie, it feels like just yesterday that they were kids, sitting in a high school class and listing out their goals. She's becoming the great doctor she wanted to be for so long. All her dreams are coming true. The longer he listens to her talk, the more he sees that all his dreams are coming true too.

They've started doing little things together: watching movies, making dinner, getting groceries. One night, while they were at Target getting food, Charlie was talking about sports when he noticed her slow down, and her attention became diverted. He saw that they were passing the baby section.

He stopped talking, studying her movement, and she turned back to him, moving the cart again, as if embarrassed to have been caught looking.

"Hey," he said, putting his hand on the cart, slowing it down. "Do you wanna stop?"

There was something different about the way that she looked at him. It was as if she was afraid, as if the minute they stopped that cart, things became real in some way that they could never turn back.

He made the decision for her and walked over to look at the clothes. Staring at the little onesies felt surreal to him, as if he'd never fully considered that one day, they'd have a kid small enough to fit into something so tiny. It occurred to him that maybe Sarah was right to be cautious, that maybe simply standing in that aisle of bottles and blankets might change everything.

She walked over to him. "You're looking at the section for one-year-olds," she said.

"You mean our kid will be even smaller than this? We're gonna need a microscope to see his little fingers!" He laughed, but in reality he felt even more afraid.

"You're pretty sure it's gonna be a boy now, huh?"

Charlie hadn't even noticed that he'd gone straight to the little boys' section. "I didn't mean to say—" He tried to shrug the comment off, not wanting to seem as if he cared about the gender of the baby one way or the other.

"I know it is, too," she said. "Funny, isn't it? How we just know?"

He smiled, and as they went around looking at tiny hats and gloves, holding them up and imagining their baby inside, he couldn't help but hope that if he were to have a little boy, that he'd grow up to be as great as his mother.

They bought a little blue blanket.

***

Later that day at the shop, after lunch, Anthony stops by to talk to Charlie.

"I've been impressed with you lately, Charlie," he says. "Your work's been fantastic, and I've noticed you haven't been late once or left so much as a second early."

He pats Charlie on the back and leaves.

"Suck-up!" TJ says, laughing.

A few minutes later, Charlie's phone rings while he's changing a tire. He doesn't move but goes about his work, not paying any attention to his phone. After a minute, it rings again.

He lets it ring, but when he finishes his task, he sets down his tools and reaches over to his phone.

The missed call is from Meghan. Right under it, there are messages from earlier in the day that Sarah left, saying she's looking forward to dinner. Haley has texted him again reminding him to be at the bowling alley as close to 5:30 as possible, and even sent a picture of Anna smiling in anticipation of the day.

He's about to set down his phone and get back to work when a notification pops up, saying that Meghan left a voicemail.

He knows he should go straight back to work, that he's just received a compliment from his boss about how focused he's been and that he shouldn't do anything to jeopardize his job. He has an education to pay for and a child on the way.

But he can't resist listening to the voicemail.

Meghan doesn't say much—just that she found out something about Wes and he should call her as soon as he gets a chance.

For a while, he tries to go back to work. All of a sudden, though, it's as if he doesn't remember how to do anything; he can't even change a tire. His hands feel tight, and he can't bend or move them without every movement feeling sharp and rough. His vision blurs, as if he can't focus on what's right in front of him.

He takes a moment to focus on his breathing. Sweat accumulates on his forehead. Trying to calm down, he closes his eyes, attempting to shut out the world.

TJ's hand touches his back, and he jumps. "You okay, man?"

"How much work do we have left today?" Charlie asks.

"What?"

"How many cars? Do we have a lot left?"

TJ looks surprised by the question. "Do I look like a psychic? How am I supposed to be able to read into the future?"

Charlie only half-listens to him. He looks down at his watch and sees that it's 3:30. Surely, he has enough to time to step out, take a phone call, and come back. He'll finish all his work for the day at five, as planned, head over to Anna's party, sing happy birthday endearingly off pitch, and then go to eat a romantic, overpriced dinner with Sarah.

"I gotta go to the restroom," he says, standing up, not paying any attention to TJ as he makes crude remarks asking why he'd need his phone for that. In the men's restroom he paces back and forth, wondering what Meghan might have found. What if she found something big? What if she found something that changed everything? He doesn't even know what that could be, though. He can't even guess. His mind feels blank, and somehow, hypothesizing only makes the pain grow.

He takes a deep breath, puts both hands on the sink, and stares down at the drain. For a moment, he wishes he could just walk straight out the door and go back to work. Today could be a good, simple day. He wants that.

But then, he looks up into the mirror. He sees tired eyes with bags of heavy weight. He reaches up, touching his face for a second, wondering when he started to look so old. All the pain in his face feels like a mask. He knows there are moments of joy, moments when people see who he really is, when the suffering of what he's lost doesn't take over every feature, but he wants more. He wants answers. He wants to escape the pain forever, and maybe answers will help that. He believes they will. He's always believed that.

As his heart hammers in his chest, he dials Meghan's number.

The way his heart thuds at a million miles per hour against his chest, pounding in his ears, makes the speed of the ringing phone feel comparatively slow. Time slows. Each second holds years, years of throwing the football back and forth with Wes in their front yard as kids, years of whispering to Sarah that he'd never love anything more than he loves her, years of spinning Anna around like a ceiling fan above his head, years of fighting under a flag, never sleeping quite right.

"Hello," Meghan says, and for some reason, her voice startles him, as if he only half believed that she'd answer. His throat tightens, as though he's being strangled. "Hello?"

"Hey, it's me," Charlie says at last, the words gushing out, rushed and unsettled. "Is now a good time?"

"Yes. I didn't mean to bother you at work."

"It's not a problem." He speaks quietly. "So what'd you find out?" His own directness surprises him.

"You know that phone number he kept? For Rylee?"

"Yeah, what about it?"

"I called it."

The sight of himself in the mirror distracts him. He looks different, even just talking about Wes, as if he's gained a kind of passion, as if his veins have been electrified.

"Are you there?" she asks. "Charlie?"

"What'd she say?"

"You should talk to her yourself."

"What do you mean?"

There's silence on the other end.

"What'd she say?"

"I just think it'd be better if you talked to her yourself."

"That bad? Was it that bad?"

"No," she says. "I mean, I don't know. Can anything be good when you're looking for answers about why someone killed himself?"

He's been trying not to think about it that way.

"I asked her if she'd talk to you. She says she'll be at her house all day if you want to stop by. I can send you the address."

He freezes, thinking about nothing. Suddenly, he thinks of that blue blanket he bought at Target, how, all week, he'd look at that blanket and imagine his baby wrapped up in it. He'd have his own baby. He doesn't know why that's what pops into his mind at this moment.

"Charlie?"

"Yeah, I'm here."

"Do you want her address?"

He doesn't reply right away.

"Charlie?"

"Yeah. Yeah, I do."

"You don't have to go if you—"

"I wanna talk to her."

He isn't sure how true those words are. He's had that number in his drawer for months, yet he never quite worked up the strength to call it. Things are different now, though. He knows, somewhere in his soul, that if he doesn't go now, if he doesn't take Rylee's address, he never will.

"Okay, I'll text it to you," she says.

"Thanks for calling."

Before she hangs up, she says, "Hey, Charlie, whatever big answer you're looking for, it doesn't exist."

"But Rylee has pieces? She has pieces of the truth?"

"Of the truth?"

"Of Wes's story."

"Yeah, but—"

"Thanks, Meghan," he says. "Thanks for the call."

He hears her take a deep breath on the other line. He can tell she wants to say something else, that she's sorry for what Wes did or that she wishes he could just move on. Instead, after a second of silence, she just says, "You're welcome."

She's the one to hang up.

A minute later, he's staring at the address that pops up on his phone. 415 Richard Avenue. He plugs it into the navigation on his phone. Twenty-three minutes away. For some reason, that makes him laugh. It's funny, really—all the answers he's been looking for might have been twenty-three minutes away this whole time.

***

Charlie drives to Rylee's house.

Everything feels as if it's gone by in a blur, going back in the shop after getting off the phone, asking TJ to cover for him as he grabbed his keys. TJ had a million questions—why Charlie rushed through changing the remaining two tires on the Volvo he'd been working on, why he suddenly had so much sweat all over his body, why he looked like he'd just seen a ghost.

Charlie told TJ that he'd explain later. He's not sure if that's a lie or not yet.

The whole way to Rylee's house, he blasts music, but he doesn't listen to a word of it. He's just trying to drown out the sound of his own heart, pounding in his ears.

When he gets close, he starts to drive slower, trying to take everything in. The neighborhood is secluded, a few minutes away from any major street. It looks like a suburb, although it's near central Houston. There's a quietness about the street, a sense of calm, that's almost contagious. It makes his breathing slow a bit.

Most of the houses are small, but nice and traditional looking. Rylee's house is no different. She lives in a quaint, one-story building with red brick and a little swing on the porch. A white picket fence, the only one on the street, surrounds her home. It's a cute place, the type of house he'd associate with a happy family. Something about that makes him nervous.

He parks a few houses down, debating what he'll say when he gets to the door. He turns the music up in his car, trying to distract himself from how uncomfortable he feels.

As he's sitting there, Sarah calls. He wants to answer, but he knows she'll ask how he's doing at work and then he'll have to explain where he is. She'll ask questions. She'll want to know more than he's ready to handle. He already feels fragile, sitting there in that car alone, and the thought of trying to handle anyone else makes him feel as though he'll break down, so he ignores the call.

He wonders who Rylee could be. Was she someone Wes had loved? Did he break her heart? Or maybe he hated her. Maybe *she* broke *his* heart. Either way, the only thing that really matters is that she knows something. What could it be? Of course, the rational thing to do would be to just go to her door and ask, but he can't work himself up for that yet, so he waits.

Sarah calls again. He stares at the screen for a second, debating what to do.

He lets it go to voicemail. Then, he sends her a text saying:

> *Can't answer. I'm sorry. It's been a busy day. Meet you at home around 7, and we can go to dinner? Love you.*

Wanting some time to himself to think, he turns off his phone.

He waits in the car longer than he'd care to admit, longer than he even realizes. It's as if he believes that simply being on the street will give him answers. Finally, he realizes how crazy he's being and gets out of the car.

He walks toward her house, and the closer he gets, the more aware he becomes that he hasn't decided what to say. He doesn't let himself stop, though. Instead, he looks down at his feet on the concrete, taking one step after another.

When he gets to the yard, he notices that the grass has just been mowed. It looks perfect. He tries to focus on that, to keep his mind moving forward as he goes up the sidewalk.

He feels ready to say everything he wants to say. He'll introduce himself, and then he'll ask if she knew Wes and how she knew him. He'll explain that Meghan called, that he's her friend. Everything will be fine.

As he stands at the front door, he stares down at the welcome mat, which says "Home". The "O" is in the shape of the state of Texas. It looks like the kind of thing Sarah would pick out. The thought of her makes him relax. He knocks on the door.

At first, he hears nothing inside and starts to worry. Suddenly, Rylee not answering feels like the worst thing that could happen. Two hours ago he didn't even know Rylee's address and he felt fine, but now things have changed. He feels that without seeing her face, he'll be ruined. He knows how irrational that is, and he forces himself to keep it together.

After a moment, he hears sounds from inside the house, but not what he expected. There's a thud, then rushed steps and the frantic unlocking of the door.

Instead of Rylee, there's a little boy standing in the doorway.

"Hello!" he says cheerfully, looking up at Charlie. He's about four years old. He has bright blond, curly hair, big, brown eyes, and a smile that fills his face. He's wearing basketball shorts and no shirt. "Are you looking for my mom?"

"Um," Charlie says, suddenly wishing he'd stayed in the car. He doesn't know why, but the little boy standing there makes everything feel different. He knows that somehow this little boy is now in the picture and that doesn't seem fair. A little kid shouldn't be any part of the answer when he's trying to find out why Wes killed himself. A little boy shouldn't be the one answering the door. "Yeah. Yeah, is she home?"

"Mom!" he yells at the top of his lungs. "Mom! Mom!"

He turns back to Charlie and smiles again. Even without being around the boy for long, he can tell the kid is happy. He's charismatic, energetic, and innocent. Charlie can see a lot of joy in his eyes.

"She's slow sometimes," the boy says. "She doesn't run fast like me."

"That's okay," Charlie replies. He studies the little boy. He can't shake the feeling that something is wrong, that he shouldn't be there.

"My mom says I got my speed from my dad," the boy says. "He was fast. He played soccer."

"Soccer?"

"Yeah, I love soccer. I've been playing since I was two and three quarters." He tries to show Charlie two and three-quarter fingers, and he struggles for a while before giving up. "Can you play?"

"No, I can't say—"

Before he can finish, a woman appears. She picks up the boy and he smiles. "Tucker, how many times have I told you not to answer the door on your own? You know it's dangerous."

"Sorry, Mommy," the boy says, only half meaning it.

She's a pretty woman with dark features. She has the same eyes as her son. Charlie can't help but notice that she's young and beautiful, with her tall frame and thin body. She's the kind of woman who could drive any man mad if she wanted to.

"Can I help you?" she asks.

The boy squirms in her arms, asking to be let down, but she just holds him tighter.

"Hi," Charlie says, his heart starting to beat quicker.

Suddenly, he can't think of what he wanted to say at all. He can hardly remember his own name. It dawns on him that she's the last piece of information he has about Wes, that if she doesn't tell him what he needs to hear, there's no one else. Standing on that porch is the last place in the world that he wants to be.

"I lost my dog," he says, before even realizing what he's doing. "Have you seen it?"

"A dog!" the boy yells. "What color? What's his name? Mom, can we help find it?"

The mom laughs at her son's eagerness. "I'm sorry," she says. "I don't think we have. Do you have a picture or something?"

"Um, yeah." Charlie pulls out his phone, and luckily, finds a picture of Haley's puppy. "His name is Eddie."

Suddenly, though, Rylee looks suspicious of him, as if she's starting to put together who he is, that he might be connected to the phone call from Meghan. Maybe Meghan described him and things are starting to click in her mind. He doesn't know how she identified him, but he can see in a shift in her eyes as she starts to recognize him. That isn't what he wants.

"I haven't seen your dog," she repeats, but now she's looking at him instead of the picture.

"Thanks for your time anyway," he says, and turns to leave.

Tucker yells behind him, "I hope you find Eddie!"

Charlie hurries back to his car, as if he's more protected inside it than on the street. He shuts the door and rests his head on the steering wheel. He instantly feels angry with himself for not being stronger, not getting the answers he came to find. In his head, again and again, he says the words "It's fine." Everything is just fine. Nothing has changed. He tries, for a few minutes, to convince himself that this is true.

The more he thinks about it, though, the more he realizes that everything is different now. He needs answers. He'll never be okay without walking up back up to that door and talking to that family to find out what he should know about Wes. He thinks about going back, about walking up and trying again.

Before he does, though, he looks down at his watch for the first time in hours. It's 5:32. He's already late to Anna's party.

***

When he checks his phone, he has more calls than he knows how to handle.

Sarah has called five times, which is uncharacteristic of her, and she's sent texts saying he needs to call her. TJ has also called three times and left two angry voicemails. Charlie listens to them as he drives.

"You did a horrible job on that simple tire change. I had to redo your work. Anthony came around asking where you went when we started getting behind. Get your ass back to the shop and do your fucking job."

Haley has called repeatedly too, asking where he is and when he'll be there.

"I swear to God, Charlie," her voicemail says, "if you aren't here with that cake in the next ten minutes..."

It's the first time he thinks about the cake.

He left it at the shop.

Suddenly, everything feels too overwhelming to bear, and he realizes how idiotic it was to try to squeeze in going to visit Rylee on such a busy day. He should have waited. Somehow, now, he doesn't feel the urgency that used to weigh down so heavily on his chest. He should never have left the shop. It was a mistake to think he could do everything.

***

The Houston traffic is hardly moving.

He wishes he could abandon his car altogether, simply run back to the shop, get the cake, and run to the bowling alley. It'd be faster. Anything in the world would be faster than sitting on stationary I-10.

Haley calls him again, and when he answers, she yells at him for not being there, demanding to know what happened. He says there was a hold up at work, but he's on his way.

"Nothing should be more important than Anna today," she says. "Nothing. Not even your job."

He knows she's right. That's the worst part. He says he's sorry again and again as Haley scolds him, and he can hardly defend himself because he knows he's the one in the wrong.

"I'm coming, okay?" he promises. "I'm sorry, but I'm coming. I'll have the cake there by the end of the party. All right?"

When he gets to the shop, he's surprised to see TJ's car still in the lot. Anthony's car is there too. He sprints inside.

His timing isn't good. Anthony is yelling at TJ about something. Charlie slows down, hiding behind a wall for a second, trying to listen.

"You never lie to me again," Anthony says. "You hear me?"

He's never heard Anthony's voice so stern. He's never heard TJ so quiet.

"I asked if you heard me," Anthony says again angrily.

"Yes, sir."

"I'll fire your ass in a heartbeat. You got it?"

"Yes, sir."

Charlie peeks around the corner and watches Anthony leave. TJ hangs his head, then goes back to trying to clean up his workstation.

Charlie comes out from around the corner, ready to go straight to the refrigerator, grab the cake, and leave. He tries to move quietly, attempting not to startle TJ, but as soon as he walks into the room, TJ's head snaps up.

He's never seen him look so angry.

"What the fuck," TJ whispers, moving toward him quickly. "Where the fuck have you been?"

"I'm sorry, TJ. I—"

"You what? You better have been fucking dying out there. You tell me to cover you with no explanation and then you bolt?"

Charlie looks down at the floor. The intensity of TJ's eyes feels too overwhelming to handle.

"No, no, no, you don't get to do that. Look at me. Look me in the fucking eyes, Charlie." His voice escalates but then cools off as he looks back in the direction of Anthony's office. "I lied for you. I told Anthony you were in the restroom, but that doesn't work when you leave for two goddamn hours and never come back! Why didn't you tell me you were leaving for good? You never tell me fucking anything, Charlie!"

"TJ, I—"

"You lost your job." TJ suddenly looks totally deflated, as if he's no longer angry but on the verge of tears.

"What?"

"Yeah, Anthony says you're fired. He said I could be the one to tell you since we're so goddamn tight. Now he's got me staying here working extra, cleaning the shop, just so I don't lose my fucking job for lying about where you were."

"I'm so sor—"

"Whatever, bro. I know you've got Rice and grad school, but I've got a mom and a brother to feed. I need this job, man. It's all I got. This is all I got, man."

"TJ—"

"You know what." TJ shoves a rag at him. "I'm done. You're the one who caused this all. You clean the shop."

"TJ, I—"

"This is all your mess, man. Not mine."

With that, TJ storms out the door, and Charlie is left alone.

***

By the time he cleans everything up at the shop, it's late. His phone hasn't stopped buzzing in his pocket. He knows it's Haley calling, but he doesn't know what to say. He promised to be there, and that's not something he takes lightly. He knows he's in the wrong, but he also knows TJ's relying on him to clean up the shop. If he doesn't clean up the shop, right then, he'll lose TJ forever, and the damage will be permanent. He cleans as fast as he can, darting around. He still has hope that he'll be able to make it for the end of Anna's party, just in time for the cake.

He doesn't.

When he gets to the party, it's over. All of Anna's friends have left, and when he walks in, he spots her immediately, sitting on the booth in her lane with her head down. Haley is squatting in front of her, trying to talk to her, but Anna isn't looking at her.

Charlie starts to hate himself. He should have been there. He starts feeling like he's in a bad dream. He feels a hand on his shoulder and looks up to see Matt.

"Matt, I'm so sorry. I didn't mean—"

Matt has always had a gentleness about him. Charlie can see it in his eyes now. He wonders if he's worthy of Matt's kindness. It's obvious that Matt forgives him, but he can also tell that Matt knows how crushed Anna is and how mad Haley must be.

"I don't think I'm the one you need to say sorry to." Matt turns and walks toward his family. When he gets to Haley, he leans down and whispers something in her ear. Haley's eyes move to Charlie. Anna's soon follow.

He won't ever forget the way Anna looks at him. He sees that she's been crying, and he has to face that it's because of him. Her shoulders lean forward, sinking in disappointment, and he can tell that he's broken her heart. He feels like crying himself.

He takes a few steps forward, wanting to talk to them, but Haley gets up and storms over to him.

"Where the hell have you been?" she asks.

"I'm so sorry. I was working and then I got a phone call, and I—"

"A phone call? Charlie, what are you talking about? What could possibly have been more important than this today? She talked all day about how excited she was to see you. All day. She didn't even have a birthday cake, Charlie! Matt kept offering to go get one, but I told him that you'd be here, that you were coming. We had to buy pretzels for all the kids, Charlie, because there was no fucking cake."

"Haley—"

"No, no, I don't want to hear it. I'm over this. I know you've been having a hard time recently, but if we can't even count on you for one day, I don't know how this relationship is supposed to work."

"Come on, now, Haley. That's not fair. You know—"

"Not fair? Of course it's not fair. But just know that you started it. It wasn't fair of you to lie to my little girl, telling her you wouldn't miss her party for the world."

"I love her, Haley," he whispers. "You know I love her more than anything."

She shakes her head. "You can't say that like it's some excuse."

He looks away from her. He listens to the chants of people in the background, cheering as they get strikes. They sound happy.

"Just go home, please," Haley says.

Charlie stares at his hands, still holding his gift and the cake.

"Can I please talk to Anna?"

"No."

"Please."

"What are you going to say to her? Huh? What do you really have to say?"

He stares at the cake in his hand, looking down at the Incredibles on the front. He thinks about the basketball inside the wrapping paper, how he'd imagined them playing outside together when he'd picked it out. He thought that maybe, just maybe, she'd take one look at the gifts and realize how wrong this day had gone. He'd wanted to make her so happy. He'd labored over every choice, the kind of cake, the color of the icing, the design on the wrapping paper.

"I just want to tell her that I'm sorry and that I love her," he says.

"That you love her?"

"And I want to give her this. I still have her present... and her cake."

"Please, just go home, Charlie."

He looks over to see that Matt is now talking to Anna, trying to get her to smile. Her head still hangs low.

"Okay," he says after a few seconds. When he looks back at Haley, he sees a glimpse of sympathy, how for a moment Haley can tell that he never meant to hurt her, that he's sorry.

"Was what you were doing more important than this?" she asks quietly, as if finally giving him a chance to explain himself.

He shakes his head.

Haley stares at him for a moment, as if temporarily curious about what happened, but the mystery doesn't dominate her. Instead of asking more questions, she just nods and walks away.

"Please just tell her I'm sorry," he says.

He walks back out to his car with the cake and the present still in his hands.

***

As soon as he leaves the bowling alley, he looks at his watch. It's 7:45, already past the time he promised Sarah he'd go to dinner with her. He opens his phone to see multiple missed calls from her and texts saying that he needs to call her.

He feels horrible. He knows there's nothing she hates more than canceled plans. He's stood her up. The thought of her, sitting in the kitchen, looking all nice and ready for a fun night out, breaks his heart.

He doesn't want to go home. He'd rather go to a bar—he needs a drink. But he knows he shouldn't do that to Sarah, so he texts her saying he's so sorry and that he's on his way home.

He lights a cigarette and smokes in his car on the way back to his apartment. He knows she'll be able to smell it on him, that it'll be another fight. He can't help it, though. He feels that everything is unraveling, even his nerves themselves, as if he's decomposing. He needs something to hold him together, and the cigarette somehow helps.

***

He shows up at his apartment with flowers that he stopped to buy for Sarah. He hopes she won't be too mad when he tells her the whole story. She knows him better than anyone. She knows how deeply Wes's death has hurt him, and maybe there'll be at least a small part of her that gets it. She has a way of seeing through him, knowing what he's feeling. He hopes she'll see how he never intended to miss a thing, how the day got away from him.

When he gets inside, Sarah's sitting on their couch, staring at a TV that isn't even on. He knows she hears him, but she doesn't move at all. She doesn't turn to look at him.

"I'm sorry, Sarah," he says, before she has a chance to say anything. "I know I should have been here sooner."

She doesn't respond but just keeps staring ahead.

"You wouldn't believe the day I had. It was—"

"Where have you been?" The anger in her voice surprises him. He knows he should have come back sooner, but she isn't the type to jump to rage so quickly. If anything, usually she gets sad and upset rather than angry.

He moves closer to her, studying her body language. She has a blanket covering her, but her arms are folded across her chest.

"I asked where you were," she repeats.

She's far angrier than he's ever seen her. He can tell how mad she is by the way her words take a long time to come out, as if she's trying to hold back from letting everything she wants to say burst from her. She won't look him in the eyes.

"Meghan called," Charlie says.

"Meghan?"

"Wes's old girlfriend. She thought she had information that could... I don't know. She thought she might have found someone who could give me more answers."

"Answers?"

"About Wes."

Suddenly, Sarah's head snaps toward him, looking straight into his eyes. Her eyes are red and puffy, and there are remnants of mascara that she tried to wipe from her face but are still clinging to her cheeks.

She turns away from him again, as if not wanting to give him any more attention.

"Did you get them?" she asks.

"What?"

"Your answers? Did you get your fucking answers?"

He's never heard her speak this way before.

"Sarah, I said I'm sorry. I didn't mean to worry you."

She stands up and moves closer to him. "You think that's what this is about?"

"Sarah, can we just... I don't know. I'm sorry I canceled dinner. I'll take you out this weekend. Anywhere you want. I promise. I'm sorry."

She says nothing.

"I brought you flowers."

She laughs. "You think that's what I want right now, Charlie? You think you can just bring me red roses and make everything better?"

"Of course not. You know that's not—"

"See, this is exactly the problem. You think you can just do whatever you want and then fix it later."

She's usually so level-headed, so calm. The only other time he's seen her like this was when she told him she was pregnant.

"What are you talking about?" he says.

"Why didn't you answer my phone calls?"

"I'm sorry. My day was just—"

"Don't tell me you had a bad day. Don't you dare tell me that *you* had a bad day."

He starts to rewind in his head, trying to figure out what's going on. This wouldn't be about dinner. She's not that emotional, that irrational.

"What happened, Sarah?" he asks.

"You'd know if you had your goddamn phone on."

"What going on?"

"What's going on is that we're not going to be parents anymore."

There's silence for a moment as he stares at her face, watching as her anger turns into extreme sadness.

"What?" he says, although the question is rhetorical. He tries to take in what she just said, but he can only half feel it. It's as if he's dreaming. It occurs to him that he's just high, that all of this is one big misunderstanding.

"I had a miscarriage," she says. "But you were too busy doing what? Playing detective? Trying to solve Wes's fucking case! Wes is dead, Charlie! He's dead, but I'm right here, and you don't care about that."

She begins to sob and turns away from him.

He reaches out to her, to try to comfort her, but she quickly steps away as soon as she feels his hand on her shoulder.

"Whatever you found out, whatever you spent today doing, I hope it was worth it to you." She moves to the bedroom. "You can sleep on the couch."

She slams the door.

"Sarah, I'm sorry," Charlie says. "I'm so sorry."

He isn't even sure if she can hear him over the sound of her own crying.

Chapter 16

Charlie doesn't sleep at all that night. He rotates between feeling horrible for what he's done to Sarah and mourning the fact that he'll never get to meet his unborn baby, that his child will never to wrap its little hand around his finger. He wonders what the child would have loved — maybe art, maybe dance, maybe sports, maybe magic, who knows. He can't think of anything but the fact that he'll never know what his child would have added to the world. He can't watch sports or eat or sleep because he just finds himself wondering if his kid would have been a Rockets fan, whether he'd like pickles, or what his breathing would have sounded like at night. When he really thinks about how he'll never hold his own child, the world feels too cold to forgive.

By missing the miscarriage, he feels he's lost the right to fully grieve the passing of his child. His right to be upset has been replaced by a requirement to feel sorry, to atone for his mistake of going to Rylee's house. He feels separated from Sarah, as though he's done something unforgivable. He can hear her crying in the bedroom as he sits outside in the living room. He can't shake the feeling that he should be in there with her, that they should be trying to talk about this, making some effort to get through things together. She shouldn't lock him out.

"Please, honey," he says occasionally through the door. "Please, let me in."

She never does.

He wonders if this is how he made her feel, if she felt just as isolated, all those nights she begged him to talk about Afghanistan.

***

A week passes, each day slower than the last. Sarah only comes out of the room to go to school and doctor's appointments. When they see each other, it's as if she can hardly see him. She's not mean, but she mostly ignores him, only telling him the most basic information he needs to know about her plan for the day.

One morning, he gets up extra early. He makes everything for breakfast that he knows how—eggs, pancakes, bacon, and sausage. He sets it out for her, spending ten minutes just arranging the items on the plate, trying to make them look nice. She comes out of the bedroom as he's hovering over the plate.

"Hey," he says, stepping back.

"Hey."

"I made you breakfast."

She freezes and stares at the plate as if it represents everything, as though she has to forgive him if she takes a bite of that food. He didn't intend to put such pressure on a meal, but he can tell by her reaction that he's made a great mistake.

"It's only breakfast," he whispers.

She nods, as if trying to convince herself of that. She sits down in front of her plate.

"Black?" Charlie asks as he pours the coffee.

"What?"

"I made you coffee."

He sets it down in front of her, and for a moment, she looks content, but then their eyes meet, and he can see all the anger in her face.

"I've got to go," she says suddenly, standing up quickly.

"Sarah, come on."

"I've got to go to school."

She goes into the bedroom, grabs her backpack and walks out the door, not saying so much as a goodbye. He's left staring at that perfectly arranged plate, not a single bite eaten.

***

His days have become quiet. He misses talking to Sarah. He misses work. He misses Haley and Anna. He misses Wes.

He struggles to come up with things to occupy his time. He cleans the house. He dusts. He sweeps. When everything's spotless, he draws. His drawings are different recently, less realistic and more abstract. He draws lines and shapes and morphed faces. He doesn't know why. When he's not drawing, he checks his email constantly. He hopes, every time he opens his email, that he'll find one from Rice telling him he's been accepted. It's what he wants more than anything. His life is still here with Sarah, and that's the life he wants. Maybe if they could just put a few of the puzzle pieces back together, everything else would become clearer, things would start to fall into place.

Above all, though, the longer he sits alone in that silent apartment, the more he thinks about Natalie. He doesn't know why, but she's on his mind all time. He realizes that he left Natalie at a time when she felt completely alone, after the accident, and the horror of the situation haunts him.

He's had a missed call from her, almost daily, since the accident. She's left voicemails which he never returned. He listens to some of them. She tells him she hopes he's doing all right and gives updates about how she is. She asks him to come over. She says she's sorry. As the voicemails go on, he can hear the hope, the passion, disappearing from her voice, as if she gets less and less convinced that he'll ever call back. He listens to the messages again and again, studying the tone of her voice. There's the same kind of emptiness and grief in Sarah's voice each morning, when she tells him goodbye as she walks out the door.

***

Instead of calling Natalie, he gets in his car and drives to her house.

It's a quaint, colonial-style, one-story home that Natalie moved into when she was twenty-nine, after saving up the profits from the bakery she'd opened out of high school. Charlie and Wes used to go to the bakery all the time when they were in lower school. Wes would always claim he hadn't stolen a cupcake, but the blue icing staining his lips quickly gave him away. Natalie would tell him not to spoil his dinner. Charlie was convinced it was the only time in Wes's life he didn't do what Natalie asked, but even as a kid, he could have sworn he saw Natalie smiling at Wes's blue teeth.

Charlie hasn't been to the house since the day Wes died. That day, he'd gone into Wes's room, right after his death. He thought going into Wes's bedroom would give him answers. He never told anyone the real reason he went there, digging around—to look for a suicide note. He thought that surely Wes wouldn't leave without any explanation at all. He searched madly through Wes's sock draws, his nightstand, his backpack. He ransacked all of it, searching for a note that didn't exist.

Instead, all he found was that slip of paper with Rylee's phone number on it. He used to think he didn't call it because he was afraid she wouldn't answer or she wouldn't know anything about Wes at all. Now, though, after standing on her front porch, he knows that all this time, he hasn't been searching for the truth; he's been running from it.

***

When Charlie knocks on the door, Hannah, Natalie's sister, answers. She greets him warmly, her face lighting up at the sight of him. She looks exhausted but enthusiastic, and Charlie admires that. There's nothing but happiness on her face, and he can hardly understand how that's possible. She doesn't seem angry at all that he's been gone so long. Hannah turns and calls over her shoulder, "Natalie, guess who's here?"

The front door opens into the living room, and Hannah invites him in. The living room looks emptier than he remembers. The lone couch and TV suddenly seem unable to fill the room. Maybe it was Wes, all along, who inserted so much life into that space.

They walk down a hallway leading out of the living room and into kitchen. Their home looks more barren than it did before. There used to be pictures of Wes all over the walls, particularly in the hallway into the kitchen, but most of them are gone now. Only two pictures remain, and they're from when Wes was younger. There's a picture of Natalie holding him as a baby, right after he was born, as she sits in the hospital bed looking at the boy bundled in a blue blanket. She's looking at him as if he's the savior of the universe. The second one is of Wes on the first day of kindergarten, smiling outside his front door with his over-gelled hair and button-down shirt. He looks happy and hopeful. Charlie wonders when that changed.

He also notices that the walls are newly painted. Natalie has changed the color from a dark blue to a light tan. He doesn't comment on it.

When he gets into the kitchen, the first thing that catches his eye is the mess. Dishes stack on top of each other in the sink, and there are more scattered around on the table and counters, seeming to be everywhere at once, almost alive. There are papers, too, many taped to the refrigerator, and more scattered on the table.

Charlie can't help but think that he should never have left the hospital. He should have been here helping. He should never have left Hannah on her own to take care of her sister, even if she never minded. He feels unsettled, unable to relax, the same way he felt in that waiting room.

"Hi Charlie," Natalie says, snapping his attention away from the mess. She's sitting at the table, with her leg propped up on a chair, a cast going from her foot all the way to her waist. Beside her is a wheelchair.

When he looks at her, all he sees is how content she appears, how her eyes and shoulders relax the longer she looks at him. He feels guilty, as if he's had some cure or medicine that could take away her pain, but he hasn't come, and that feels unforgivable.

"Hi," he says. Being there makes him feel as though he's found his way home, but he's no less angry at her for being in that car.

"I'm sorry for the mess," Hannah says, frantically moving about the kitchen, attempting to bring all the dishes to the sink. She tries to bunch all the papers into a single massive pile, something that could be tucked away. "Things have just been crazy, you know, with all the medical bills, and trying to get everything sorted out with my family too, and —"

Charlie walks over and puts his hand on her shoulder, and she stops talking.

"I'll do it," he says. "I'll clean it all up."

She slows down enough to relax, and all of a sudden, the circles under her eyes become more evident, as if she's been working in overdrive to the point that she forgot about her exhaustion. Charlie insists on handling things for a while and suggests that she should rest. After he's reassured her a few times that everything is under control, Hannah sets the dishes down, thanks him, and walks out of the room.

Charlie sits down at the table with Natalie. There's silence for a while as he tries to think of the right thing to say.

"The house looks different," he says.

Immediately, Natalie's eyes dart to the dishes, as if that's what he's talking about.

"The paint and the pictures," he clarifies. "They've changed."

"Oh." She seems caught off guard, as if she hadn't expected him to notice. "Yeah. They have."

He doesn't let her off the hook so easily. "Why did you change them?"

"I don't know." She looks at the walls and he sees fear in her eyes, as if she expects monsters to pop through the drywall at any moment. "I think... I think that sometimes I just feel like this place is haunted."

"Haunted?"

"The walls, the paint, the pictures." She keeps looking around. "All of it."

He understands that. Right after Wes's death, he had a hard time even breathing because the air felt as though it shouldn't belong to him, as if each breath somehow meant taking air that Wes could have breathed. He knows he'd sound crazy if he ever tried to articulate such a thing out loud, but he can tell by one look at Natalie's face that she'd understand.

"That's not entirely a bad thing, though, is it?" he asks.

She looks at him deeply for a second, as if he's just told her a riddle. "No, of course not," she says. "Of course it's not."

He can't help letting his eyes linger on her scar, the way it dips down toward her eye. He wonders how lucky she got that the cut wasn't lower, that the metal didn't hit her eye, taking away her ability to see forever. Then again, maybe he was thinking of it all backward. Maybe it was her inability to see things clearly that caused the crash in the first place.

"Why'd you do it?" he asks.

"What?"

"Why'd you crash your car?" His voice is sturdy and heavy.

She sounds surprised by his question, but he also knows she must have seen it coming. She always knows what he's thinking. "It was an accident, Charlie."

"Why were you on the road?"

"I don't know."

"You don't know?"

"Yeah, I don't know."

"You don't know why you were on the road at two in the morning?"

"That's what I just said, isn't it?"

Charlie looks down, away from her face and at her cast. His compassion starts to morph into something else, anger maybe.

"You don't know what it's like," she says.

"What?"

"You don't know what losing him was like."

"You don't think I lost him?"

"He was my son."

He can't decide whether that's a fair rebuttal. Part of him gets it, how Wes grew inside her, making them one in a way he'd never be. But Wes was like his brother, and it doesn't seem a fair thing for her to say, as if all the time they spent together could never be equivalent to the relationships with the people who shared his DNA. He gets it, but the statement also feels horribly illogical and degrading.

"Hannah said you were at the hospital the whole time, and then you left right before I woke up," Natalie says. She doesn't ask any questions, but he can feel the way she studies him, as if she's trying to get an answer out of him.

"Yeah," he says, "I did."

"You left me." Each word comes out slowly and reluctantly, as if it's something she's thought about saying a million times in her head

- 145 -

but never has. Her words are accusatory. He can see she feels betrayed, and that she's trying not to get upset, but he can hear her sadness seeping into each word.

"I left you?" he repeats. "You think I left you?"

"Yes, you did."

Charlie has an instinct to get up and leave right then and there. He wants to get up and walk out of the door, and tell her she doesn't get it, but he knows that isn't fair. She's right. He did leave.

"You could have died in that accident, you know," he says. "You could have left me forever."

She looks confused, as if she doesn't get how that's related. "I didn't, though. I'm fine. I'm right here."

Charlie can't look at her, and his heart race increases. Even considering whether she's fine seems too much to handle.

"What you did what reckless," he says at last.

"What was? Driving a car?"

He pauses for a second before replying. "There was a witness to the accident. The lady that called 9-1-1 said you didn't turn the wheel."

Natalie takes a minute to analyze his words. She shakes her head. "My God, Charlie, is this really what we're going to talk about? You think I did this on purpose?"

"Did you?"

She looks as if the question is a betrayal.

"No," she says at last.

Suddenly, though, she isn't looking at him. He takes a moment to study her body language, the way her head leans down, the way she's looking at her cast as though it's a mystery to be solved.

"I don't think I believe you."

He waits for her to say something back. Instead, she just keeps looking at her cast.

"Say something," he says.

"Is there anything to say?" she asks. "If you've already made up your mind, there's nothing to talk about."

They sit in silence for a while.

"I don't know if I think you actually tried to crash, or if you were just indifferent to it," Charlie says. "But something happened in that car, something terrible. I think you gave up."

When Natalie looks up, her eyes look glassy and distant. "I left because I couldn't be in this house anymore. I hadn't slept in days. I couldn't breathe inside these walls where he used to be. I just couldn't,

Charlie." She takes a deep breath, composing herself. "I was exhausted, but I had to leave. I guess I was more tired than I thought. That's it. That's all there is to it. I promise. Okay?"

She's looking him in the eyes again, and Charlie starts to believe her. Part of him doesn't want to believe it because then his absence over the last few weeks becomes unjustifiable. Maybe there's more to the truth that even she can't see. Maybe inside her exhaustion was some sense of surrender. But then again, maybe not. The longer he thinks about it, the less it matters. All that matters is that he's there, in this house, sitting across the table from her.

"I'm moving, Charlie," she says, looking out the window. When she works up the courage to look him in the eyes, she's crying. "I'm leaving. Hannah's gonna let me stay with her family for a while in Kansas. I'm selling everything: the bakery, the house. It's happening fast."

Charlie freezes, saying nothing.

"This city was home to me *and* my son, and without Wes, it's impossible to feel like I belong here."

He finds it hard to listen to her words, to think about the way she constantly hurts. Of course, he knows she's been feeling this way, but hearing it out in the open is terrifying.

But he also can't help wondering if she's a fool. The problem doesn't lie in her city, or her house, or the bakery. The pain is all in her soul.

He begins to formulate a speech to convince her to stay. He could tell her how she helps him. He could tell her it's her job to look over the people she loves, and she should take this opportunity to watch over him in the way that she'll never be able to look after Wes again. He could beg her to stay and say, *Don't be another person who leaves me like Wes did.* That would really do it. She'd immediately choose to stay.

"My baby is dead," she says. "He's really dead, Charlie."

The horror in her voice, the pure terror, won't stop ringing in his ears. He can tell by the way her eyes go wide, by the way she looks as if she's been struck by lightning, that she doesn't expect this to be something he'll ever get.

She starts crying again. After a moment, Charlie moves closer to her, scooting his chair to be next to her. She leans her head into his chest and wraps her arms around him. He holds her.

"I know," he says, trying to comfort her.

"I'm sorry," she says. "I'm sorry I'll be leaving you."

"It's okay. Everything is gonna be okay."

The longer she cries on his shoulder, the more her words replay in his head. *My baby is dead. My baby is dead.*

"It'll be all right," he keeps saying, even long after she's stopped trying to speak, and only her crying fills the silence.

As they sit there, Charlie looks around the kitchen at the piles of dishes and papers, and he wonders if it's even possible to clean up such a mess.

***

Later that night, after spending most of the day at Natalie's house, he waits on the couch for Sarah to get home. His eyelids feel as though they weigh a million pounds. He's exhausted.

When Sarah arrives, she tries to go straight into their room. It's what she's been doing every day for the last week.

Things are different today, though. He won't let her get away so easily.

"Sarah, can we please talk?" he asks as she sets her backpack down on the counter. She takes her shoes off, as if getting ready to bunker in for the night.

"I don't know, Charlie."

She begins to move toward the bedroom. Charlie positions himself between her and the door.

"I can't do this right now," she says, looking away from him.

He looks at her, waiting for her to make eye contact. She tries to move around him. He steps in front of her, slightly bumping into her, and she takes an aggressive step back, as if just touching him is too much.

She becomes visibly upset. "Don't touch me!"

"Whoa, whoa, I'm sorry, Sarah. Okay? I'm sorry."

She looks at her arm where his chest grazed her skin. He hates the way she looks at it, as if it's contaminated.

"God, I can't even touch you?" he whispers.

She looks down, and when she looks back up, he sees tears in her eyes. He knows she doesn't want to feel this way.

"The baby," she says quietly.

"What?"

"When you touch me..."

He can see in her eyes how she will never be able to separate him from their dead child, how they created something, someone, together, who will never exist.

He moves closer to her, mindful of keeping his distance.

"Okay," he says, trying to be as understanding as possible. He gets it, to an extent. Part of him is terrified to kiss her again, as if it might lead to something more, as if it might lead to more death.

"You don't have to touch me. All right?" he says.

She nods, wiping the tears from her face.

"But please, please don't do this anymore."

She looks up at him. "What?"

"You can't keep doing this to me," he says. "I see the way you look at me out of the corner of your eye, the way you can't even make eye contact with me."

"Charlie, I—"

"You blame me. Maybe for getting you pregnant or something, but the way you look at me makes me feel like I'm the one who killed him. You look at me, like, like... I'm evil or something."

She looks shocked.

"I know you were the one who went through this," he says. "I know you were alone. I know I wasn't there. But, God, Sarah, you don't know how sorry I am. I loved that baby too. I still do."

It was bad enough to lose their baby, and now he's losing her too.

"Just give me one answer. Do you think I meant to hurt you?" he asks. "Do you really think I'm that cruel?"

She shakes her head no.

He wants to reach out and hold her. His hand even starts to move toward her. He remembers, though, the way she backed away a second ago, as if he was dangerous. He puts his hand back down. "I wish things were different, but our child is dead, Sarah."

"Don't say that."

"But—"

"Just don't say it, okay?"

He can see she doesn't want to acknowledge it. She wants to run away. He studies the way that her chest moves sharply and unpredictably, as if breathing itself is a laborious process.

"All right," he says. "I won't. I won't say anything."

She doesn't say anything else either. She just stares into space. He wonders what she's seeing. It looks as if she's seeing something horrific, as if she's seeing the death of the child, and he thinks that whatever she's seeing is only the second worst sight in the world. The worst is her face in that moment. He looks at her red eyes, peeled widely in constant shock, growing dry and heavy, drooping downward. Her uncombed hair is shooting in five directions, and her skin is splotchy and patched from where tears have hardened and dried.

He's about to say something, to apologize again, when he looks in her eyes and sees that it's not about him, that in this moment, she's not grieving what they've lost, but something greater, something he can't ever fix.

He walks over to the couch, where he's been sleeping lately. He sits down and stares blankly ahead, like she does.

They're quiet for a long time.

Then she comes and sits down, still a foot or two away from him.

"I bet it was a girl," she says.

"What?"

"I bet we were going to have to a girl," she repeats. "The things you're most sure about are always the things that are wrong."

She won't look at him.

"It was a boy," he says, almost in a whisper.

"I guess it doesn't matter anymore." Even as she says the words, he can tell how her lips barely let the words out, how everything on her face shows that nothing could be less true.

"It was a boy," he repeats. "We knew it was a boy."

She hasn't moved. He wonders if she's even breathing.

For a few minutes, the two of them just sit, not saying anything. Eventually, she reaches out and touches his hand.

Charlie looks at her for a second, trying to figure out what that means. Before he has time to read into it, she takes her hand back, stands up, and goes to bed.

He's left alone with his thoughts, and he can't help but wonder what he would have named a daughter.

Chapter 17

Another week goes by, and with each day that passes, not much changes. Sarah keeps to herself and doesn't tell him much about her day. He tries to ask all the time, but her answers are short and empty. Sometimes he asks if she's okay. She says yes and that she just needs a little space. Once she kissed him on the cheek before she went to sleep, and he was overwhelmed with such a tremendous sense of hope that he felt pathetic to feel such joy over something so small.

When he isn't trying to mend his relationship with Sarah, he's calling Haley. She never answers. He leaves voicemail after voicemail saying that he's sorry, asking when he can come over. She hasn't called him back. He thinks about telling her about Sarah's pregnancy and how she lost the child. He knows that would get Haley to listen, that she wouldn't ignore him then, but he never mentions it. He doesn't want Haley to forgive him for not being at Anna's birthday party simply because other things were going wrong in his life. He wants to be sorry and earn his way back into their good graces. Mentioning the baby would be using it as a sort of leverage in a way that he'd never want to do. So, day after day, he listens to her ringing phone and finds a new way to phrase the same apology.

In a similar manner, he's called Anthony, begging for his job back, almost every day. Anthony refuses. He says he's sorry, but the shop can't handle the instability of not knowing where he is or when he's coming back.

Charlie has a choice between thinking about missing Haley and Anna or missing his job. He chooses to think about work because it's less painful. The more he thinks about Anthony's words, the more he wishes he could have just one more chance. Finally, instead of calling again, he gets in his car and heads straight to the shop.

As he parks and turns off his car, it feels so long ago that he worked here, as if it's been years. For a moment, he thinks he shouldn't go inside, that he should try to hold onto that sense of distance.

He needs a job, though. Being alone at home, day after day, makes him feel hollow. He waits in his car until he starts sweating, and he realizes that it's been too long, so he gets out.

When he walks in, TJ is off task, laughing at something with the other guys, but when he sees Charlie, his face slowly neutralizes. TJ looks down and swallows. Charlie can tell he feels guilty, but of course, nothing that happened is TJ's fault. He hopes TJ knows that too.

Charlie waves at the guys, but without saying much, he goes straight in to talk to Anthony.

Anthony is on the phone when he knocks on the door, and he quickly glances up, looks down, and then does a double take when he realizes it's Charlie standing there. He's silent for a moment.

"Sorry, yes, I'm still here. Can I... can I call you back?" Anthony says. "Okay, thanks Rob. Talk to you later. Yeah, sounds good."

Charlie can see by Anthony's lack of eye contact and fidgeting hands that things aren't going to go well, but Anthony tells him to sit down.

He tells Anthony the full story, everything about Wes, about Meghan, about Sarah.

Anthony is understanding but unwavering. "I wish you'd explained everything sooner. You've had multiple chances and warnings. I'm already in the process of hiring someone new."

"I understand," Charlie says.

"I wish you only the best," Anthony says, as Charlie stands up to leave. "You know that, right?"

Charlie nods. "Yes, sir. I do."

He wants to say something else. He wants to thank Anthony because, somehow, despite everything, he still feels grateful for the time he's spent here. When he thinks of speaking, though, he feels choked up. He says nothing, shakes Anthony's hand and leaves.

On his way out of the shop, TJ yells at him, "Wait up!"

TJ tells the others he's taking his lunch break. It's only 10:30 AM, but TJ grabs his brown paper sack anyway.

Charlie and TJ sit in silence for a while, in the same place they always used to have lunch, a vacant hallway with nothing but a vending machine and old, thin, blue carpet. Charlie likes it because it's quiet and peaceful.

"We've missed you this week," TJ says at last. "It's not the same without you here."

"You wait until I leave to start complimenting me, huh?"

"Couldn't let you get too cocky around here."

Charlie smiles. TJ takes a bite of his sandwich, chewing for a while without saying anything.

"You're still lucky, you know," TJ says.

Charlie turns to him, trying to study his eyes, to piece together what he does and doesn't know. Sometimes, he feels as if TJ can read his mind and already knows everything.

"I know," Charlie says after a pause.

TJ stops looking at him. After a minute he says, "You shouldn't come back here anymore. You shouldn't ask for your job back again."

"What?"

TJ works up the courage to look at him. "I said, you shouldn't ask for your job back."

Charlie feels a wave of anger.

TJ can read him, and he interrupts before Charlie blows up. "Do you remember that perfect girl I met? The girl from the grocery store?"

Charlie doesn't see what that has to do with anything. "What about her?"

"I liked her. I really liked her."

"Okay." Charlie still can't grasp his point.

TJ's momentum in his story has slowed now, as if he's thinking carefully about each word. "You know something about me, Charlie? I'm gonna be in this shop my whole life. I thought about going to college, and I believe I'm smart enough, but I can't get a score on the SAT that's better than a goddamn average middle schooler. I just can't. Plus, I've got a family to pay for now, that needs the bills paid. This shop is where I belong. I'm not sad about it. I'm not angry or mad, but this is the best it gets for me."

"TJ, that's not—"

"Please, don't argue. All I'm saying is that she was different. She had a law degree from UVA, and all these plans to be the best lawyer in the country, and the whole world was at her fingertips."

"So you left her because of that?"

"Yes."

"What do you mean? That's crazy, TJ."

"I mean that we were different."

"I don't think that's—"

"You don't have to disagree. I'm not trying to make you feel sorry for me or anything. I'm happy here." He looks down at his feet. "My point is that just because we can hold onto something doesn't mean we're meant to."

When Charlie looks at TJ, he sees something he's never seen before. TJ looks sad and desperate for Charlie to understand him.

"Get out of here, Charlie," he says. "Go to Rice. Go to fucking Harvard. Go somewhere. One day, a couple years from now, you're gonna be walking back through those doors telling me all about how getting fired from this little shop was the best goddamn thing that ever happened to you, and I swear to God, I'll be the first one to say I told you so."

TJ puts his hand on Charlie's shoulder, keeping it there until Charlie looks at him.

"Sometimes you gotta leave things behind even when you don't want to. You know that, don't you?"

"Yeah, I do."

"Sometimes it's just what's right. It doesn't always feel right, but it is."

Charlie doesn't say anything, trying to decide what he feels. Before he can figure it out, though, TJ switches the subject altogether. He starts rambling about sports and pretty girls. He asks Charlie if he watched any of the football games over the weekend, and he goes out of his mind retelling all the highlights. He could be an announcer with that amount of detail and enthusiasm.

Sitting there, talking to TJ, makes Charlie wish he could take his job back and stay, but part of him knows, somewhere deep down, that TJ is right, and it's just not where he's meant to be.

***

That night, Charlie goes to his art class. He hasn't told Erin about the miscarriage. One of the things he likes about being around her is that she's a break from everything. She doesn't expect things of him in the same way other people do. She doesn't need anything from him, and that makes him feel safe around her. He also understands, though, that there's something artificial about their friendship, because no relationship is really authentic when people don't need anything from each other.

He's been getting to class extremely early the last two weeks, to the point that he's usually already sketched a full picture by the time anyone else arrives. He likes taking it all in: the quiet stir of the air conditioner, the cold frame of his chair, the tree branches bouncing off the glass window. He pays attention to everything and sitting there brings him comfort.

Today, Charlie decides to draw a planet. For a while, he debates which one to pick, and then he starts drawing lines and swirls on the inside, carefully sketching out Venus.

He doesn't even notice that Erin has arrived until she's standing right beside him. At this point, he's almost done with the whole picture, Venus sitting on a canvas of stars and blackness.

"Venus, goddess of love and beauty," Erin says, smiling. "You feeling extra in love today or something?"

"Or something," he replies, returning her smile.

She takes off her backpack and sits down next to him, beginning to study the picture again, as if looking for the reason behind his desire to draw that planet.

"Did you know that Venus spins at the speed of a snail compared to Earth?" he asks.

Erin laughs a little. "You're just all ready for trivia night, now, aren't you?"

"A day on Venus would be equivalent to 243 days on Earth. It's by far the slowest rotating planet in the solar system."

He looks back down, studying his drawing. He remembers when he was little, he liked to draw pictures of Venus. He used to spend a lot of time studying the planets, and he doesn't know why, but he always liked Venus best.

"Did you know that there's hardly any difference in the temperature of Venus during the night and day?" he asks.

"Charlie," Erin says, laughing a little again, "I don't know a thing about space."

"Well, you're missing out."

He watches her studying his picture, and he can see how she's looking for something, searching for his secrets.

"Venus is your favorite planet?" she asks.

Charlie nods.

He can see she's hypothesizing why. Maybe it's the stillness and stability that appeals to him, that makes him feel as if he'd belong there. Maybe this world seems to spin too fast sometimes, and he wishes everything would freeze, just for a minute.

"Mine's Neptune," Erin says at last.

"Why's that?"

"Because it's the prettiest color." She laughs, neither proud nor ashamed by the lack of intellect behind her answer.

Charlie smiles. "You need to look into planets more often and come up with a real reason," he teases. "There's only been one probe to ever visit Neptune. You should like it because of that. Like Neptune because of its mysterious factor."

"All right," Erin replies. "Next time someone asks me about my favorite planet, demanding a scientific reason, I'll make sure to present a compelling case for mysterious, unexplored Neptune."

"That's all I ask."

Charlie goes about finishing his drawing, and Erin doesn't say much else. She watches him, though. He can feel her eyes on him.

"I used to want to be an astronaut," he says after a minute. "And don't get me wrong, if someone gave me the chance, I'd get on the space shuttle in half a second. There'd be no thought necessary."

"But you'd rather be an engineer?"

"Yeah. I don't know. I want to be the one figuring out how to see things we've never seen before. You know? I want to be the reason, the mind, behind how we can find out more about what's out there."

He can feel a certain life, a fire, in his own voice that's been missing for a while. It relieves him. It's the type of passion that you can feel in the air, that's magnetizing.

"So you're telling me you want to send more probes to Neptune?"

Charlie smiles. "Hell yeah. I'm gonna ruin all your mysteries."

"That's what you want?"

"Of course. I want answers."

When she doesn't reply, he looks up to study her eyes. He can tell she doesn't know what to make of that. He can't understand what about that comment confuses her so much, but he can see the gears in her head spinning as she repeats his words in her mind.

"You remember that picture that I gave you?" she says. "The one of the face in the tree? You know how you could never figure out what it meant?"

"Yeah."

"It just meant that sometimes I feel like I'm alive in everything. Sometimes I feel like I'm inside of everyone and everything. Any tree, any planet, any person. I can't help but want to be part of it. I feel connected to everything. You know?"

"Sounds exhilarating."

"And exhausting," she says. "It's exhausting."

Something in his mind clicks. He can see in her eyes, suddenly, what's always been there: she wants to be a part of him.

**

When class is over, a few of Erin's other friends start talking to her. It's the first time Charlie really pays attention to how other people interact with Erin. She can get anyone to talk to her. She's dynamic and engaging, drawing people in, and everyone orbits around her. She's the sun.

Charlie gets up to leave, and as he walks out with her, he wonders how he's never noticed before how she takes the time to talk to every person. She's asking the other students about their lives, how their dogs are doing, how their tests have been, asking the old lady in the front row how her husband's knee surgery went. As they walk out of the room, everyone has something they want to say to her, and she says hi to them all.

"You know everyone?" he asks.

She shrugs. "I can't help it."

Another boy from the class comes up to her and says they're going to a bar. He asks Erin to come. Charlie sees a group of people from the class huddled around, talking and laughing, as they wait for the guy to come back. He's young and attractive, and his long hair is mostly covered by his beanie, only the tips curling out at the bottom. He's wearing a green t-shirt and jeans that are slightly too big, but most of all, he looks happy. The whole time he's talking to her, he's smiling.

"Sure, Tate, I'll go," Erin replies. He starts telling her about the bar, where it is, what it's like, that it's new.

"You want to join, man?" Tate asks, turning to Charlie.

His instinct, immediately, is to say no. He doesn't know why, but it doesn't even cross his mind to say yes.

Before he can say no, though, Tate adds, "Come on, it'll be fun."

He can't remember the last time he's gone out with anyone, and he feels a sense of belonging and peace from the simple offer to tag along. He looks over at the group of laughing people, and he remembers how easy that used to be for him, how before the war and Wes's death, being happy felt easy. As he watches them, he starts to think about Sarah's miscarriage. It's as if he can't figure out how to leave it behind, even for a night, as if having fun would somehow be a betrayal to the child he never met.

"I don't—"

"First drink on me," Erin interrupts.

He thinks about Sarah, how she never comes home early anymore. He knows she'll still be at school, and that his choices are between going home and being alone or going to out the bar with them.

"I can't turn down a free drink," he says.

"Words to leave by," Tate says, smiling and gesturing for them to come over to the rest of the group.

***

The bar is crowded, loud, and smoking friendly. There's a perpetual cloud of smoke hanging in the air, dancing under the dimmed lights. Most of the people there are men, covered with tattoos, drinking beer.

Tate gets them a table for seven. All three of the women at the table are young, about mid-twenties, and the men are too, apart from one who's about forty and tags along without inhibition. He's chatting and laughing as if he's the youngest one there.

Charlie quietly observes most of the time, only speaking when he orders his beer. Erin sits next to him, and she orders the same thing he does.

"So, I'm fourteen years old, skinny as hell, standing on the stage with a guitar that's as big as I am, right?" Tate says. "And I feel something drip in my eye, so I'm thinking it's not a big deal, and I go on to introduce myself on the microphone. Of course, I'm scared to death of what the older, cooler, middle schoolers are thinking. But then, I feel another drop and another, so I go to wipe my forehead, when suddenly for the first time, I realize that I'm covered in sweat. I look like I dove into a fucking swimming pool."

Charlie smiles, and he looks over to see Erin giggling.

"And of course, the most beautiful girl in the school, Diana Rivers, is sitting in the front row, and I can see her friends whispering to her, surely wondering how it's even possible to sweat so much, and I swear to God, I almost turned around and walked straight off that fucking stage." He stops to take a sip of beer. "I could have used a beer then!"

Everyone laughs.

"But I don't know. I just looked at my guitar, and I started playing and singing, and that was it. That was when I knew that no matter what went wrong, as long as I had that guitar, I'd be fine."

As people ask Tate more questions about his band, Charlie's mind starts to wander. He's had a couple things in his life, a couple people, who made him feel the way Tate felt about his guitar — as long as he could hold them, he'd never lose what's important. Somehow, though, he wonders if those people are slipping out of reach.

"You okay?" Erin asks him quietly.

Charlie immediately feels bad, knowing he should at least try to engage, to laugh when the others laugh and throw in a few comments. He nods. "I'm fine."

The others all talk, about their careers, their lives, their boyfriends and girlfriends and wives. It's nice imagining all their peaceful lives, thinking maybe one day he could have something like that. The married man shares a story about how he always fights with his wife about forgetting to take out the trash. Charlie hopes, more than anything, that one day that'll be his biggest problem. He'd give anything for Sarah to yell at him for not taking out the trash, something simple, something fixable.

"Charlie, you're quiet over there," says Adrienne, one of the girls. "Tell us something about you."

Suddenly, all the eyes are on him. Even with the background noise of the bar, the place seems silent to him in that moment as they all anticipate his answer.

He thinks about all the things he could say. He could talk about Sarah, or Wes, or Afghanistan, or the child he's lost. They'd empathize with him. They'd be interested and compelled, and they'd want to know more than they'd ever actually ask. Things would be different, though, after that. They'd see his past, and that might start to become the only thing they'd see at all.

"I want to be an aerospace engineer," he says finally.

Everyone's faces light up, and he feels relieved. When he looks over at Erin, she's smiling.

The others ask him a lot of questions, and he explains what he can. He talks about space, all the fun facts he knows that no one else does, and he can see in their eyes an excitement about his future that feels electric and contagious.

After that, Charlie lightens up. He participates in the conversations. He makes a few jokes. The others start to engage with him. He feels as if he belongs.

***

Around eleven, when they leave the bar, everyone heads in different directions to their cars, yelling their goodbyes along the way. Charlie doesn't leave yet, though. He stands in front of the bar with Erin.

"It was a good night, huh?" she says.

He looks down for a second at his shoes and taps his toes up and down. "Charlie?"

"Yeah, it was. It was a good night."

He looks back up at her, suddenly aware of the way the moonlight bounces off her skin, the way she looks as though she belongs right there. She looks so beautiful that he wishes he could freeze time and draw her.

"What?" she asks.

"What?"

"You're staring at me. Do I have something in my teeth or something?" She suddenly seems shy.

He laughs. "No, no. It's not that."

The street is totally quiet, apart from the background noise coming from inside the bar, which reaches a crescendo when the door opens and few belligerent drunks stumble through the doorway.

Erin takes a step closer to Charlie, and nervousness overcomes him. He thinks about turning around and going home, but he stays where he is. He doesn't know why.

Slowly, she moves closer to him.

"Erin, I—"

Before he has time to say anything else, she wraps her arms around him, leaning her head on his chest. For a moment he stands there, not moving, as she holds onto him. He starts to feel embarrassed, as if she'll be able to hear his heart hammering in his chest.

After a moment, she steps back and smiles at him. He can see that she cares for him. It's a selfless kind of caring, which he used to believe was the only type, but he knows better now.

"Goodnight, Charlie," she says, and walks away.

On his way home, he thinks that there was something so genuine and personal about the way she held him that it was almost worse than cheating. Part of him wishes she'd kissed him instead. Then she'd be at fault. Erin would be the bad guy. Instead, though, he can feel his stomach turning at the simple memory of her head on his chest. The innocence, the purity of it, makes it worse. It makes it real.

The rest of the night, he can't shake the feeling off. As soon as he gets to his apartment, he takes off his shirt, trying to get rid of what she touched. Of course, he feels no different. The problem isn't the shirt. The problem isn't even on his skin. The problem is that Erin doesn't see his past, and because of that, Charlie feels like someone new, someone different. At home, though, when he looks at the pictures of him and Sarah, he doesn't want to be someone different. He wants to be the same man he was. He thinks he still is. He remembers the first time Sarah touched him, how her touch had lingered on his skin for hours. He wishes she were home. He wishes she'd hold him like that, even just for a second, so he could remember what it felt like, and everything would be fine.

He waits for Sarah at their kitchen table, hoping maybe she'll come home soon, maybe she'll be done studying. He waits and waits. After a while, he falls asleep in the chair, still waiting.

Chapter 18

The next morning, Sarah isn't there. He wonders if she ever came home. He tries not to think about it.

As the day goes on, he gets more inside his own thoughts. He doesn't do much of anything. He turns on the TV, but he can't even focus on that. He can't relax. Things feel different. He can still feel the gentle pulling on his skin where Erin held him, and he realizes that it isn't even about Erin at all. It's about the fact that she comforted him, that she got through to him at a time when he couldn't get through to Sarah and Sarah couldn't get through to him.

Later that afternoon, he gets a call from his father.

For a moment, he just stares at the phone beside him on the couch, the laugh-track of *Friends* playing as white noise in the background. His dad hasn't called him in months. Maybe years.

He doesn't want to answer. His dad might be the last person on earth he needs right now. Then again, it's his father. He answers.

"Hi Charlie. How's your day going?" His dad rarely asks him this.

"Fine, thanks," Charlie answers shortly, trying to figure out why his dad called. "What's going on, Dad?"

"I was wondering if you wanted to have dinner with me today."

"Dinner?"

"Yeah. Maybe around six?"

Charlie says nothing.

"Maybe earlier? Or later?" His dad backtracks, as if that's the part of the proposition that tripped Charlie up.

"Yeah," Charlie replies. "Yeah, sure. Dinner at six would be fine."

"Great. I'll send you the location."

"All right."

"Okay."

His dad doesn't say anything else. Charlie feels the need to fill the silence, but he doesn't know with what. He doesn't have anything else to say.

He can hear his dad breathing on the other end of the line for a second, and then it goes quiet as his dad hangs up.

"What the hell was that," he says, speaking out loud to the empty apartment.

He starts wracking his brain, trying to figure out what's going on, when he puts his phone down on the table beside him and something catches his eyes.

In the stack of mail piled up beside him, there are letters from Rice and Duke.

***

His dad makes reservations at Capital Grille. When Charlie gets there, arriving early, the lighting is just bright enough to make everything visible, like the tail end of sunset. He orders a bottle of red wine, knowing they'll need it. There's an older man with bleached white hair playing the same classical song on a piano over and over, and Charlie watches him as he waits for his dad to arrive. The man never takes his eyes off the keys, and smiles to himself a few times as he plays. Charlie wonders what it'd be like to have his life, to never quite be the center of what's going on, to always live in the backdrop of conversations, in the periphery. He gets the feeling he'd be happy there, that maybe that's the key to a happy life after all.

His dad walks in at a brisk pace, as he always does, as if on a mission. When he gets to the table, Charlie stands, but then he suddenly realizes that he doesn't have a plan after that. His dad isn't really a hugger, and shaking hands would be so formal it'd create an unrecoverable distance between them. Charlie doesn't want that—he never has.

His dad gives him a half smile, saying he's sorry for running late, but they both know he's not late at all. As his dad takes off his jacket, Charlie sits back down. A few seconds later, his dad sits down too. He puts his napkin on his lap, moves the plate an inch to the right, looks at the wine. He pours himself a tiny bit and takes a sip. Then he's still.

Charlie's dad has never been the sort to make small talk. In fact, it's something he's let his wife do for so many years that Charlie wonders if he could even make it through a full dinner conversation on his own. When Charlie was younger, this wouldn't have been a problem. He talked to his dad about football, all the time, and that was enough to fill any silence. They'd debate plays, yell about referees' calls, predict trades in the NFL. That doesn't feel like the same life anymore.

"Good wine choice," his dad says.

Charlie can't help but wonder if there's something going on, if his father was trying to get on his good side before revealing some horrible new information. He studies his father's eyes, how they won't look directly at him. But his dad isn't the type to look away when he has something bad to say. Charlie still remembers the day his grandpa died when he was only eight, still so young. His dad had sat him down, looked him directly in the eyes and said, *Son, my father passed away.* That was it. One sentence. His jaw was clenched shut. His eyes were direct. Not a single tear on his face. That was all his dad said, and then he leaned forward and hugged Charlie. In that moment, Charlie would have given anything to see his dad mourn. It was as if he needed proof that his dad was strong but still emotional. Later that night, his dad put him to bed, tucking the cover tight around him, and kissed him goodnight. Twenty minutes later, Charlie crept back downstairs for a glass of water, and on his way, he saw his dad sitting on the sofa in the living room, his face in his hands, crying. Charlie watched for a moment from the stairwell, looking at his dad as he grieved. When he had enough proof, more than he could ever need, of his dad's vulnerability, he went back upstairs. He never saw his dad cry again.

"Everything all right?" his dad asks.

"Yeah," Charlie replies automatically, not even stopping to think if the words are true. "Yeah, why?"

His dad shrugs.

The waitress comes by and introduces herself. His father's shoulders relax, as if he's relieved to have a break even for a moment, as if he needs time to think about what to say. She asks if they'd like anything else to drink.

"Charlie? Anything?"

"No, I'm fine."

"I'll take a scotch." His dad hands the drinks menu back to the waitress. She walks away.

"I thought you liked the wine," Charlie says.

"I do."

Charlie nods and pours himself another glass.

His father asks him a series of questions, and there's something strange about all of them. They're all about such trivial things — what Charlie's thinking of ordering, what he thinks the weather will be like for the rest of the week, what sorts of side dishes they should get. He tells stories about times he came to this restaurant with business clients. He says he has a friend who spilled wine all over his suit during an interview. He laughs at his own story. He talks as if they go to dinner weekly, as if there's nothing weird between them at all. It makes Charlie angry. He doesn't like being part of something that so closely resembles a façade.

The waitress takes their food orders. His dad gets the filet mignon and Charlie orders a salad.

"He'll take a steak too," his dad says to the waitress. "The salad and a steak."

"Dad—" Charlie says.

"Come on. You love steak. I know you do."

The waitress smiles and writes another item on her pad. "Seems like you have quite the dad. Don't you?"

Charlie sees the joy in her eyes, the grin on her face only spreading as she walks away. He doesn't smile, though. He looks at his father, and the minute their eyes meet, the smile on his face vanishes.

"What's going on?" Charlie asks.

"What do you mean?"

"I don't like it when you order for me. I'm old enough to order the food I want."

"You really just wanted a salad?"

"Yes."

"Really?"

"Yes."

His dad takes a deep breath and sits back in his chair. He puts his hands behind his head.

"Just say it, Dad," Charlie says after a second. "Whatever you're thinking, just say it."

His dad shakes his head. "I know you like steak, and I don't know why you won't just order it."

Charlie looks at the man playing the piano. He'd give anything to be him in this moment. He'd give anything to be anywhere else.

"Why'd you ask me here tonight?" he asks at last.

"I wanted to talk to you."

"About what? About my opinion on different foods? About your business dinners?"

"No."

"Then what?"

"I don't know."

Charlie laughs. "Dad, that's the biggest lie. You have a reason for everything."

"I wish you'd let me buy you a steak."

"Oh my God, Dad, enough about the food."

"You're not listening to me."

"I am."

"No, you're not listening to me." he says sternly. When he looks up, Charlie sees that his dad is looking right at him, but not with that same, calm, together, unbreakable look. His dad's eyes are red, and his eyelids droop down just a bit. "It's not just this. You've never let me do anything for you."

"What are you talking about?"

His dad squirms in his seat, visibly uncomfortable, and he leans forward, putting his elbows on the table and then taking them back off, as if he can't get comfortable.

"This wasn't what I wanted," he whispers, so quietly that Charlie barely hears him. "I didn't come here to fight."

"Then why are we here?"

"Because..." He watches as his dad tries to find words he doesn't have.

"Because what?" Charlie pushes him.

"Because I wanted to fix things."

"Fix things?"

"Us. I wanted to fix us."

"You think buying me a nice meal is going to fix us, Dad? You really think that can fix anything?"

"I don't know."

Charlie shakes his head, as though that's the most ridiculous thing he's ever heard.

"You didn't write to me, you know," he mutters. "I went to Afghanistan, and you never even sent a letter."

"I know."

"That's horrible, Dad."

"I know."

"Did you really care that little?"

"That *little*?"

"Did you?"

When his dad looks at him, he sees something he's almost never seen before. His father's eyes are filled with tears. He looks sadder than he when he lost his father. Maybe the pain of losing a son is worse.

"That's what you think?" his dad asks. "You really think that I care about you only a *little*?"

The way his dad sits back in silence is different from before. It's as if someone's just punched him, knocking the wind straight out of him, as if the words have been punched from his throat.

"I wrote you hundreds of time," he whispers at last. "Hundreds of letters that I wrote and then crumpled up. None of them sounded right. None of them were enough. I couldn't. I couldn't..."

"You should have sent those letters."

"I know."

"It didn't matter what they said —"

"I know," he interrupts. "I know. But I was so angry and sad, and I just... I just couldn't figure out what to say. First you think to yourself, I'll write tomorrow. It's just for a day. I'll figure out the right thing to say soon. But then it's been a week, and next thing you know it's been months since you've called your own son, and he's asking what you want from him when you just want to sit and have a nice dinner."

Charlie takes a moment to digest his words. "That's what you want? A nice dinner?"

His dad shrugs.

They listen to the piano, running up and down chords, crescendoing from silence to mayhem and back down.

"You know, my father could never give us much. I loved him, more than anything in the world, but he worked a near minimum wage job, and he could hardly feed his four kids. I remember being six years old, looking up at my dad, and telling him that I was hungry when he tucked me in, and it broke him. It broke his heart. That look in my father's eyes was the most horrific thing I've ever seen in my life. And I just... I remember, in that moment, I swore I'd be a different kind of dad. My dad was a good man, and I loved him with everything in me, but I didn't want to be like him. I wanted to give my kids whatever they wanted to eat, whenever, and I wanted them to be able to go to school without working two jobs, and I just... I never wanted the pain of having my kid look at me the way I looked at my father that night... like they needed something I couldn't give them."

He stops playing with his fork and looks at Charlie. His voice drops to a whisper. "But you do." The words aren't an attack; they're a confession. "You look at me like that all the time."

"Dad —"

"No, no. Please let me finish. Please."

Charlie is quiet again.

"Ever since you enlisted, I realized I couldn't save you from everything, that you weren't gonna have the easy life I'd imagined for you so many times. I wanted... I wanted... I don't know. I don't know what I wanted, but when I watched you suffer, I just... I was so mad. I was mad for what you'd put yourself through. How dumb is that? What sort of a father does a thing like that? What kind of a dad gets mad at his kid for his own suffering?"

Charlie doesn't reply.

"I know you think I care about you going to college, but I don't," his dad continues. "I never did. I just... I wanted you to be happy, and you just... you picked such a hard path for that, and I could see it. I could see the future of things I couldn't save you from, and it killed me. I worried about you all the time. I still do. I know that's not fair to you. I know it's not." His dad takes a deep breath. "Then, you told me you were gonna be a dad, and... I realized how wrong I'd been for so long, that I couldn't do that again, not with another kid. I want you to know that I won't make the same mistakes as a grandpa. I won't. I'll do better by both of you."

Charlie suddenly feels paralyzed. He wishes he could just say nothing and accept his dad's proposal.

"Dad, there's something—"

"Look, you don't have to say anything if—"

"Sarah had a miscarriage, Dad."

Charlie no longer has to wonder what his dad felt like as a kid, looking up at his father as his heart broke. He gets his own personalized version as his father crumbles apart right then and there. Somehow, after everything he's been through, nothing hurts him more than that moment.

"Oh," his dad says.

"I'm sorry. I should have called you."

"There's no need to apologize."

But he can see on his dad's face how disappointed he is that Charlie didn't tell him something so major had happened. It's just the way things are, though.

"That's where you're wrong," Charlie says. "I did owe you a call. I did. Right?"

His dad studies Charlie's eyes for a second, and then nods. "Yeah. You're right."

Charlie watches his father take in every ounce of his pain, like a sponge, feeling every part of it. Maybe, all along, the distance in his father's eyes, the pain he felt when they were around each other, was nothing more than a mirror of what he felt in his own heart.

When their food arrives, they eat mostly in silence, but Charlie finishes every bit of his steak, stuffing himself past the point of being full.

"You were right, by the way," he says.

"About what?"

"I didn't just want a salad."

His dad sets aside his scotch, pours some more wine into his glass, and takes a sip.

It's not much, but it's something. It's a start.

Chapter 19

Instead of going home after dinner, Charlie goes to Haley's house. He knows it's around Anna's bedtime, so he knocks instead of ringing the doorbell.

Matt answers a few seconds later.

Charlie can tell by the look on his face that he didn't look through the peephole before answering. Suddenly, Matt seems stuck, as if it's too late to close the door, but he's also not sure whether Haley wants to speak to Charlie.

"Hey," Matt says after a moment, stepping aside to let Charlie in. He offers a small smile. Charlie knows Matt has an unwavering kindness, and as Matt looks over his shoulder, searching for Haley, Charlie can tell that if it were up to him, Charlie would be forgiven already. Matt never oversteps, though. He knows it's not entirely his situation to forgive.

"Hey," Charlie replies.

Matt shakes his hand. "I'll go get Haley."

Charlie waits anxiously for a minute until Haley comes out into the foyer.

He can tell that their time apart over the last two weeks or so has given her some distance, some space, and because of that, she's less mad. He wants to be the first to speak, but Haley beats him to it.

"Sarah called me," she says. "A few days ago, she called me to ask if you were okay, and I went on some tangent about how you should have been there, and she was agreeing with me, and we were just ranting until suddenly, I realized that we were talking about different things. I was talking about a birthday party, and she was talking about a miscarriage that I knew nothing about."

This isn't the conversation he expected to have right off the bat. The only thing running through his head is the speech he made up in the car on the way over, about how he was sorry, how he had no excuse not to be there, that he gets how important birthdays can be.

"You didn't even tell me she was pregnant."

Charlie takes a deep breath. It's starting to feel like a pattern — every time he tries to make up for something he's done wrong, he makes another error.

"I'm sorry," Charlie says.

"Why didn't you tell me?"

"I don't know."

"Well, try to come up with something... because I don't understand."

There's silence for a moment.

"My relationship with Sarah has been..." Charlie searches for the right word. "Fragile lately."

"Fragile?"

"I don't know."

Truthfully, it was because Sarah and Charlie were happy for a while. Lately, he'd felt as if they were living in a bubble, as if any sudden movements, any changes, might pop it, but inside, where it was just them, they were happy.

"The miscarriage isn't why I wasn't at the party. I didn't know any of that then."

"Charlie —"

"I'm just saying. I came to say I'm sorry, not to hear you say it."

As he stands in front of her, he starts to feel as though all the pieces inside of him are crumbling, as though he's one second away from falling apart, and that's not what he wants.

"I'm sorry for not being at Anna's party," he says. "I'd really like to talk to her, to tell her myself, if I could."

He can see on Haley's face that the birthday party now seems like something small, like something not even worth being mad about. Charlie wishes she didn't feel that way. She looks at him as if it's cruel to be mad at him for missing her child's party when his own baby would never get a single birthday. Not a single party. Not a single gift.

"Can I talk to her?" he asks.

"Yeah," Haley says. "Sure, you can."

Charlie begins to turn away from her, to go upstairs toward Anna's room.

"Wait," Haley says, taking a few steps toward him. She reaches out and hugs him.

He can tell that as she holds him, she's imagining a lot of things. She's thinking about the fragility of life, how with one bit of bad luck, she might never have had him as a brother. What she's saying is that she loves her family more than anything, and that he'll always be hers.

"I love you, Haley," he says, and he lets her hug him for as long as she likes. When she finally lets go, he goes upstairs.

***

"Mommy?" Anna asks when he knocks on the door.
"No, it's me. It's your Uncle Charlie."
He opens the door a little, peeking his head in. Anna sits up in bed, saying nothing at first. She's wearing light-pink cupcake pajamas that match her walls.
"Can I come in?" he asks.
She leans over and turns on the lamp on her nightstand.
The floor is a mess. There are Legos and dolls everywhere, making the ground a minefield. When he gets to her bed, he doesn't know what to do. He leans down, to squat beside her, but she moves over and motions for him to sit next to her. He takes off his shoes and climbs in bed beside her.
Anna squeezes her teddy bear. Charlie hates how uncomfortable she is. She looks as if she doesn't know how to be around him anymore. The last thing he ever wanted was to hurt that little girl, and he can see that he did.
"My mom told me about your baby," she says after a moment.
"She did?"
"She said sometimes babies don't make it out of their mommy's tummies, that sometimes they die."
"Yeah," he says.
The way she looks up at him is desperate and terrifying. He doesn't know how to explain any of this to a kid, a child who he doesn't want to break any more than he already has.
"Is that why you weren't at my party?" she asks.
"No. No, it wasn't that exactly."
"Then what was it?"
He wishes he'd lied, that he could just give her some simple explanation that'd be easy to understand.
"You remember my friend, Wes?"
She nods.
"Well, he was my best friend in the world, and then he chose to die."
"What does that mean?"
"He killed himself. He was sad and he... he wanted to die."

INDIVISIBLE

As soon as the words come out of his mouth, he wishes he'd said something different. Telling the truth feels like the worst idea ever.

"Why?"

"Well, I don't know exactly, but there was this woman, and I thought she might know why, so I went to see her instead of going to your party."

"Did she know anything?"

"Kinda," he says, trying to summarize, trying not to be too specific.

She looks at him in a way that he didn't know, until that moment, was possible for such a little kid. She looks at him with such grace, such deep empathy.

"Are you sad like Wesley, Uncle Charlie?"

Her innocence is overwhelming.

"No. God, no, Anna," he says, feeling an immense guilt for making her wonder such a thing.

She looks relieved. She relaxes, leaning back on her pillow. She begins to study her teddy bear.

"I just... I came here to tell you that I'm sorry," Charlie says. "I made a mistake. I should have been there for your birthday."

"You told me you'd be there," she says, not afraid to look him in the eye.

"I know."

"You promised me, and then you didn't come." Her voice is soft and gentle, not attacking, but hurt.

"I'm sorry, Anna."

She takes a deep breath and pulls the covers up over herself, all the way to her neck.

"I thought I could make you happy," she says.

"You do."

"I thought that if you came to my party, you wouldn't look so sad anymore."

"Honey, I'm so sorry. I don't mean to look that way." He tries to comfort her, but he's growing more and more mad at himself.

"I know you're upset," Anna says. "I know you're sad because you lost your baby and your best friend."

"Anna, I—"

"But I could be those things."

He stops for a second. "What?"

"I could be your best friend, and I know I'm not your kid, but I could be kind of like your kid. Couldn't I?"

"Anna—"

"Then you might not be so sad."

He puts his arm around her, and she leans into him. "Why do you think I'm sad, honey? I'm fine. Okay? You don't need to worry about me."

"You used to sing to yourself," she says, looking away from him and down at her bear. "And you used to jump out from behind walls and tickle me. And you used to surprise me and just be waiting in our kitchen when I got home from school. You used to hardly be able to stop smiling when you read to me at night. And now... I don't know. Wes died, and now you don't sing, or jump out to tickle me, or read to me at night. You never surprise me anymore. You're not even here usually. I don't know... maybe I'm the one who's sad."

He doesn't know what to say, so he says nothing at first. Instead, he just holds her tightly, letting her head rest on his chest. She holds him back, and her grip gets tighter and tighter, as if she's afraid to let go.

"I'm sorry, Anna," he whispers, suddenly realizing that the birthday party was only the smallest part of what he has to apologize for. "I'm so sorry."

"I could make you happy," she says. "If you were around more, I could."

"You do. I promise."

"Are you happy now?" she asks, looking up at him.

"Yes," he says. "Of course."

She watches the tears filling up in his eyes. She seems to be trying to figure out which is true, his words or those tears.

"I love you," he says. "I'm not going anywhere, okay?"

She nods, but she doesn't say anything else. He can tell that she must feel safe, that she must still trust him, because she falls asleep a few minutes later—her head still on his chest, her arms still wrapped around him tightly.

***

A little later, after sleep has softened Anna's grip on him, he kisses her forehead, pulls the covers up tightly, and puts her bear in her arms, at the spot where he had been. He leaves a note by her bed saying that he loves her more than anything, and then he drives home and falls asleep on his couch.

He's woken up a few hours later, when he feels someone gently shaking his shoulders. The shaking gets more and more forceful the longer it takes him to come out of his sleep.

"Sarah?"

He blinks repeatedly, pulling his head up, waiting for his vision to focus. He's disoriented, looking around the kitchen, trying to get the kink out of his neck.

"Hey," she says, "Yeah, it's me."

Once he sits up, she sits down next to him.

"Can we talk?" she asks.

There's an urgency in her voice that makes him move a little faster, sit up a little taller. He notices she has red eyes, as though she's been crying, but she's pulled it together now. She doesn't look like she did after the miscarriage, though. She looks at him with sympathy and even a bit of fear.

"I'm sorry," she says. "I'm sorry to wake you, and I'm just... I'm sorry."

"Honey, it's fine," he says. He reaches out to try to touch her hand, to calm her down. She pulls back and quickly turns away, unable to look at him.

He watches as she squirms, as she tries to make eye contact but can't. He identifies what it is on her face that he's never seen before: guilt.

"We need to talk," she says at last, finally looking him in the eyes.

Chapter 20

She didn't mean for it to happen. She starts by repeating that a million times in a million different ways. He gets increasingly nervous the longer she doesn't tell him what's going on. Instead, she talks about how she's been having a tough time with the miscarriage, that she needed someone to talk to, that she's spent so many late-night hours just trying to stay on top of her schoolwork.

Then she asks if he remembers her lab partner, Max.

"He kissed me," she says, without waiting for Charlie's response. "I didn't kiss him back."

He wonders if that's true. He remembers how nervous he was the first time he kissed Sarah, how he'd stared at her eyes and lips for seconds on end before leaning down. He wonders if Max stared into her eyes too, looking for permission. He wonders if she gave it to him.

At first, Charlie chooses not to process what she says enough to really consider how he feels. He tries to withdraw from the situation, to let everything unfold in small, manageable pieces. He starts by trying to gauge how she feels about everything. He studies the sweat on her forehead, the way she plays with her thumbs, anticipating a response.

The longer he stays quiet, the more she fidgets.

"Please say something," she says at last.

He doesn't. He studies her, trying not to think about how he feels. He knows that if he really lets it in, he'll have so many questions, so many things he needs to know. He's not sure if he's ready for all that.

She reaches out to touch his hand. He thinks about how, over the last two weeks, this is all he's wanted, for them to be even partially together. He lets her touch him.

"Please, Charlie," she repeats. "Talk to me."

"Did you want to kiss him?" he finally asks.

"No, of course not."

He can hear the desperation in her voice, how worried she is that he won't understand.

Part of him wants to brush the whole thing off, to let her off the hook. Maybe, if he forgave her, she'd have to forgive him. It'd be an exchange, and things could reset to how they were when there was no one to blame for anything, when they were happy. Then, another part of him wants to explode. He wouldn't do this to her; he really believes that. To let her off the hook would be to equate their actions, and he doesn't know if that works in her favor or his.

"So it didn't mean anything to you?" he asks.

She opens her mouth to reply, but nothing comes out. He can tell that this surprises her, that she expected the answer to be easy.

In that moment, Charlie feels everything crumbling. He can feel the way his heart breaks apart, stinging with a growing pain the longer she waits to reply.

"No," she says at last, shaking her head, partially at herself, as if wondering what took her so long to say something. "No, it didn't."

"What was that?"

"What?"

"That pause."

"I didn't mean to pause. I don't know why I did." She suddenly looks appalled by herself, as though there's someone else in her body that she can't control. "You know this isn't simple. You know we're not simple."

"What's your point?"

"I don't have a point. I'm just trying to tell you the truth."

He takes a second, trying to decide what there is to say to that. "Let's hear it."

"What?" she asks.

"This big truth. Whatever you're not saying."

"There is no—"

"Whatever's going on in your head, I wanna hear it."

"Charlie, there's nothing I haven't—"

"There is. Otherwise you wouldn't have paused."

They're silent for a moment. She stares at him as if waiting for him to say something else, but he doesn't.

"Do you remember Brett?" she says at last. "He lived in my dorm during my sophomore year of college."

"What about him?"

"When you came home to visit, you told me to be careful of him because he liked me, and I thought you were crazy. Then one night, he tried to kiss me, and it was so startling to me, so out of the blue, that I told him he should be embarrassed. The idea of kissing him just had never even occurred to me. I'd never in a million years have thought of him that way."

"And you're telling me this now because why? Because this was different? You wanted Max to kiss you?"

"No, of course not."

"Then what?"

"I didn't want him to, but the reason why was because I was thinking of you."

"What is that supposed to be? A compliment? An insult? What?"

"It's not anything, Charlie. I'm just trying to talk to you."

He can feel everything spiraling. He knows that if he yells, if he presses, he could win. She'd never win this debate because she's the one at fault. He can feel the ice beneath them thinning, and because of that, he backs off. He doesn't want them to break. The last thing he wants is for them to end up yelling at each other, saying a bunch of things they mean far too much.

They both look away for a while, and Charlie tries to think, but nothing comes to his mind. He can sense that her brain is doing the opposite, running at a million miles per hour.

"Sometimes I feel like we're spinning in circles," she whispers.

He feels thrown off; of everything he expected her to say, that wasn't on the list. "What do you mean?"

"You and me. Sometimes I feel like we're stuck in this unending loop of fighting and making up, of being close and then being apart. We have a different version of the same fight over and over again."

He pulls his hand back, away from her.

He didn't know it until the words came out of her mouth and he read her face, but now he understands that those words are the worst thing he could possibly hear. He realizes that she's changed the course of the conversation. They're no longer talking about one isolated event. It no longer has to do with her kissing Max. It's about them, and whether or not they work.

He looks at her for a second, hoping he's read the situation wrong.

"What are you trying to say?" he asks, the anger building back up. He wishes he'd waited longer, that they could have finished talking about Max first.

"I don't know."

"You don't know? You don't know what?"

He takes a breath, trying to slow everything down while making sense of what he feels. He can't decide whether he's angry or if he understands her side of things, and that makes the conversation impossible to progress.

"What is it, Sarah?" he says.

"Can't you just give me a single second to process?" she asks.

"Oh, you're the one who needs time to process?"

"Charlie, please —"

"What is it? Please just tell —"

"Fine. You want to know what I'm thinking? I'm wondering if we're meant to be together."

He's silent. He can tell that the words shock her almost as much as they do him. She didn't mean for the conversation to go this way; he can see it on her face.

"What?" he asks.

"Are you sure about me? Are you sure you want to be with me?"

"Of course I'm sure, Sarah."

Truthfully, they've been here before. They've asked these same questions.

He stands up as if he's about to start pacing around the room. She does too. There's something about her mimicking him that he doesn't like. He sits down again, trying to get some space from her.

"Oh come on, don't do that," she says.

"Don't do what? Be mad that after six years you want to just walk away?"

"Don't start that with me."

"Start what?" He stands back up. He feels as though he can't stop moving, as though the adrenaline in his veins is moving far too quickly.

"I don't want to —"

"You just said you're not sure whether you want to be with me. How'd you envision this conversation going down?"

"Charlie, please just —"

"What? Calm down? Did you think we'd sit down and have a nice conversation and hug at the end?"

"No, that's not —"

"What was it, Sarah?" he asks. "Losing Wes? Losing our baby? That's my fault now? You're gonna blame it on us being together?"

"Stop. That's just not fair. You know that's not what I'm saying."

"What, then? Were you waiting around to break up with me and you thought now's the perfect time, right after I upset you by not being there for the miscarriage? What was kissing Max? Some kind of revenge?"

"Charlie, I know you're hurting, but —"

"Hurting? Hurting doesn't even —"

"Stop. Please, stop."

"Was it revenge?"

"God, no, Charlie," she says. "You've got it backwards."

"Backwards? What the hell does that mean?"

"It means that—"

"What?"

"Please, just give me a second! Please..."

She carefully grabs his sides, trying to get him to stop pacing, trying to get him to look her in the eyes long enough to see how much pain she's in. He can tell how badly she wishes he'd just try to understand. That's the last thing he wants to do.

"You know that ring you were telling me about?" she says. "The one you saved up for in high school?"

"What's that have to—"

"Why didn't you propose to me? All these years, why'd you never do it?"

"That seems a little irrelevant, right now, doesn't it?"

"No," she replies. "It's not actually."

"Don't try to turn this on me. Don't try to make it my fault for not proposing."

"I'm not. I'm just asking—"

"You want to know why I didn't propose to you, Sarah?" he says. "Maybe it's because I've been sleeping on the couch, because we haven't talked in weeks, because you can't even look me in the eyes long enough for me to get the full sentence out!"

He hates that he's yelling. He's never been the yelling type, especially not with Sarah. He can tell she's getting heated, that she wants to yell back, but she bites her tongue, and he envies her restraint. He'd do anything to feel restrained.

"So what was your plan?" she asks quietly.

"What?"

"Your plan. If we've been so horrible together lately, if proposing has seemed so outlandish, how were we going to fix it?"

"Time."

She laughs. "Time? We've had six years together."

"That's not what I mean."

"Well, it should be. After six years, it shouldn't be so hard. You shouldn't have to feel like depending on the week, it's a wild card whether you'll be proposing or sleeping in the other room."

He's silent for a moment while he takes in what she's saying.

"So you want this to be simple?" he asks. "You want something simple and easy?"

"That's not what I mean. I hate it when you do that."

"Then what do you mean? You mean that this is too hard? It's been too much?"

"I couldn't love you more than I do. I love you more than I can put into words. I love you enough that I'd move mountains for you. I'd take a bullet for you. I'd suffer endlessly for you if that's what it came down to. We've suffered so much for each other."

"What's your point?"

"That maybe it's not kind of us," she says. "Maybe we shouldn't put each other through this anymore."

Suddenly her face is blank, but he knows it's just a moment of rest before she starts arguing again.

"Put each other through this?" he says. "That's how you've felt? Like I've been putting you through something all these years?"

"No," she says. "You know that isn't what I meant."

He says nothing.

"Sometimes, I feel like we're so different," she continues, "that so much has gone wrong between us, that we're fighting fate so extremely that we're just breaking, crack by crack."

"That's what love is, sometimes, Sarah. That's—"

"I know," she says. "I know. And I'd... I'd stay with you forever. I'd love you forever, and I'd completely break for you if that's what it took. I would." She looks down away from him. "But is it what we want? Because we are breaking, you know. We are."

She turns away from him again, as if trying to collect herself.

"We'd do anything for each other, Charlie. I waited for you to come back from war. You promised to go to Rice to stay close to me. I quietly lay by you, night after night, after the war when you couldn't sleep without seeing ghosts. You slept on the couch when I was too upset to talk to anyone. We'd do anything. We've done everything."

"You make it sound like a problem. That's what it means to care for someone."

He can tell she's wondering if he's right. Maybe she's crazy. Maybe everything she's saying is way off base, and she'll regret all of it in the morning.

"I don't get what you're saying," he says.

All her energy is visible. She's turned half away from him, and they're both on the verge of tears.

"Do you remember when I met Erin at the art gallery," she says, "and she was smiling while looking at all your art?"

"Oh my God, don't drag her into this."

"Why not, Charlie?"

"Because she's irrelevant right now. Compared to you, she's irrelevant."

"Do you think you could love her one day? Is she the kind of person you'd love?"

"We had a class together one night a week. You think I... what? That I'd throw away what we have for that?"

"But what if there is someone else out there that—"

"What if not?" he asks. "What if there's not someone simple and easy and perfect? Huh? Then what? Is that what you're looking for? Simple, easy, and perfect?"

"No."

"Then what are you looking for?"

"I'm looking for someone who makes things feel simple and easy and perfect, even when everything is falling apart."

"You sound childish."

He can see she's letting his words sink in, analyzing what he's saying.

"You think that's childish?" she says. "Do you get how sad that is? Do you get how sad it is that you see love and ease as two things that can't exist simultaneously? They should, Charlie. They should."

He stops for a moment and looks around their apartment, out of the side of his eye, and he wonders if he feels the same way about this place that Natalie feels about her house. He wonders if, for him, these walls are filled with ghosts that haunt him. He wonders if this apartment will always hold memories of how things were, if they'll hold the past in a way that makes it impossible to move forward.

He studies Sarah's face. She looks so much like she did six years ago, and in some ways, he feels as if it was just yesterday that he was the boy sitting in Algebra II, trying to come up with something to say to the smartest girl in the room to grab her attention. He remembers, still, the way she'd sit in the front, seeming to notice no one but the teacher, and how he felt as if there'd never be any way to get her to see him. He feels similarly now. She'll never see his side of this.

"If I'd asked you to marry me," he says, "what would you have said?"

"What?"

"What if I did right now?" he says. "What if, right now, I fell to my knee and asked you to marry me?"

"I don't think—"

"Would you?"

"Charlie—"

"Would you have said yes?"

"Could—"

"If right now—"

"Yes," she replies quickly, without giving it any more thought. "I would have said yes. I'd say yes."

"Then marry me," he says. "All this crap, we'll figure it out later if you just marry me."

"Charlie—"

He slows down, takes her hand, and presses his forehead against hers. "I love you, Sarah. I want to be with you for the rest of my life. Okay? I swear. I even have the ring."

He starts looking around for his jacket.

"Stop," she says.

He's darting around the living room, as if everything will be okay if he can just find the jacket that has that ring in the pocket. He moves all the pillows on the couch, frantically searching.

"Stop!"

"Why?"

"You asked me if I'd say yes, not if I wish I would."

He freezes, not saying anything. He's starting to feel something other than anger. He becomes sad.

"If I said yes," she says, "would it be the best day of your life?"

"You're being cruel."

"I'm being serious. Would it be? Would you call your parents and not be able to stop smiling? Would you call Haley and Anna? Would you start thinking of our wedding every time you eat a cake?"

"Yes."

"Stop," she says. "Don't answer so quickly. I want you to really stop and think. Really try to imagine it. Do you feel just simply happy?"

He takes a moment to do what she asks.

"Love isn't simple," he says. "For the millionth time. We're just going through something right now."

"I think you're wrong."

"You want to live in some fairy tale?"

"I think that after six years, you should be able to kneel down with a ring in your hand, and I should be able to say yes without us both feeling like the idea of that is too complicated. I don't think that's asking for a fairy tale. That's just asking for some sense of clarity, just a slice of peace."

Her eyes become distant again, as if she's trying to take a break from the conversation.

"I love you," he says. "I'm sure of that. That's clear to me."

"I know. I've never doubted that."

"Do you love me?"

"Yes."

"Then what else do you want? That's all I have. That's all anyone has."

He can tell she understands every word he's saying, that it's something she's thought of already. He hates that.

"Love isn't enough for you?" he asks. "Is that what you're saying?"

She studies his eyes. "I wish you wouldn't do that. I wish you wouldn't make what I'm trying to say sound so dark."

"It is."

"It isn't. I'm trying to say that I care about you more than anything in the world and that, at some point, we have to care about each other enough to wonder if we're too broken to put back together."

He knows there have been moments when he's looked at her and couldn't see the perfect life they had planned, that they wanted more than anything. There have been so many moments when he could see the disappointment on her face, when he could tell he'd failed to be the man she wanted. There've been nights when he was with her that he could no longer see her as the one either, but he'd thought it only natural.

"Maybe," he says. "But I'm not done fighting. I'm not done trying to put the pieces back together."

He takes a step closer to her, and he can feel it all over again, how this is the moment where she'd usually agree with him, where she'd start to believe they'll be all right. He remembers once, when they were younger, they were walking through a park, hand in hand, trees surrounding the walkway, birds chirping, children running around them. They walked past an old couple, sitting on a bench, talking and laughing, and Charlie thought that one day that'd be him and Sarah. It feels like just yesterday, and somehow, even as he's standing there listening to her say she thinks they need space, when he thinks of himself as an old man, she's still the one he sees sitting next to him. She's the only one.

"Well, I am," she says. "I'm done."

He stares at her, only half taking in what she's said.

"I'm tired, Charlie," she adds. "Aren't you exhausted?"

"You're not serious," he says, shaking his head. "You don't get to be serious about this."

"We're not happy," she says. "It's that simple. I can't make you happy anymore. There's too much — "

"You're not serious. You can't be serious."

Suddenly, panic sets in, as if he's coming out of a nightmare. The layers of anger and sadness disappear, and he's left standing there, pleading with her, begging her to say it's a bad dream.

"Remember when you were sick in high school, and you were in the hospital, and you felt horrible and had that terrible fever?" she asks.

He says nothing.

"I told you I'd always be there to make you feel better," she says. "And I... I want that more than anything. I want you to always feel better, but it's like I can't cure you anymore, and you can't cure me. It's like we're just too sick."

She takes a step closer to him. He still can't fully process what she's saying.

"I wish we could go back in time," she whispers.

He doesn't know if he wishes that or not. It's almost more painful to wonder if they would have been fine if they'd made different decisions or had different twists of fate. What if he'd never gone to war, or what if she'd never gotten pregnant? He still wants to believe in a love that can conquer anything, even horrible luck, a love that's greater than circumstances. He also thinks it's impossible to love anyone more than he loves her.

"I'd do anything to rewind," she says.

He remains quiet, as if waiting for her to say this is all some prank, that she's not really breaking up with him.

"Did you mean any of it?" he asks quietly, just above a whisper.

"Any of what?"

"All the times you said you loved me. Did you mean it?"

"Yes, Charlie. Yes. You know I meant it."

"What about all the times we promised each other we'd be together forever? Did you mean that?"

"Of course. Of course I meant it."

He looks at her, and he can see the sincerity in her eyes. Somehow that sincerity feels like the entire problem.

"How can you say that?" he asks. "You didn't mean it, or I wouldn't be about to walk out the door."

He can sense her breaking, as though she wants to crumble completely. He thinks about trying to take his words back, but he doesn't.

"I can't be here," he says, backing away. "I'm leaving. I'm leaving now."

"Please, don't," she says quietly.

"Well, I'm not staying."

She's crying now, and he wishes she'd stop. It's not her right to be upset when she's the one causing the whole mess.

"Please, don't leave like this," she says.

"Are you serious? I mean, do you hear yourself?"

He packs up whatever he can into his duffle bag. She follows him as he walks across their living room, grabbing everything that's his.

"This isn't what I ever wanted," she says. "It's not."

He's tempted to just go numb, to try not to think about any of it too hard, but he doesn't let himself. He feels every second of it.

"You're out of your mind," he says, hurrying toward the front door.

"Please just slow down," she says.

"I don't know what you thought would happen." He opens the door.

"Please, just—"

"I hope you were sure about this," he says. "I hope you were really, really sure, because if we weren't broken before, we are now."

He'll never forget the look in her eyes. She's staring at him as if they're standing on the edge of a cliff, about to jump, without knowing whether there'll be water or rock below.

Then he closes the door.

Chapter 21

Charlie doesn't know what to do or where to go, so he goes the only place he can: home.

The whole ride there, he feels as though he's in a dream, as though his life isn't his own. His hands are so sweaty on the steering wheel that he feels he can't grip it, but his desperation to hold on only makes him sweat more. Sometimes, when he's staring at the road, it's as if there are gaps in time, as if he's drunk. One minute the stop signs are a hundred yards away, and then, one blink later, they're behind him. Other moments, he feels as if he's moving at the speed of a snail, as if the car isn't even going. Time doesn't seem to be grounded in any equation, anything factual, but just fluctuates as it pleases.

He gets home safely, though, and when he arrives, standing on the front porch of his parents' house, he can't help but feel young. He takes a moment to look at everything, to study the familiarity of it. Years ago, the trees were all the same, the stars peeped through the clouds the same way, the bugs still buzzed around the porch light. It upsets him how familiar things look but how different things feel. He takes a deep breath and knocks.

At first, no one comes. He looks at his watch. It's nearly 2:00 AM.

He rings the doorbell.

A minute or two later, he hears the door unlatch, and his mom is standing there. Her curly hair, uncombed and puffy, shoots in a million directions, and her eyes are barely open. When she sees him, though, she perks up. She even smiles.

"Charlie," she says, suddenly seeming wide awake, as if it's Christmas morning. "What are you doing here?"

"Can I come in?"

"Of course."

Charlie steps through the door, but before he's even inside, his mom wraps her arms securely around him.

He can tell how happy she is just to see him, and it makes him feel bad for not visiting more. He's never known how much his visits meant to her. He watches as her expression rotates between lighting up at the fact that he's home and worrying about what's brought him here.

"Is everything okay?" she asks.

"Can I stay here tonight?"

He watches as his mom tries to read his face. She tries to figure out why he didn't answer her question.

There've been many instances in the past where Charlie felt that his mom was absent, and because of that, she's never fully known him. However, in that moment, in the kindness of her opening the door and welcoming him home, all of that disappears. He feels secure. He feels safe.

His mom helps get his room ready, folding down the sheets, as if he's a kid that can't do anything on his own. She even lingers in the doorway when telling him goodnight.

"Hey mom," he says as she's leaving.

"Yeah?"

"I love you."

The smile on her face vanishes for a second. It's as if she can hear desperation in his voice, how desperately he needs those words to mean something again.

"I love you too, Charlie," she replies.

He nods and gives her a little smile. He turns away from the door. He can tell she's still standing there, trying to come up with something to say, but a minute later, she walks down the hallway, back to bed.

***

Charlie sleeps terribly. He's in his own room, but nothing about it feels familiar. He's exhausted, but it seems that every time he falls asleep, his body is jolted awake, as if he's been shocked with electric paddles. His stomach flips and his nerves feel as though they're on fire every time he realizes Sarah isn't near him. At one point, he feels the need to go running. Maybe that'd calm him down or exhaust him enough that he'd be able to sleep. But he knows that disarming the alarm system would make it beep and wake his parents up, and that doesn't feel fair. He doesn't want to disturb them again or cause them any worry about why he'd run so late at night. At every second, he wonders what Sarah is doing. Did she just stay there, standing by that door? Did she call her parents or her friends? Maybe she called Max.

Maybe Max could comfort her in a way Charlie never could. He hates thinking about it, and he hates the idea of Max ever being around her again, but he's not entitled to that thought anymore. She's left him, and Max isn't his to hate at all.

He's relieved when, around 6:00 AM, he hears noises downstairs. He wants to be around other people, near someone, rather than lying in bed awake with no one.

In the kitchen, his dad is making coffee while his mom makes pancakes.

She greets him with a friendly hello and says, "I hope you still like buttermilk with chocolate chips. It's a nightmare for anyone on a diet, but delicious none-the-less."

His dad studies him, trying to figure out what's going on.

"It's so nice to have you here," his mom goes on. "Things haven't been the same since you moved out all those years ago. It felt like you took a part of me with you."

His father interrupts. "What's going on, Charlie?"

The room freezes. Charlie watches his mom's face harden, angry at her husband for his bluntness, as she stands over the stove.

"What?" his dad says, turning to his wife, letting his voice grow soft. "It's just a question. My son shows up at 2:00 AM, and I can't ask what he's doing here?"

Charlie's mom shakes her head, and he can see she's about to fight him, to tell him that Charlie is welcome any time he wants, with or without explanation.

"Sarah had a miscarriage," Charlie interjects. "And then she left me."

Both of his parents look at him, eyes wide, but they say nothing.

He tries to say the words passively. He feels so deeply hurt, so purposeless, like a moon released into the solar system without a planet to orbit. He knows that if he really tries to tell his parents how he's feeling, he won't make it, so he sticks to the facts.

They continue to stare at him in shocked silence. His mom suddenly seems scared to speak, as if he's made of glass, and one little wrong movement or word might shatter him if it's not gentle enough.

After a moment, his dad looks down. "Are you okay?" He tries to go back to making his coffee, as if nothing is wrong, but his voice is tight with vicarious pain.

"Should I be?" Charlie says gently.

Neither of them answers that question.

His dad sets his coffee down, excuses himself, and walks out of the room. Charlie sees the pain in his father's eyes, though. He sees that his dad feels everything he does.

His mother's eyes haven't come off him, and he can see how she's thinking about everything he's been through, how she's wondering what it would have been like if she'd never gotten to have him as a child. He watches her imagine his broken heart. It's a horrible look to see in his own mother's eyes.

"I'm fine, Mom. Really."

It isn't until the burning pancakes start to smell and smoke that she realizes she's forgotten to flip them. When she does, they're completely black and ruined.

For the rest of breakfast, she apologizes again and again for the pancakes. "I should have paid more attention to them, then they never would have burned."

He can't help but wonder if what she's really saying is that she's sorry for all the time she was away from him, that she's sorry if she hasn't been there enough.

"It's okay," he says, over and over. He means it, too. The last thing he wants is another broken heart.

***

Both his parents offer to take the day off work to stay home with him. His mom even rattles off a list of things they could do that might be fun. Charlie insists it's not necessary, that he'll be just fine. He says it'd make him feel worse if they changed their schedules for his sake.

His father caves before his mom. Charlie can see that his dad wants to stay, that he wants to be there for him, but he can't quite figure out what to say, what would actually help his son feel better. As much as his dad wants to be there, he also desperately wants to leave.

Charlie tells his mom his plan for the day.

"I'm hoping to get a new job," he says. "I'm gonna spend the day applying for things, so it's best if I'm alone. I need the time to myself."

Eventually, they give in. Both his parents leave for work, and the house is his.

He does just what he said he would. He fills out applications to be a waiter, just for a few months, until school starts. He looks for gyms that need personal trainers, searching for anything he feels qualified to do.

The applications take forever because a stinging in his chest stops him every minute. Every once in a while, it takes him a long time to breathe, and sometimes he feels as though he has to focus on the fact that his lungs are there to even get a breath out. It's as if, without Sarah, he's missing his entire heart, his entire chest. He starts to feel as if the humid Houston air is too thick to take in, but he forces himself to breathe, in and out, again and again.

In the middle of his applications, without giving it too much thought, he picks up the phone and calls Rice.

***

That night, Charlie's mom makes a home-cooked meal of chicken parmesan and green beans. They eat together, but it's a quiet meal. Sometimes, Charlie's mom talks about her day, about different things going on with her business, but he can tell that her heart isn't really in it. She's just trying to fill the silence. His dad hardly says a word the whole meal, but it's a different kind of quiet than normal. It's as if he's too sad, too afraid of hurting Charlie, to say anything.

After the meal, his mom takes a business call, and Charlie and his dad do the dishes together. They stand side by side, working in total silence. They finish up, putting the soap in the dishwasher and pressing start. They wash their hands. Charlie can practically hear his dad thinking, can feel how badly his dad wishes he could figure out the right thing to say. He never says a word, though.

"Hey Dad," Charlie says.

"Yeah?"

"I have something to tell you."

His dad freezes, then turns off the water and slowly faces him. "Okay, what is it?"

"I got into Rice and Duke."

The look on his father's face is something Charlie's never seen before. He looks as if he's been given the world, yet he doesn't want Charlie to feel any pressure, so he keeps his face neutral.

Charlie smiles, just a little, to let his dad know that it's okay to be happy. His dad smiles and throws his arms around him.

"I'm proud of you," his dad whispers. "Whatever you do, I'll be proud."

"Why doesn't this feel easier though, Dad?" Charlie asks. "Can't just one thing feel simple?"

His dad steps back, looking him in the eyes. "You'll be okay. Whatever you pick, you'll be just fine."

Charlie isn't sure whether that's the type of statement worth acknowledging.

"How do you know?" Charlie asks.

"Because brave people find a way to be at peace."

"Yeah?"

"Yeah," his dad says. He sounds so sure.

Charlie can't decide if his dad's answer is wise or crazy. Maybe there's no difference.

Chapter 22

The next few days, his family seems normal, happy even. His dad returns to being quiet and private, but in a thoughtful sort of way. He still laughs at stories during dinner and shares a few things from his day. He tries to be more engaged, and Charlie tries to do the same. There are times where he ends up laughing with his parents, and he feels as though things are sliding into place somehow. The problem is that he doesn't feel completely sane sometimes. Every once in a while, he thinks he sees Sarah out of the corner of his eye, but of course, when he turns, she's not there. For a split second, he convinces himself that the whole breakup was just a bad dream. He feels out of his mind.

One night, he's watching a movie with his parents when his phone rings. He only notices when the scene goes dark and he sees the light of his phone glowing in the room.

It's Sarah.

At first, he stares at the screen for a long time, blinking, his heart rate accelerating. He closes his eyes for a while, as if making sure this isn't another thing he's imagining, but when he opens his eyes, the phone is still buzzing. He turns it over, putting it down on the couch beside him, as if somehow that'll make the call disappear. He goes back to looking at the movie, but he doesn't hear a word of it anymore. All he can hear is the vibrating of the phone on the cushion.

Anger overwhelms him, as if, all this time, it's been building in him, and he hasn't realized the extent of it, how little he's forgiven her. Just the sight of her name makes him feel as though he's spun around in circles and then tried to sprint.

The phone stays face down. He doesn't answer.

The next few minutes, time trudges forward as if it's pulling a parachute behind it. Everything in the room blurs, making him feel dizzy. He closes his eyes again. He starts to feel as if he's suffocating, so he picks up the phone and walks out of the room. He hears his mom ask if everything's okay. He says yes and that he's going to use the restroom.

When he gets to the bathroom, he turns on the lights and sets his phone down. He splashes water on his face, trying to make it colder and colder. He takes a deep breath and looks at himself in the mirror. His eyes look different than they did a few months ago. He's not numb anymore. Instead, he feels everything. He can see it in his face, how suddenly, he's completely present, how the past and future have left him alone, just for a minute, and he's bare. It's too much for him. He turns away and picks up his phone.

He finally looks at the screen and sees that he has a voicemail from Sarah. He wishes he could just delete it, but that's the last thing he wants to do, which is the entire problem. Instead, all he can think about is what he hopes it'll say. He doesn't know. What if she called to say he needs to come get his things? He'd hate her for that. What if she wants him back? He'd hate that even more.

His sits down on the bathroom floor, puts the phone to his ear, and hits play.

There's a long silence at the beginning of the voicemail, as if she had to decide whether to speak or to just hang up.

"Hey," she says. As soon as she speaks, the hair on his arms stands up, and he leans forward, feeling sick. "It's me. I know you're mad. I just... I haven't really been okay since you left. I can't sleep, or eat, and I know that's not your problem or anything. I know that. It's just that I keep hearing your voice as you left... Man, I swear, I practiced what to say before I called, but I just can't think straight. I guess that's the whole point of calling. I just... I can't even think without you... I don't know why I called really. I think I just wanted to hear your voice again. I'd give anything to just hear your voice. How dumb is that? I know I'm not being fair: breaking up with you and then asking for you to talk to me because... what? Because your voice might fix me? God, I'm sorry. I shouldn't have called. I'm so sorry, Charlie."

He keeps the phone next to his ear for a while, not moving. He's never heard her sound like that before, so all over the place, so anguished. For a while, he doesn't notice anything else around him. It's just him and the silence. He wonders if what he said to Sarah was unfair. That voicemail is proof of something he's tried to deny. He wants, so badly, to turn her into the villain, someone who made him suffer so she'd be happy, but happy is the last word he'd use to describe her voice. She sounds as bad as he feels. Maybe worse. For a second, that brings him some comfort, as if the world has a sense of justice. But that feeling fades as quickly as it comes. It leaves him feeling her pain too, making him feel twice as bad.

Knowing he has to do something, he stands up. He walks into the TV room and tells his parents that TJ called and wants to hang out. They look unconcerned and tell him to have a good night. He puts on his shoes, grabs his jacket, his pack of cigarettes, and heads out the door.

On the way to his car, he pulls out his lighter, but just on cue, rain starts sprinkling down. He steps aside, trying to cup the flame under his hand, trying to keep his cigarette from getting wet. The rain only picks up, though, and his hands shake from the adrenaline running through him. He can't stay still. He feels as if he's been drugged, as if his heartbeat is inconsistent and the muscles in his body are only half connected to him.

"Come on," he whispers to himself, trying more and more to get the cigarette to light. "Come on."

Sarah's words run through his head, telling him that he shouldn't smoke, that it's a terrible habit. With every unlit flame, he feels as though she's winning, as though God is siding with her. He gets madder and madder, and finally throws the cigarette to the ground, gets in his car, and turns on the music as loud as he can.

***

He's never been to this bar before. When he gets inside, he asks the bartender for three shots of tequila. Everything around him is extremely hectic: the loud music, the drunk men, the dancing women. He hardly notices. He feels as if there are two worlds, theirs and his.

He keeps to himself completely, taking the shots quickly and ordering more drinks right away. New bartenders shuffle in, and he switches up who he orders from, as if he can trick them into not noticing how much he's been drinking. Slowly, he feels the world distancing itself from him, although he can't feel the way he wants to. He can't feel numb. Even as the world blurs around him, the pain in his chest just gets stronger and stronger.

A woman comes up to the bar, slightly bumping into him, and he's suddenly pulled out of his own head. He looks down to see all the empty shot glasses in front of him. He's pushed some to the side to try to make it look as if they weren't his, but he can't fool himself. The woman brushes into him again. He looks up at her.

She's a tall, slender, African American woman with a beautiful smile and soft features. She apologizes for bumping into him, giving an unnecessary explanation of how she was pushed.

"It's all right," he says.

"I swear, if it were any more crowded in here, we'd have to start walking on top of people's heads," she says.

Charlie gives her a slight smile. He likes her. He can tell, just from her spirit, that she's a nice woman, someone who sees the good in things, who brightens the world.

"Sometimes it makes me wanna leave," he replies. "All the chaos."

"Oh no," she says, laughing. "This is the first night I've had off work for a long, long time. I'm soaking up each moment of it. I just want to have a good night. A really fun night. You know?"

He smiles again.

A second later, a man walks up behind her. He's an attractive guy with light features, pale skin and blonde hair. He's wearing black jeans and a tight black t-shirt. His ears are pierced, and he has tattoos on his forearms in a language Charlie doesn't speak. He whispers something into her ear, and she smiles. Then he puts his arms around her.

"Can we get two gin and tonics, please?" she says to the bartender.

The bartender nods.

Charlie goes back to minding his own business. The more he drinks, the more his head feels as if it's on fire. The world around him is becoming more fictional than real. He likes that. It's what he wants. He reaches out, studying his hand, and he can't even tell if it's shaking anymore. His muscles feel as though they don't belong to him, but that relaxes him. He feels as if he's outside his own body, only half there.

He looks over again at the couple beside him, trying to focus on something other than himself.

"What's your name again?" the guy asks, trying to talk louder than the music.

"Kerry."

"You sure are beautiful, Kerry," he says. He doesn't speak personally, though. His words sound scripted, as if it's something he's said a million times, as if they're part of his plan.

"Thank you," she says.

Charlie looks up at her, to read her face, to try to see if that kind of compliment means anything to anyone. She's not really smiling, but she doesn't look unhappy either. She looks as though she's trying to do math in her head, calculating something.

"Where have you been all my life?" the guy asks, putting his hand on her waist. He moves up closer behind her.

"I don't get to go out a lot. I work at the hospital. I'm a pediatric doctor, actually."

INDIVISIBLE

"Best looking nurse I've ever seen."

Charlie waits for her to correct him. She doesn't.

Charlie looks away from his drink, studying the guy. He's not even looking at her, not really. Charlie hates the way he dismisses her. He's not listening to a word she says. He looks at her body as if she's soulless.

The guy's hand slides down to her thigh.

"Hey," she says, trying to laugh it off as she brushes his hand aside. "You need to keep your hands free for your drink."

"Oh, come on, you don't like the feeling of my hands?"

Charlie turns more blatantly toward them. He looks at Kerry directly, and a few seconds later, she makes eye contact with him. His vision is a bit blurry, but he sees something odd in her eyes, something like embarrassment. He looks a bit longer, trying to read the scene better. His head feels heavy. He's suddenly aware of how drunk he is, how the world won't stay still.

"How about we ditch the drinks?" the guy says. "Get out of here."

He kisses her neck and puts his hand back on her thigh.

"Can't we just stay?" she says.

"Come on. Why?"

His hand grips her tighter, and she tenses up a little, seeming to be in her own world now.

Charlie stands up next to them and puts his hand on the guy's shoulder.

"Hey," he says, "Back off."

Suddenly, Charlie sees how big the guy is—easily 6'4" and built.

"Excuse me?" the guy says, a little smile coming across his face as if there's something funny about Charlie standing up to him.

"It's okay," Kerry says to Charlie, trying to defuse the situation. "I've got it."

Charlie takes a step closer, getting slightly in the guy's face. He looks at Kerry. She doesn't seem to know how to react. He turns back to the guy. He has eyes that don't look at people directly, as if everyone else in the world is invisible to him.

"Fuck off," the guy says. He shoos Charlie away as though he's an insect, and he puts his hand back on Kerry.

This time, Charlie grabs the guy, pulling him off her by the back of his collar.

"I told you to back off," he says.

"What the hell is your problem? You looking to make a scene?"

Charlie looks around, seeing that other people are starting to turn to them. He watches the confusion on the strangers' faces grow, as if they're trying to determine whose side they should be on.

"Get your own girl and leave me the hell alone," the guy says. Charlie's never had anyone look at him like that, as if he's a ghost, as if he's powerless.

Charlie turns to Kerry, seeing her face grow worried.

"She just wants a nice night," he says.

"Who the fuck do you think you are?" The guy reaches back to put his hands on Kerry's waist.

"Hey asshole," Charlie says, tapping his shoulder, getting him to turn back around. He takes a breath. Next thing he knows, he feels his fist clenching.

He starts a fight.

***

He waits on the curb outside the bar for Haley. He keeps his eyes closed and leans gently into the brick, his hand on his side, trying to ease some of his discomfort. Kerry stays for a while after calling Haley and explaining what happened. She brings him ice and a cup of ice water. Her sitting there, waiting, makes him feel both better and so much worse.

He sips on the water, trying to keep to himself. Kerry seems to be able to sense how he's not quite in the same world as she is, how little he can engage with her.

"What on earth did you do?"

He looks up, and as he turns, pain shoots through his side. He winces.

Haley is standing there in sweatpants and her threadbare Vanderbilt hoodie that she's worn each night since she turned eighteen. She doesn't sit down beside him. She just hovers over him. He can hardly see her face because of the streetlamp glowing behind her head. He looks away, the world starting to spin again.

Haley exchanges a few sentences with Kerry, but it's muffled. He only half attempts to hear their conversation. A minute or two later, he hears Haley thank Kerry, and then Kerry hugs him and leaves.

"A fight?" Haley says quietly. "A fight?"

"You don't understand what happened."

"You mean your .20% BAC? What is there to understand about that?"

"Haley, please listen." Charlie looks at his sister, trying to understand what else she would have expected him to do. "I did what I had to do."

She's silent for a second. She sits next to him, and for a while, it's as if they're the only ones in the world. Nobody goes into the bar. Nobody comes out. It's just the two of them, sitting on the street, a light rain sprinkling on them, the moon barely visible under the clouds. It's the kind of night that almost feels romantic, even in spite of everything.

"Charlie, you beat the guy so badly he needs stitches."

"You should have seen the way he was looking at her, the way he talked to her."

"What?"

"He was looking at her like she was worthless."

"I know, Charlie."

"I would never look at someone that way."

"I never said you would."

"Then why are you talking to me like I'm the bad guy here?"

"I'm not."

"You are. You are, Haley." He feels himself getting more worked up and the pain in his chest increases.

Haley puts her hand on his arm. "Okay, okay, I'm sorry. All right, I'm sorry."

They're silent for a while.

"What happened to you?" she asks. "What's going on with your side?"

Charlie tries to explain how he got thrown into a table during the fight, and every breath feels noticeable and painful. She asks him to raise his arm so she can see. She lifts up his t-shirt and even the gentle touch of her finger on his skin makes him jump.

"I think you have an injured rib," she says. "It might be broken. Keep an eye on it and take things easy for a few days."

He just nods as he listens to her advice. Soon, though, she's silent too.

"I know about Sarah," she whispers after a few minutes. "Mom told me."

He watches the rain, how it sticks on the lights, how it sings as it hits the ground, making a gentle ring. He wishes it would rain harder.

"I think I hate her," he replies.

"That's not true," she says.

"That's the thing. It is."

"Charlie—"

"I never would have left her."

"I know."

"I never would have done this to her. Never."

"I know."

"Please stop saying that."

"Then what do you want me to say?"

"Just not that."

She leans closer to him, leaving her hand on his arm. It's unusual for her to hold him like that. It makes him nervous, and he looks her in the eyes.

"Do you want me to say that you would have?" she asks.

"What?"

"What if you would have left her, Charlie? Would you feel better? If this were something you chose, would you feel better?"

"What are you talking about?"

"You know what I'm talking about."

The anger starts coming back to him, and he wants to yell all over again, but before he does, Haley takes her other hand and puts it in his.

"I would have understood," she says.

"Understood what?"

"If you did something imperfect. If you fell out of love with her. If it got too hard. I would have forgiven you."

"That's not what happened." He pulls himself away from her.

"I'm not saying it is."

"Then I don't know why you're bringing it up."

He starts to wish the pain in his ribs would grow. Maybe it'd become the only pain he could feel.

"Sarah's strong," Haley says at last.

"Why are you doing this?"

"Because I love you, Charlie."

"Are you taking her side?"

"No. Of course not."

"Then what are you doing?"

"I'm trying to get you to see it."

"To see what?"

Haley takes a deep breath.

"To see what, Haley?" he asks again.

"How angry you are. How it's not like you to be this angry."

It's an ironic thing to say to someone. It's the kind of thing that'd make anyone mad, yet somehow, getting mad in that moment would only prove her point.

"You don't think I have a right to be mad?" he asks.

"You have a right to be, but that doesn't mean you should be."

"The guy in the bar had it coming—"

"This doesn't have anything to do with him."

"It does, though."

"What do you mean?"

"I'm just..." He tries to collect his thoughts. "I'm tired of all the people that go around thinking they're not gonna hurt anyone. I'm tired of all the people who just think they can do whatever they want without caring about anyone else."

Haley takes a minute to internalize his words. "Sarah is nothing like that man, Charlie. Neither is Wes."

He doesn't reply for a second. He stares her, trying to see whether she really believes that or not.

"I know," he says quietly. "But sometimes they feel the same. To me, they do. Right now, they do."

For the first time since he started drinking, he begins to feel the numbness wearing off, and suddenly he's exposed again. He feels the same as he did when he held the phone in his hand, listening to Sarah's voice.

"She didn't love me the way I loved her," he says.

"You don't know that."

"I do, though. I do. Everything feels like a lie."

Haley says nothing.

"Everything that could possibly break inside of me has broken," he adds.

He doesn't cry. He doesn't even feel like crying. It feels so true, so real to him, that it's just factual. It's almost scary how even, absent emotion, he feels so sure that he's damaged.

She leans over and puts her head lightly against his shoulder. She takes his hand and puts it in hers. They sit for a while, just being still, and he closes his eyes.

"I don't know what to do, Haley," he says. "I just don't even know what to do."

The wind blows into them, chilling everything.

"Let's take you home," she says. "Start by going home."

Chapter 23

He wakes up to a giggle.

"Mommy, Uncle Charlie drools when he sleeps!"

"Shhh, honey, leave him alone," Haley says. "He's trying to get some rest. He had a long night."

Charlie opens his eyes to see Anna in front of him, sitting on the coffee table by the couch. He ignores his pounding head and empty stomach.

"No, Mom, he's awake!" Anna says as he bats his eyes. "Good morning, Uncle Charlie!"

"Good morning, Princess," he whispers, waiting for his eyes to adjust so he can see her properly.

He begins to sit up. He's covered in pink blankets, and Anna has set her bear by his side, keeping him company.

"All right, come on, Anna," Haley says as she shuffles around the kitchen. "You've gotta eat your cereal now or you're gonna make me late for work."

"Uncle Charlie, what happened to your face?" Anna says, studying the marks on his forehead, slowly reaching for them.

"I, uh—"

"He got hit playing football," Haley answers.

Anna looks confused. "Playing football? You play football? Aren't you a little old to play football?"

"Yeah, Haley," Charlie says, turning to his sister. "Aren't I a little old for football?"

"Apparently, because you can't help getting hit," Haley says. "Now, come on, Anna, we gotta get you to school."

Anna drops the subject and runs over to her bowl of Fruit Loops.

Charlie gets up, too, and walks over to the kitchen. Haley scrambles, trying to do the dishes, muttering under her breath that she's going to kill Matt for forgetting to do his chores.

"Let me do it," Charlie says, standing up. His head aches, and his upset stomach feels unstable. He tries not to pay attention to that.

Haley stops. "What?"

"All of it. How about you let me do the dishes and take Anna to school?"

"But your car is..." she stops, not wanting to explain to her daughter how Charlie got so drunk that she had to drive him.

"We'll walk," he says. "Right, Anna?"

Anna looks up at him, smiling, as if that's everything she's ever wanted. "Yeah, please, Mom? We can walk."

For a minute, Haley stares at the two of them, as if trying to see if this is some sort of scheme. After a second, though, she gives in and thanks Charlie. She kisses them both goodbye.

While Anna eats, he asks about what her day has in store.

"We're playing soccer in PE," she says. "I think my team's going to win today."

While she talks, Charlie gathers the Fruit Loops that fall out of her mouth and onto the table as she tries to shovel the sugar inside her body.

"For such a cute little girl, you sure do turn into a monster when you eat," he says.

She just laughs.

By the end of the breakfast, he has quite the collection of Fruit Loops, and he arranges them all into a little colorful heart, keeping the cereal box between them so Anna doesn't see it.

"Hey, Anna," he says, pulling the box to the side, revealing the heart. "I love you."

She looks at it and smiles.

She reaches inside the cereal box to grab some of her own, and she begins to make a sun out of all the yellow ones.

"Look, Charlie!" she says, pointing to the rays, laughing, as if those Fruit Loops were the exact center of the universe. Maybe they were.

***

On their way to school, they walk hand in hand. She walks too close to the sewer drain sometimes, and Charlie pulls her away.

"You don't want to get too close," he says. "That's where the ninja turtles live."

"What?" She laughs.

"You don't know about the turtles? Your mom never told you?"

Charlie tells her a long, made-up story, about how the slime on the street is the slime of the turtles' bellies when they come out at night, roaming the streets, keeping people safe from whatever danger comes their way. Anna loves every word. She always loves his stories.

"Did you hear about the butterflies that live in the trees?" she asks when he finishes.

"No."

"They help the turtles. They lift people away from danger."

Charlie smiles, listening to her go on, making the story up as she goes.

They talk the whole walk, and by the time they get to school, Anna is late. She doesn't care. Neither does Charlie.

He kneels down in front of her when they get outside her door. Her smile has been ever-present. He adjusts her backpack and straightens out her uniform.

"I wish every morning was like this," she says.

"I do too," he says, leaning forward and kissing her cheek. He wipes the hair out of her face.

All of a sudden, though, the smile on her face wavers, just for a second, as if she's being pulled back into a reality she doesn't like as much as the world she'd just been inside.

"It could be," he adds, after a second.

"What do you mean?"

"I could walk you to school. Every day."

"But you don't live with us."

"I could drive to your house."

"Uncle Charlie—"

"I'm serious, Anna. I could."

For a moment, she just stands there, and then she leans forward and puts her arms around him, holding him tightly. He closes his eyes. She doesn't let go. For a long time, they stand like that in the hallway.

"Okay," Anna says.

"Okay," Charlie says. "I'll be there, then. Every morning."

He'll never forget the way she smiles, as if she has everything she could ever want in that moment.

The longer he stands there, holding her, the more he realizes that he isn't just doing this for Anna. It's for himself too. He can feel the way she fixes him. Finally, after so much time, he's done fighting the truth that he does, in fact, need to be put back together.

***

"We have the best science department in Texas," says the tour guide, Ben, pointing into a classroom, showing all the students hard at work in the lab. His voice is about an octave lower than Charlie would have expected. When Charlie first met him, he was struck by how young he looked, how childish his frail frame and thin face seemed. Ben has a nice smile, though, a passionate smile.

The trip to Rice was incredibly last minute, something he did on a whim after dropping Anna off. He felt the need for direction, to make an assertive choice, to quit living in such an unknown space. He wanted something certain, something real and tangible, so he put on nice clothes and drove himself to Rice.

As they stand there, Charlie examines the way all the students turn to the professor, frantically trying to store every word she says in their minds. Some of them scribble down each word, some stare straight ahead, as if trying to take in the instructions. He wonders, as he looks at them in their white coats, how long they dreamed of being in that spot and whether it's everything they dreamed it would be.

"What class is this?" Charlie asks.

"General chemistry."

Ben goes on a tangent about the chemistry department, about the wonderful opportunities Charlie could have there, but Charlie only half listens. He never doubted the prestige of the program. He didn't come on the tour needing affirmation of that. He looks around the building, studying the white tile beneath his dress shoes, staring up at the tall ceilings and glass windows, trying to imagine whether he could become one of those students, whether he could be happy here. The more he looks at them, the younger all the other people look. He feels slightly out of place, as if he'd only half belong. He wonders if maybe, just maybe, that feeling will never escape him for the rest of his life.

"The lab is cool, right?" Ben says.

"Yeah," Charlie replies. "It's unbelievable." He studies the machines, wondering what it'd be like to fully understand each device. It makes him feel powerful.

"It's my favorite place in the world," Ben says.

Charlie turns to look at him, and he sees Ben smiling to himself as he watches the kids in the lab. "Yeah? You want to be a researcher?"

"Not just a researcher," Ben replies. "I wanna be the one who changes everything."

He looks at the lab the way Wes looked at the football field, as if it held everything.

For the first time on the tour, Charlie realizes that Ben isn't as young as he once thought.

When Charlie looks back, away from Ben, he sees his own reflection in the glass. He's smiling. Something about that moment freezes in his mind, and he knows, as it's happening, that he'll never forget it. This is the moment he decides that he can see himself here, at Rice, day after day.

He finishes out the tour, listening to Ben talk about his experiences, and he hears about all the things he'd be able to do there. They end up back at the admissions office door.

"Thanks for giving me a tour on such short notice," Charlie says. "Sorry I didn't schedule it further in advance."

"Thanks for coming," Ben says. "Is there anything else you'd like to see before you leave?"

Charlie expected to say no, but for some reason, that's not what comes out of his mouth. "Actually, yeah, I'd like to see the art department."

When they walk in, Charlie looks around at the room. It's spacious with large glass windows overlooking the campus. There are paintings, drawings, all over the walls, photographs hanging everywhere. Ben is completely quiet. Charlie walks around, looking at everything, trying to recreate the lives of the people in the drawings and of those who drew them. He comes across a drawing of man, completely disfigured, reaching out in front of him, but melting down.

"Sorry," Ben says after a few minutes of silence. "I'm a little out of my element here. I don't know what to say about any of the work."

Charlie smiles. He finds that to be part of the beauty, how nothing needs to be said. He watches the way Ben stares at the work, as if it's in a language he doesn't speak, as if he's trying to see the stories that Charlie sees in those pieces but can't.

"Are you an artist?" Ben asks.

"I don't think I'd go as far as to say that," Charlie replies, although the words don't feel entirely truthful.

"But you draw?"

"Yeah." He nods. "Yeah, I do."

"I would never know where to start. I'd stare at the blank page for hours, never making a mark." Ben laughs to himself. "I'd probably never even get far enough to realize that I should start over."

Charlie smiles, too, but for the rest of the day, the week, the month, long after he's left Rice, that comment sticks in his head. He just can't shake it.

He can't help but wonder if that's all life is: a series of getting far enough to realize that we're meant to start over.

Chapter 24

For the next month, Charlie begins to pull himself together. He follows through on his promise and walks Anna to school each day. He even starts picking her up from school sometimes. She loves it. Every day, they make up new stories, taking their time as they stroll. Even in the rain, they walk, hand in hand, under the umbrella, Anna tightly pressed against his leg. He's happy when he's with her. It's easy. Finding joy feels simple.

He also starts spending more time around his family. He stays home for his mom's meals, and in return, she's around more. She even decides to skip out on a business trip so they can all go to an Astros game together. At the game, Charlie's dad never shuts up, rambling on about the statistics of every player. Charlie loves it. He feels at home. Everything about his life starts to feel more like an open book. Things that used to feel hard start to get a little easier. He sings in the car when he drives. He dances by himself when he cooks. He even gets a job as a waiter at an Italian restaurant until he starts school. He can feel himself moving forward.

When he tells his family he's decided to go to Rice, he can see both pride and relief on their faces. It's as if, all along, he's failed to study their faces enough to know what they wanted, how scared they were that he'd pick up and go across the country, leaving them behind. It's as if Sarah was the brightest star in the galaxy, blinding him to everything else with her radiance, maybe even blinding him to himself. He doesn't blame her for that, though. The more time passes, the less he blames her for anything. She's tried to call him a few more times, but he doesn't answer. He still can't face her. Thinking of her makes him feel blinded again. She leaves him messages sometimes. He deletes them. He doesn't know what he thinks might be in the messages, but he knows he's afraid. He's afraid that, no matter what she says, he's not strong enough to handle it.

***

One day, he's walking through the grocery store, trying to pick out what kind of granola he wants, when he hears a voice.

"Charlie?"

He looks up, taking a moment to find where it came from.

"Erin," he says, smiling a little. He sets down the bag in his hand. "Hey."

She walks over to him, holding a basket with only Oreos and ice cream inside.

"Looks like you've got lunch there," he jokes.

"Did I not tell you that my fallback career was a nutritionist?"

"That explains everything."

She stares at his cart, nearly filled to the brim. "Are you hibernating or something? Loading up for the winter?"

He catches her eyes as they linger on the boxes of Fruit Loops and the mountain of Lunchables stacked upon one another.

"More like grocery shopping for my sister's family," he replies. "She has a six-year-old."

"Oh, I thought you were just a Lunchables sort of guy."

"I am. Those are mine, actually."

She smiles and is quiet for a moment. He finds that he's having a hard time looking at her.

"Have you been busy lately?" she asks.

"What do you mean?"

"You haven't been around the last few weeks. In class. I kinda got the feeling you weren't ever going to come back."

He says nothing. He rearranges a few of the items in the cart, trying to avoid eye contact.

"Was I wrong?" she asks.

Part of him wants to lie, but when he looks at her, he just can't. She looks at him so earnestly, so completely, that he can't deceive her even a little.

He takes a deep breath. "What would you say if I offered to buy you a real lunch?"

She studies him for a second, as if trying to gauge everything that's going on in his head.

"All right," she replies. "I'd say all right."

***

Charlie explains everything to Erin — everything that happened between him and Sarah, with his family, with Wes. He leaves out one small part. He leaves out the part where, as Sarah broke up with him,

Erin's name came from her mouth. He doesn't think that'd be a fair thing to put on her.

She listens closely. She asks question after question. He answers each one, but he focuses mainly on his food, trying not to look at her directly. He spins his pasta around his fork again and again.

When he finishes telling her about all of it, they sit in silence. He can tell she's replaying his words in her head.

"I wish you'd say something," he says.

For a moment she doesn't reply. Then she asks, "Why won't you look at me?"

Just for a second, Charlie finds the question funny. After all the things he's shared, that's what she wants to know. But the minute he looks at her face, that feeling vanishes. He can see the pain in her eyes, how she wanted him to look at her so he'd understand how deeply she felt for him, so he'd understand all the words she couldn't say.

He looks away again. He closes his eyes for a second, and he starts to feel that coming to this lunch was a mistake.

"Are you mad at me?" Erin asks.

"Mad at you?"

"You seem mad."

He shakes his head, although as he does, that feels untrue. "I'm not." Silence.

"Why didn't you come back to class?" she asks.

He tries to think of an answer but realizes he doesn't have one.

"Was it because of me? Did I do something?" she asks.

"No." He doesn't stop to wonder if that's true or not.

"Why didn't you come back then?"

"Because I needed time," he says.

"Time for what?"

"Time to wait."

"For what?"

He's quiet for a moment, and suddenly, he feels as if he's at a tipping point, as if everything rests on his answer.

"I knew that if I saw you, you'd try to fix me," he says.

She looks completely confused, as if she doesn't understand how he can turn a compliment into something that kept him away. "I don't get it."

The truth is, he doesn't get it either. He just knows that every time he thought of going to art class on Monday nights, he never went. "I didn't want to be fixed. I still don't."

"What does that mean?"

"I don't know."

For a second, she looks at him as if deciding whether to let him off the hook. She doesn't. She leans on the table, moving a few inches closer to him. "Yes, you do."

Once again, she's looking at him as though she can read his mind. She makes him feel so transparent. He can't tell if that scares him or relieves him.

"If I came to you damaged," he says, "you would have given me pieces of yourself until you fixed me."

"You mean I would have been there for you?"

"I would have taken what I needed without having anything to give you in return. I was empty. I'm worried that I still am."

Again, she's quiet, and she looks at him as if she's trying to figure out what he's getting at, as if he's speaking some slightly unfamiliar language.

"I wouldn't have needed anything," she says. "I don't know what you think I would have needed."

Her expression makes him feel as though he's playing a game of chess, as though they're each waiting for something, some clarity about what the other person is planning on saying next. He can't tell whether she understands or she's angry. She doesn't look as if she understands, but she won't say anything. Instead, she turns and looks out the window, away from him. He hates that look on her face, as if she's trying to decide what she has the right to feel. She must decide that there's not much left to say because in the end, when she looks back at him, she still doesn't have words.

"I'm sorry if—"

"Tyler came back," she says. "My ex."

He waits for her to go on, feeling a vague sense of relief or regret. He doesn't know which.

"He got on a plane from New York. He flew down here. He showed up at my door with flowers. He asked me to go back to New York with him. He said he made a mistake, and that's a big deal for him. He doesn't even believe there's such a thing as mistakes, usually."

He takes a moment, trying to digest her words. "So you're going back?"

She begins to play with her glass, rubbing her finger along the rim as she thinks. Then she shakes her head. Suddenly, she's the one who doesn't look at him.

INDIVISIBLE

"All my things are packed," she says. "All of them."

She doesn't say anything for a long while. He studies her face, the way she looks as if nothing else exists except what's going on in her head.

"I just never thought I'd be this kind of girl."

"What kind of girl?"

"The kind of girl who packs up all her things when a man shows up at her door." She looks up at him, finally. "Am I being weak?"

"Loving someone is never weak."

"That's not true."

"I think it is."

"You haven't thought hard enough about it, then."

They look at each other for a while, as if waiting for one of them to give in.

"I don't know if he can make me happy anymore," she says. "We used to have these moments in the morning where I'd look at him while he was sleeping, and I just felt like the luckiest person in the world. He'd wake up, and we'd look at each other for a long time, and then he'd kiss me. It was perfect. We were perfect together."

"You should get on the plane then."

"It wouldn't be like that now. I know it wouldn't. I'd look at him in the mornings, and every perfect moment would be tainted by the memory of him leaving me once. I'd never feel fully safe again. Knowing that he could walk away, that walking away was in him, it'd change everything. He'll never be the same person to me again."

"Then don't get on the plane."

She smiles for a second, as if to acknowledge something, but he's not sure what. "If I don't get on that plane, I'll always wonder what would have happened if I had."

"So you're leaving?"

"Yeah. I'm leaving. I just don't know that I'll be happy."

"No one knows if they're going to be happy."

"That's not true, Charlie."

"Bliss is always slightly ignorant. That's just how it is."

She looks at him deeply. "Don't ever say that again. I know you don't believe that. I know that deep down, you don't believe that."

"What do you mean?"

"Bliss can be unqualifiedly easy."

He wonders if she's right.

"I love him," she says. "I always will, too. I know in my heart that I always will."

"I know."

She's never looked at him this way before, as if she hangs on his every word, as if she desperately needs something from him. She's so still.

"Am I making a mistake?" she asks.

For a minute, he wonders what he should say. He wonders what the truth is. He wonders if she is making a mistake, if Tyler is the same man who broke her. He wonders if she'll spend the rest of her life waking up to a man who's only a shell of who she once loved. He wonders if sometimes a shell is enough. Then again, nothing could be more beside the point.

"No," he replies.

She studies his eyes, and he doesn't move. He's rock solid.

"You don't think I'll regret this one day?"

"No."

"I feel like an idiot. I feel like an idiot in advance of a choice I haven't even made, and I'm still going to make it. How dumb is that?"

"It's not dumb," he says.

"Then what is it?"

"I don't know. Faith maybe."

"Faith in what exactly?"

"Faith that maybe one day, he'll be exactly who you thought he was, and you'll wake up next to him, and he'll look you in the eyes, and bliss will just be unqualifiedly easy again."

He sees her relax, and her breathing slows. She even gives him a smile, ever so slightly.

What he feels in that moment is not in itself romance. He doesn't have the energy or the heart to think of her that way, and he knows that she, too, only has room in her heart for the man on a plane. What he feels, though, may be something greater than romance. It's comfort.

"You were wrong before, you know," she says.

"About what?"

She doesn't answer. Instead, she sits back, looking at him as if trying to figure out how to put it into words.

She doesn't have to have to, though. He can feel it.

In that moment, with her, he feels anything but empty.

Chapter 25

That night, he can hardly sleep. He's thinking of so many things, of all the ways he needs to heal, of how he wishes he had all the pieces of himself, how he still feels only partially present. He wonders what he would have said to Erin, if he would have been able to find something more, if he'd only been complete, all on his own.

The next morning, before he walks Anna to school, he decides to go for a drive.

He ends up at Rylee's door.

***

He doesn't wait outside like he did before. He doesn't even stop to think about how early in the morning it is, how he might be disturbing them. If he thought about that, he might talk himself out of walking up to the door. He doesn't think about whether he wants to hear what Rylee has to say. He knows, now, that he does, because whether he wants to or not, everyone around him needs him to move on, and he needs to find out whatever Rylee knows in order to do that.

Rylee answers the door.

"I lied before," he says immediately, hardly giving her a second to process who he is.

"What?" She looks totally thrown off, and he can tell she's in the middle of getting ready for work. She's wearing scrubs, and he can hear Tucker running around upstairs as he yells down, asking who's at the door. She looks flustered.

"I didn't lose my dog," he says.

She studies him again, and then a look of understanding sinks in.

"My name is Charlie. You talked to Meghan about my friend Wes. I just... I came to ask if you knew anything about him."

For a moment, she is still. Then she moves aside and lets him in.

***

They sit down at the kitchen table. The room is small, and the walls and cabinets are so white that the room looks sterile. The table crowds the room in a way that makes it hard to navigate around it. Tucker runs down, darting around the chairs, and Rylee tells him to be careful or he'll hit his head on something. He doesn't slow down one bit.

"Did you find your dog?" he asks.

Charlie looks to Rylee as if asking for permission to lie. She remains expressionless. "Yeah, I did."

"Can he play fetch? I bet he's good at it. My dad used to always want a dog that could—"

"Tucker, honey, eat your breakfast," his mom interrupts.

"But I'm done."

"Three more big bites, okay?"

Tucker sighs and shoves another bite of Captain Crunch into his mouth, a little bit of milk slipping out of the side of his mouth.

"I'm sorry for coming here uninvited," Charlie says.

"No, no, any friend of Wes's is a friend of ours."

"Wes?" Tucker says, with a mouth full of cereal.

His mom suddenly looks as if she's made a mistake, as if she shouldn't have said that. "Honey, why don't you go to your room, okay?"

"You're Wes's friend?" Tucker asks.

Charlie tries to read the kid's face. He can't tell whether this fact makes the boy happy or sad.

"Tucker, I'll be up in a few minutes, okay? Go get changed for school."

"But I thought you wanted me to eat my cereal?"

"Just go change, okay?"

He doesn't move at first, but eventually he reluctantly walks away, his energy seeming gone as he goes up to his room.

***

Rylee starts at the beginning.

She says Wes was in the same unit as her husband when they served in Afghanistan. He came to visit her, to tell her more about the war, things her own husband never could. Wes told her what things were like for them over there.

Her husband's name was Tim, although he often went by Timmy. Rylee shows Charlie a picture of them together. Tim is a skinny, scrawny, young man, but he's still handsome, and he has a big smile.

She looks happy with him. They're gazing at each other as though their heartbeats are synched. She's holding a baby close to them, wrapped warmly in a blanket. Timmy has one arm around her and the other gently rests under the baby's head. They look like a family that has everything in the world to look forward to.

Rylee says that Timmy had grown up in a poor family, never knowing if there'd be food on the table, something that seemed just as scary as war. Despite his struggles, when Timmy was with her, he was charismatic and charming, but according to Wes, in Afghanistan, he rarely talked to anyone. The only time he ever spoke in front of everyone was one day when he told the whole unit that all he wanted in life was a little white house for his family with air conditioning and a white picket fence. He had the biggest smile on his face when he spoke of his goal. He was so happy, Wes had told her, it was almost sad.

Apart from that one story, Wes said that while he was at war, Timmy seemed relatively emotionless. When people tried to talk to him, he'd just stare blankly back, as if he had his mind on a million other things. He would nod and say "Yes, sir" to their commanding officer, but nothing more. Most of the time he looked perpetually pensive and sad.

One day, it was so hot that Wes spent the whole day just hoping not to pass out. To fill the silences, a guy called Jason kept talking to Timmy about random things, but Timmy didn't say a word. So finally, Jason said, "If only we had some goddamn air conditioning out here, right?" A huge smile spread across Timmy's face, and everyone laughed. Wes said he'd never forget that million-dollar smile, as if someone had just handed Timmy the world. After that, no one called him Timmy anymore. Everyone called him AC. Wes was never sure if they meant for the nickname to tease him or if they meant for it to be endearing, but whenever they called him AC, Timmy smiled a bit to himself.

AC was fine during the day, but at night, he'd cry. For months, Wes would fall asleep to the sound of him sobbing. A few of the guys in their unit decided to sleep with earplugs just to avoid listening, and other people would hold their pillows over their ears. Some guys would yell at him to shut the fuck up. Of course, there were nights he didn't cry, when he was too exhausted, but in some ways those nights were the worst because Wes would lie there and imagine him crying. Imagination can be a horrible, horrible thing. It brought Wes so much pain to imagine his crying.

One night, everyone had fallen asleep except AC and Wes. Wes told Rylee that he'd tried to make a game of the situation by thinking of every little thing that could be a possible reason for his sadness. Maybe AC's mom had died, or maybe his father had forced him to go to war, or maybe he was afraid of what his future held in store for him. Maybe he was afraid of dying, or maybe he was afraid of living. It was nearly three in the morning, but Wes couldn't stop listening to him cry. He couldn't take the wondering anymore, so he got up and went to sit by him. AC wiped away his tears and started apologizing for keeping him up.

"Why do you always cry?" Wes asked, skipping any small talk.

AC looked down at a note in his hands. It had been folded and unfolded so many times that it looked more like a used tissue than a piece of paper.

He never answered Wes's question, but instead, he asked, "Do you think we're going to live?"

"Yes," Wes said. He told Rylee he had never been more uncertain of anything in his life, but he sounded sure. He wanted more than anything to be sure for AC. He'd never seen anyone look so sad.

"We have to live," AC said firmly. "I have to get back to her and my son. We're going to be so happy. I promised her that. I promised she'd be happy one day."

AC opened up the paper, in front of Wes, and in neat, girly cursive were the words, "One day." That was all it said. It was a note from the love of his life, and somehow those two words captured his entire future. Rylee had written that to him the night before he left, as a promise for all the things that were to come. He held onto it as closely has he held his gun.

Wes pulled out the picture of himself standing with his mom and Charlie, a picture he'd kept in his pocket, and without saying anything, he handed it to AC. AC stared at it for a long time, and he ran his finger over all of the crevices, and when he handed it back to Wes, he looked at him as if they were friends, as if Wes understood something about him that he didn't think anyone could.

Then AC pulled out another sheet of paper, and he wrote down *Rylee* and her phone number. He asked Wes if he'd call her if anything ever happened to him. Wes said he would, and then he took another piece of paper from him and wrote down Charlie's name and phone number and asked him to do the same. He said Charlie was his brother.

Seventeen days later, their unit was walking on a dirt road, and all of sudden, Wes heard an explosion, and there was dust everywhere. He couldn't see a thing, but he could hear screaming and cursing as he waited for the dust to settle. When it finally did, Wes saw AC lying on the ground. Someone yelled that they needed to get a medic ASAP, and Wes rushed to AC's side to see that his limbs had been completely torn off his body, and he was bleeding everywhere. Jason was yelling, and everyone started to move carefully because they realized there were IEDs on the path, and if anyone took a wrong step, an explosive device would blow them up.

Wes stood over AC, completely terrified, not saying or doing anything. He was twenty-two years old. He couldn't think enough to move. AC was gasping for air, and he couldn't scream because he was in shock and couldn't get enough air in to let out any sound. Some of the other guys kept telling him to hang on, and that he'd be okay, but Wes didn't say anything. He just stared at AC with horror. AC was looking around at everyone's eyes and then came to Wes's and kept his gaze there, as if Wes was the only one he trusted. Wes couldn't hide the horror on his face. AC's arms and legs weren't on his body. He was fully aware that AC was going to die, and he didn't get why everyone else was ignoring that. They could fight all they wanted to keep him alive, but AC's body was already severed and dead. In that moment, AC was just a soul, waiting to be taken by God, and what was left of his consciousness was nothing more than a lag in time between life and death.

AC seemed to know this too, and his eyes got heavy and sad. He started to cry because he realized he was never going to get to live in that little white house with a picket fence and air conditioning that he'd been dreaming about for so long. He'd broken his promise to Rylee. He'd never make her happy. In fact, he'd do the opposite. His death would break her heart, and that was the worst part of it. He seemed, as he died, to know that his death was not the end of the suffering, and that he would now bring eternal pain to the one he loved most in the world. He hated himself for dying.

"Don't you die on me, AC," Jason yelled.

But AC's eyes kept closing.

"Hang on. You'll be fine," Jason said. "You'll be fine soon."

They all knew that wasn't true.

Wes knelt down, close to AC, and said, "I'll call her, okay? I'll call Rylee."

AC nodded, still crying, but suddenly he looked slightly more at ease, as if those words offered him a hint of peace.

He died seconds later in the midst of chaos.

The guys didn't stop trying to bring him back. Jason kept screaming and punching on his chest. The other men ran around looking for a doctor. Wes did nothing, though. He just sat by him and prayed. No one could get him to move. He had to be dragged away, and even then, he never stopped praying. For days, Wes sat in the corner and prayed. Charlie would have given anything to hear what he said in that prayer.

***

When Wes got home, he called Rylee as promised. She tells Charlie that the conversation was slow at first, that Wes didn't know what to say, as if that conversation was as volatile as the dirt road with IEDs.

"I don't know what Tim would want me to say," Wes said. "Maybe just that he loved you. He loved you so much that he hated himself for dying. He hated that it'd hurt you."

Rylee pauses in her story for a second, as if affirming her awareness of what those words would mean to Charlie. Charlie wonders if what Wes said to Rylee on the phone that night were the exact words he'd say to Charlie now if he could rise from the grave.

"When we were on the phone, I told him he could come meet me if he'd like," Rylee says. "He could come meet Tucker and me."

She pauses for a second.

"Wes, well, he... he had a hard time after he got home. But he came around here all the time. He played with Tucker. Sometimes he'd help watch him when I had work, and they'd play football in the yard. He gave me money when he could, too, for groceries and things, back in the beginning when I was struggling to make ends meet."

She sounds strong, as if she's cried all her tears out, as if she's now unbreakable.

"Wes was a good man. A really good man. He even went outside, and he made our white picket fence for us, just as Tim always wanted. He built it with his own two hands, just out of the kindness of his heart. No one asked him to. He just did it."

The more she goes on, the less Charlie feels he knows about Wes. He wishes Wes had told him any of this, about Timmy or coming over here all the time.

"I knew he was sad, though," Rylee continues. "Once, he told me he thought Tim's death was his fault somehow, as if he should have been the one to die instead. He blamed himself. It wasn't a logical sort of blame, but he felt it so completely. Sometimes, when he worked on that fence, he'd have to take long breaks, go on walks, try to cool off. He had a temper. It wasn't us he was mad at, of course. He was angry at the world for taking

Tim. He said it wasn't fair to us, that Tucker was a good kid who deserved his father, that I deserved my husband. He said that a world that crushes dreams is a terrible place. He took it very personally. I tried to ask him about himself to figure out why, but he didn't say much. He just looked sadder. Once he mentioned something about football, how he thought he wanted to be a coach, but a few weeks later he said he thought coaching would just remind him of the dream he lost. He told me that he had to go, and the next I hear of him is a few weeks later, when he hasn't been around, and I find out that he killed himself. Just like that."

There's a long silence.

Charlie tries to analyze what Rylee's told him. He thinks about why Wes enlisted in the first place, how he was trying to create a new future for himself, how he wanted meaning and passion after his injury took away the life he'd always imagined for himself.

He wants to say nothing, to shut off, like he has so many times when talking to Sarah, but he forces himself to respond.

"The war... it was numbing," he says. "It still is, I guess."

She looks at him, trying to understand what he's saying.

"First day I got there, I was quiet. Hardly spoke to anyone, like Timmy. I only had one conversation, and it was with a guy about how we both hated the smell of the mud. That was it. That was all he said, but I liked the guy for it."

Charlie's never told anyone this story before, and suddenly, he remembers why. It's because every time he tries, his throat closes in on itself, the words unable to slip out. He waits for himself to calm down.

"The next day, he was shot in combat, and I remember looking at his body, and all I noticed was that it was covered in that mud. Just covered."

He stares at the table, and Rylee doesn't say anything. Tucker isn't making any noise upstairs. The world is quiet.

He can tell that Rylee doesn't know what to make of this story, that she can't get the point of what he's trying to say. He wonders if there is one.

"It's not fair," he says at last.

"What isn't?"

"How our nightmares have a way of coming true."

She looks away from him.

After a moment, she reaches out with two hands and holds his hand. He can tell that she's kind, that she didn't think of herself while he was telling his story. He can see that she's good and loving.

The silence lasts almost a minute, and he tries to process everything, to come up with something else to say.

"I know it's not my place to speculate," she says.

She stops herself, studying his face, trying to see if she's overstepping. She's not, though. One look at Charlie, and it seems she can tell how desperately he needs her to say something else, anything else.

"But Wes couldn't see past what was in front of him," she says. "He couldn't get past the idea that sometimes our lives don't turn out the way we once envisioned."

At first, Charlie doesn't know what to make of that.

"Our nightmares do come true, sometimes, but so do so many other types of dreams."

"I think you might be braver than I am."

"That's not true." Her voice is firm, and he can see that her eyes are strong and sure. "It's just not."

He nods, trying to internalize her words.

"Wes wouldn't be dead if he'd just... if he'd just been able to see what I saw when I looked at him," she says. "Do you ever feel that way?"

He nods again.

"He was so good, wasn't he? He was such a good man."

"He left behind such a mess."

"You're right."

"He shouldn't have left us."

"But he did," she says.

Charlie looks away, not knowing what else there is to say.

"Sometimes, the goodness of what's left seems small," she says. "But it's enough. You can make it enough."

He's about to ask what it was for her, what her little remaining piece of unbroken love was. Then he hears Tucker's footsteps upstairs, stampeding around, shaking the ceiling as if he's accompanied by herds of angels. He watches as she looks up at the ceiling and smiles. Then, there's nothing left to ask.

Chapter 26

Later that day, he goes to Natalie's house.

He knocks on the door incessantly, and finally, Hannah opens up. She's sweating, and he can see boxes piled up behind her.

"Can I come in?"

"Well, don't you look nice," Hannah says, as she steps aside and lets him in.

Charlie's wearing a black button-down shirt and khaki pants with dress shoes. He thanks her and walks into the living room where Natalie is sitting. She looks at him for a moment, and a smile spreads across her face.

"Charlie, what are you doing here?" she asks.

"Would you mind changing?"

"What?"

"Hannah, can you help her change into something a little nicer?"

They both stare at him as if he's gone crazy.

"Why?" Natalie asks.

"Because I'm taking you to church."

Both of them are shocked. Natalie's face doesn't move at all, and when it does at last, it's to shake her head no.

"Come on, Charlie, I told you I didn't want to go back there."

"I know."

"It's not somewhere—"

He walks over to her and squats down so that he's about her height. "It's 11:23 right now. There's a daily mass at noon. If we hurry—"

"You're not even religious, Charlie. Why would you—"

"You go one time with me, and if you never go to church again, I won't say a word about it."

Natalie is quiet, not moving a muscle. He can tell how much she doesn't want to go.

"Come on," he pleads. "You're about to move to another city, and I just want to spend another hour with you. Won't you go with me?"

At last, she nods, reluctantly.

Hannah drops them off at mass. Natalie looks pretty with her make-up done and wearing a long, loose dress that covers her cast in the wheelchair.

They're a few minutes late, and Charlie opens the door to the church, which is quiet apart from the priest talking alone at the front. He hesitates for a moment. He looks around, at the statues and stained glass, and tries to focus on the fact that it's beautiful. If he knew nothing else about this church, if this were his first time inside these walls, he would undoubtedly find it gorgeous. He thinks about religion, about how incredible it is to believe in things you can't see, to believe in a glorious future awaiting you, even when it's something you can't currently feel or hold. Whether he has faith or not, he tries to focus on that, the idea of it all.

Charlie rolls Natalie up the middle aisle. The church is nearly vacant, and almost everyone there is elderly. He can tell that the young priest, who ran Wes's funeral, is temporarily distracted by their entrance.

"Charlie," Natalie says, turning to him. "I don't... I don't know if I can do this."

He ignores her and goes near the front, to the pew where he found Wes. They stare at it for a second. There's new fabric on the seats, and if they didn't know any better, they'd think Wes had never been there at all.

Charlie sits down.

"What are you doing?" Natalie asks, visibly upset. "This isn't a joke, Charlie. I don't want to be here."

He doesn't move.

"Charlie," she says. "This isn't—"

"One mass," he says. "One mass."

For the next twenty minutes, Natalie stares at the floor. Charlie doesn't. He looks up at the priest, who's dressed in a green garment with a cross down the front, and he tries to listen to the words of the other people as they read from scripture.

He feels a bit out of place, observing the way everyone else knows when to stand and sit, and what to say back to the priest when he speaks. But he follows along and tries to engage.

What catches his attention, though, isn't the words of the priest. The sun appears from behind a cloud, and the stained glass from the side of the church causes light of every color to come in. He looks down at his skin, which is now tinted blue, and when he looks up, he sees a blue dove, illuminated by the light.

"May the peace of the Lord be with you," the priest says.

Charlie looks around the church to see people reaching out, shaking hands, hugging, mumbling words he can't make out.

He looks at Natalie and sees that she, too, can't help but notice the light on her skin, the beautiful way that suddenly, the church itself seems to light her up.

When she turns to him, he can tell that she's falling apart. She begins to cry.

For the rest of the mass, she cries quietly to herself, unmoving. Long after the mass has ended, she doesn't move. They sit in the pew, frozen. At one point, she reaches over and holds Charlie's hand.

It occurs to him that in this church, Natalie's found what Wes failed to find the morning he sat there with that gun. There, in that pew, holding onto Charlie's hand, letting the stained glass paint her different colors as the sun moves across the sky, he can tell that she finds her piece of unbroken love. She finds comfort in God and in the embrace of the son she still has sitting next to her.

"What Wes did was unforgivable," Charlie says. "I won't ever understand it."

Natalie is quiet.

"But I think we might have been wrong about something."

"About what?"

"About why Wes came here."

She looks at him.

"Maybe he came here because he wanted us, when we found him, to fall to our knees and pray. Maybe, even when he couldn't find faith himself, he wanted to make sure we could find it. Maybe the hope, the faith, has been right in front of us all along, and we just forgot to look for it."

Natalie doesn't take her eyes off him. "I don't know about that," she whispers.

"You don't have to know," he says. "That's where the faith comes in."

She looks at him, trying to study his eyes, trying to figure out what she should take away from everything that's happened.

As they sit, Charlie starts to think about Sarah. He thinks about all the messages she's tried to leave him, about how he never even listened to them. He decides that when he leaves the church, he'll go see her. He'll stand outside her door, knock, and when she answers, she'll look at him and cry. He won't know what to do at first. He'll study how thin she is, how heavy her eyes look, how her body shakes just looking at him. He won't know what to say, but finally, he'll reach out and hold her. There she'll be, in his arms, like she's been so many times before. She'll break down. She'll say she's sorry while she cries. She'll sob and sob. He'll be angry and sad and broken. He'll cry too, but he'll still hold her. He'll say he's sorry also. He's never been so sorry about anything in his life.

"I loved you," she'll say. He'll feel her grip on him tighten, as if knowing that she'll never hold him again. A part of that will make him mad. A part of that will make him wish she were strong enough to keep hanging on. But, then again, he knows that this has nothing to do with strength. He wishes it did, but it doesn't. She'll repeat the words again and again. "I loved you. I loved you. I loved you."

"I loved you, too," he'll reply, at last. He'll have so much more to say, but he won't say it. "God, I loved you too."

While he holds her, he'll wonder one last time what their life would have been like together. He'll think about all the mornings he would have woken up by her side. In his head, these mornings would be perfect. He would have spent every day watching the sun stream in through their bedroom window, lighting up her face, her smile slowly spreading.

"Wake up," he'd say as he kissed her, letting their arms and legs intertwine, but her smile would just widen in her sleep.

"Not yet," she'd say, and together, they'd keep their eyes closed. "Let's just stay like this a little longer."

So they would. Everything in this vision feels peaceful. It feels heavenly.

One day, though, he knows they'd have to come back down to earth. One day, they'd have to open their eyes.

***

"I thought coming here would just break me," Natalie says.

Her voice is different, though, than it was when they walked into the church. He can tell by the way she looks at the cross that she believes in something again.

"Maybe," she says, "the things that break us are also the things that put us back together."

He watches as she turns and looks up toward the light. She stares at the stained glass, each sharp piece coming together perfectly to create something soft, something peaceful, something artistic, something secret. She stares at the soaring angel whose wings outstretch across the sunlight, and Charlie knows, in that moment, she sees her son.

---WE HOPE YOU ENJOYED THE STORY---

But... don't stop here. Please keep reading for our Back-of-the-Book Content, including an interview with author Julia Camp.

INTERVIEW WITH THE AUTHOR

Q. How long have you been writing?

A. I wrote my first full-length novel when I was twelve. We had a class assignment as part of national novel writing month to write 5,000 words in four weeks. Our teacher told us that she had to give us a "kid" version of the challenge because we wouldn't be able to do the "adult" version, which was to write 50,000 in a month. I didn't really like the assumption that we were too young to write that much, so I wrote 55,000 words and told her I did both the "kid" and "adult" challenge. I'd always liked writing, but that was how I found out that I particularly loved novel writing.

Q. What made you decide to write a book about a veteran?

A. My desire to write about war started because of what I loved reading. *The Things They Carried* is my favorite book of all time. After reading it dozens of times, I decided to branch out and read other war novels as well. I loved *The Yellow Birds, Billy Lynn's Long Halftime Walk,* and *The Narrow Road to the Deep North.* Eventually, reading a bunch of war novels made me want to write a book that was about the intersection of war, love, and loss. So I did!

Q. Was it nerve-wracking writing about the experience of a veteran without being a veteran yourself?

A. Of course. In fact, I almost didn't write the book because I was so nervous about misrepresenting someone's experience. In the end, though, I believed I had a story worth sharing, so I had to kind of put that fear aside.

Q. Do you hide any secrets in your books that only a few people would find?

A. I think it's impossible to make art that isn't filled with your own secrets. At one point in the book, Erin even says to Charlie, "Isn't that all art is? A bunch of people's secrets." I tend to believe that. The whole book is a secret in a way.

Q. Are there any characters that either of you placed a piece of yourself into or feel more connected to?

A. To piggy-back off the answer to my last question, I think it's impossible to write without having the characters hold parts of you. I definitely feel as if all the characters have a piece of me in them. On a whole, I think I'm probably the most similar to Sarah. My default when coming up with her dialogue was to think of what I'd personally say if in her shoes. However, I think there are times, particularly near the end, where I could see myself being more like Charlie. There are parts of Wes, as well, that I think are a lot like me. I feel like I'm cheating the question by answering with too many characters, so I'll stop myself.

Q. Which character did you enjoy writing the most?

A. Probably Erin. I honestly still can't decide how I feel about her. I partially hate her and partially love her.

Q. What was the hardest part of writing the book?

A. Deciding the ending. At one point, I had two entirely different versions of the last 100 pages written. I had many sleepless nights trying to choose between them, so let's hope I made the right call.

Q. How many unpublished or half-finished books do you have?

A. I have five more books that I've written but not published, although most of them were written when I was young. I wouldn't be eager to let anyone read them. I have zero, though, that I've started and not finished. Finishing everything I begin is important to me, as a general life philosophy.

ACKNOWLEDGEMENTS

A special thank you to Andrew Porter for all the time he spent helping me with this book. It really means the world to me!

ABOUT THE AUTHOR

I'm currently (as of 8 September 2020) a law student at the University of Texas at Austin. Prior to law school, I taught creative writing at John Hopkins' Center for Talented Youth program and worked as an editor for *1966: A Journal of Creative Nonfiction*. I'm a graduate of Trinity University, where I majored in English and minored in creative writing. I've always had a passion for writing literary fiction, and after continuously reading and rereading my two favorite novels, *The Things They Carried* by Tim O'Brien and *The Yellow Birds* by Kevin Powers, I decided to write my own story about a soldier's return home from Afghanistan.

For more, the author online at:
Facebook: Julia Camp
Twitter: @JuliaCampAuthor

MORE FROM EVOLVED PUBLISHING

We offer great books across multiple genres, featuring high-quality editing (which we believe is second-to-none) and fantastic covers.

As a hybrid small press, your support as loyal readers is so important to us, and we have strived, with tireless dedication and sheer determination, to deliver on the promise of our motto:

QUALITY IS PRIORITY #1!

Please check out all of our great books,
which you can find at this link:
www.EvolvedPub.com/Catalog/

Thank you!

CPSIA information can be obtained
at www.ICGtesting.com
Printed in the USA
LVHW022343121020
668643LV00004B/983